Women's Fiction by Jacquelin Thomas

Jezebel
Redemption
Defining Moments
Singsation
Have a Little Faith*
Shades of Gray
Saved in the City
Soul Journey
A Change Is Gonna Come
Prodigal Husband

And check out Jacquelin's Young Adult titles

It's a Curl Thing*
Divine Match-Up*
Divine Secrets*
Divine Confidential*
Simply Divine*

*Available from Pocket Books

THE IDEAL

Wife

Jacquelin Thomas

POCKET BOOKS

New York London Toronto Sydney

Pocket Books
A Division of Simon & Schuster, Inc.
1230 Avenue of the Americas
New York, NY 10020

Designed by Jamie Lynn Kerner

Manufactured in the United States of America

ISBN-13: 978-1-61523-647-3

Acknowledgments

To my husband—we've had a wonderful eighteen years together. I can't thank you enough for your continued support, your friendship, your wealth of knowledge, but most of all your love. We make a great team!

A special thank-you to the brave women who responded to my inquiries and were candid about their marriages; I pray that God will continue to strengthen you and give you wisdom.

To my readers—thank you so much for the never-ending support you have shown me throughout my career. I hope you will be blessed by this story.

By the king's command each guest was allowed to drink in his own way, for the king instructed all the wine stewards to serve each man what he wished. Queen Vashti also gave a banquet for the women in the royal palace of King Xerxes. On the seventh day, when King Xerxes was in high spirits from wine, he commanded the seven eunuchs who served him— Mehuman, Biztha, Harbona, Bigtha, Abagtha, Zethar and Carcas—to bring before him Queen Vashti, wearing her royal crown, in order to display her beauty to the people and nobles, for she was lovely to look at. But when the attendants delivered the king's command, Queen Vashti refused to come. Then the king became furious and burned with anger.

ESTHER 1:8–12
NEW INTERNATIONAL VERSION

THE IDEAL

Wife

Chapter 1

THE LONG, SLEEK BLACK limo rolled to a stop in the driveway of the Tuscan-style, four-bedroom, six-bath paradise that was now her home. Jana had fallen in love with the grand estate the first time she'd come to have dinner with Lawrence Collins—her husband of one week.

The modest three-bedroom house where she'd grown up, on Fourth and Jefferson in Los Angeles, had been nothing like this Hollywood Hills mansion, although she had loved growing up in the house that had once belonged to her parents. After their premature deaths, her grown-up sister Robyn and her husband had moved in to care for Jana, who was twelve when they died.

A touch of sadness filtered through her as she thought about her sister. Robyn had always wanted children but had suffered three miscarriages; she'd finally had a hysterectomy. Despite her personal grief, she had been a wonderful mother to Jana.

Lawrence's fingers brushed Jana's collarbone and lingered there for a moment, bringing her out of her reverie.

"Welcome home, Mrs. Collins."

She shivered a little every time he called her that. Jana was still trying to digest the fact that at twenty-four years old, she was now a married woman. "I love hearing you call me that," she murmured softly.

"You belong to me now," Lawrence responded before placing a kiss on her lips.

Their driver parked in the circular driveway, then got out to open the door for her. Lawrence came around and helped her out of the car.

He led her by the hand through widely arched wooden double doors, a foyer with high ceilings, marble inlay floors, past a balustrade staircase to the formal living room.

"This house is so beautiful." Jana broke into a wide grin. "Living here is going to take some getting used to, but I'll have you know that I'm up to the challenge."

Lawrence laughed.

She loved the sound of his laughter. The truth was that she loved everything about him. Jana had always had a secret crush on Samuel Jackson, and Lawrence looked so much like the actor that they could pass for twins. He was tall and had big, beautiful eyes and a bright smile that simply warmed her all over. He sported a bald head that Jana found incredibly sexy, and he looked much younger than his thirty-six years.

Hugging Lawrence, Jana whispered, "I love you so much."

"I'm glad to hear it," he responded. "Especially after all the money I spent on our wedding and the honeymoon."

She gave him a playful shove. "I told you we could've had a smaller wedding. It wouldn't have mattered to me."

Jana's mind traveled back to April 4, the day she'd married Lawrence. It had been a perfect spring day designed especially for their wedding—a gift from the Lord. Her sister had had the church decorated with lilies and exotic greenery throughout. Her brother-in-law had officiated over the ceremony while her uncle had escorted her down the aisle.

Her wedding day couldn't have been more special.

"That's not what you really wanted and you know it. You wanted a big wedding—all women do." Lawrence's hand slid down her arm and tightened around her wrist.

"You're right," Jana confessed. "I used to dream of the kind of wedding I wanted. Lawrence, you gave me the wedding of my dreams. Thank you for that, honey."

He looked her over with a seductive gleam in his smile. "Now it's your turn to make all my dreams come true."

"It'll be my pleasure," she murmured. "But first I'm going to need to put something in my stomach. I'm starved."

Hand in hand, they walked toward the back of the house.

Jana loved the gourmet kitchen, with its granite counters, alder cabinetry, and a center island. "All this really inspires me to cook."

"There's not much here," Lawrence stated. "You're going to need to do some grocery shopping. We'll probably have to eat out tonight."

Jana checked the pantry and the refrigerator. "I'm pretty sure I can piece something together." She turned toward him. "I don't feel like going back out, Lawrence. I just want to stay home with you and enjoy our evening together—just the two of us."

She glanced over into the family room at the huge stacks of gifts on the sofa and on the carpet near the fireplace. "We have a lot of wedding presents to open," she commented. "I guess we'll eventually get to them sometime tomorrow. I don't want to wait too long to send out the thank-you notes."

"Then we should probably do it today," Lawrence suggested with a hint of sternness. "We're having dinner with Ron and Lela Boykin tomorrow night. I'd like to be able to thank them personally for whatever they gave us."

Stunned by the news, Jana said, "I thought maybe we'd spend some time alone when we first got back. I didn't know you'd accepted a dinner invitation." She didn't really want to go anywhere.

"Ron is one of my partners and he is my best friend. We went to college and law school together. One of the reasons our law firm is so successful is because we are a family. We spend a lot of time together."

She knew they were close, especially since Ron had been the best man at their wedding. The two men acted like brothers. "I understand that," Jana responded. "But—"

Lawrence interrupted her. "No buts, sweetheart. They invited us over and we're going. What did that Bible college you attended teach you? Didn't it tell you that you're supposed to be submissive to me? Didn't you agree at our wedding to obey me?"

Lawrence was a bit of a control freak. She'd known this about him and had married him anyway. After all, she wasn't perfect either. His good qualities far outweighed the negative as far as Jana was concerned.

She released a soft sigh. "Okay, Lawrence, I get it already. We're going to have dinner with Ron and Lela Boykin instead of staying home and cuddling."

He kissed her, trying to lessen the sting. "We're going to make it a quick dinner, and then we'll come home and enjoy each other."

"Thank you," she murmured.

Jana eyed her handsome husband's six-foot four-inch frame as he scanned a stack of mail. Lawrence was twelve years older than she was, although he looked like he was in his late twenties. He was a senior partner in the prestigious Beverly Hills law firm of Collins, Boykin, Richards & Lennox. Lawrence worked out every morning to keep his body toned and muscular.

She glanced down at the two-carat, yellow diamond engagement ring and wedding band. God had blessed her with a husband who was not only handsome but also financially secure. Jana never had to worry about working another day in her life. He'd even convinced her to withdraw from the Los Angeles Bible College so that she could focus on being a full-time wife. Jana already held a bachelor's degree in psychology, but she'd been working on a second degree in Christian counseling. Her goals had changed when she'd met Lawrence.

Her sister hadn't been thrilled with the idea of Jana's dropping out of college, but she'd respected Jana's decision. Robyn and her husband had not been just guardians as Jana was growing up; they'd also been role models. Robyn owned a clothing boutique, which she'd named after herself, on Third Avenue. Daniel Barker was the senior pastor of Jefferson Street Baptist Church. Despite a ten-year difference in their ages, Robyn and Daniel were very much in love and devoted to making their marriage a happy one.

Lawrence opened an envelope and handed a credit card to Jana. "This is for you," he stated. "Your American Express card is in my office. I'll give it to you later."

"Thank you," Jana responded. "But you didn't have to do this, Lawrence. I do have my own credit cards—two of them."

She and Lawrence had discussed finances before the wedding, but he'd never once mentioned his plans to acquire credit cards for her. If he had, she would've told him not to bother. She wasn't a fan of credit cards.

Lawrence glanced over at her and said, "You're married to me now. I'm sure the credit limits on your cards don't come close to the ones I opened for you. Jana, you can keep the ones you have, or simply pay them off and close out the accounts. It's your decision."

He placed the pile of opened envelopes on the breakfast counter. "Oh, you'll also have an allowance of two thousand a month for your own personal use. This doesn't include household expenses or your clothing allowance."

The idea of allowances staggered her. "Clothing allowance?"

"Jana, as my wife . . . we'll be attending a lot of functions, and, well . . ."—Lawrence's eyes strayed to her pants—"denim of any kind won't be appropriate."

She glanced downward. Her pants were practically brand-new. "I love my jeans."

His fingers were warm and strong as they grasped hers. "I know that, but they won't cut it at the Oscars."

Jana broke into a slow smile. "It just hasn't been done yet. Who knows . . . I might start a trend."

Lawrence didn't crack a smile, and Jana could see the tensing of the muscles in his face. He could be so serious at times.

"Honey, I'm kidding," she assured him. "You of all people should know that I don't have any problems when it comes to shopping. I was the buyer for my sister's boutique. I have some nice stuff in my closet. I'm just more comfortable in jeans."

"I've asked Lela Boykin to take you shopping one day during the week," Lawrence announced.

Her eyes narrowed. Did Lawrence really find her taste in clothes so terrible that she needed a chaperone? "So what other plans have you made for us?" she asked pointedly. "In case you didn't hear me, I'm going to repeat myself. I was the buyer for Robyn's Boutique. I'm pretty sure if I can buy for an entire store, I can manage to pick out my own wardrobe."

"I never liked anything I saw in your sister's shop," Lawrence stated firmly. "They're fine if you're looking for something to wear to church or a corporate function, but that's not how I want my wife to dress."

Distracted by a name he saw, Lawrence held up an engraved invitation. "On Thursday, we're having dinner with John Lennox and his wife. It's Rose's birthday."

She withdrew her hand from his quickly and turned away, trying to control her temper. *"Is there anything else?"*

"There's a party on Saturday night." Lawrence eyed her. "Why? Is there a problem?"

Jana shook her head. "Why don't you give me an idea of what I need to buy when Lela and I go shopping?" Deep down, she was seething.

Lawrence was making plans without checking with her. Moreover, he had suddenly decided she needed fashion advice from his best friend's wife.

Her 36 double Ds, twenty-four-inch waist, and thirty-six-inch hips had drawn Lawrence to her. Now that Jana really thought about it, she realized that he'd always commented on her body—even to the point of saying that he expected her to keep her shape after having children. Lawrence had even given her a gym membership as a pre-wedding present.

Old memories resurfaced that she'd thought were long buried.

From the moment Jana's body had begun to mature, men, both young and old, had tried to get her into bed. She was more than that, but why couldn't anyone see that? Why couldn't Lawrence?

Seeing her distress, he reached for her, pulling her close. "Jana, I'm sorry if I offended you. It's just that I want you to dress for me. I don't want you dressed like some frump or old maid. You're too fine for that."

His kind words melted her anger. Jana wrapped her arms around him. "Maybe I overreacted. I'm sorry too."

"Why don't we open our gifts?" His large hand took Jana's face and held it gently. "When we're finished, we can go upstairs and take a nap."

"Sounds good to me," she responded. Jana turned back toward the kitchen. "If you're not hungry, I'm going to make myself a sandwich."

"I'm fine, sweetheart."

Jana strode into the kitchen and pulled out a pack of deli ham, a jar of mayonnaise, and a loaf of bread. She could feel her husband's eyes on her as she made her sandwich.

Without looking up, Jana asked, "Why are you staring at me like that?"

"I still can't believe how lucky I am. I never thought I'd get married again after Gia and I broke up. After everything she put me through, I wasn't sure I even wanted to remarry."

Jana didn't respond. She had never met his ex-wife and could not contribute to the conversation. She bit into the soft bread and honey ham and chewed slowly.

"I'm sorry. I guess I shouldn't be talking about Gia like that. She's my past and you are my future."

When he and Jana had first met, Lawrence had talked about his life with Gia, and how her drinking had ruined their marriage. He hadn't been able to get her to face the fact that she'd been an alcoholic. A drunken driver had killed Jana's parents, so she knew firsthand how easily alcohol could destroy lives.

She finished off her sandwich and cleaned up before joining Lawrence in the family room to open their wedding gifts.

Lawrence marched over to select a wedding present. "Open this one first—it's from Ron and Lela."

"How do you know?"

"When I arranged for the presents to be brought here, I told my secretary to make sure Ron's was on the top, because I knew we were having dinner with them when we got back. I also told her to put all the gifts from everyone at the firm on the sofa."

Lawrence was organized right down to the wedding gifts.

Jana sat down and began opening the present.

He joined her, paper and pen in hand. "I'll write down everything so that we won't make a faux pas by sending a thank-you note to the wrong person for the wrong gift." Lawrence gave her a reassuring smile. "Don't worry, baby; I'm going to teach you how to be the ideal wife."

Her mouth dropped open at the sight of what was in the gift box. "Lawrence . . ."

He glanced over and laughed. "That Ron—he's crazy."

Jana eyed her husband. "What kind of man gives his friend lingerie like this for a wedding present?" She held up the skimpy, sheer material. Her sister had given her a lingerie-themed bridal shower, but none of the gifts she'd received had been as risqué as the teddy she was holding.

Lawrence was still laughing when he held up the thong briefs. "His-and-her lingerie—only Ron."

Jana thought the gift was highly inappropriate and wasn't amused at all. What kind of people were Ron and Lela?

Chapter 2

Ron and Lela Boykin lived less than ten minutes away, in a walled and gated country English mansion that featured a breathtaking view of the city. Ron, a tall, muscular man with skin the color of peanut butter, greeted them. His dark, wavy hair was cut close to his scalp. He was wearing a pair of rust-colored linen pants and an ivory silk shirt with a pair of brown leather slip-ons.

Lela looked stunning in a ruby red strapless dress and silver sandals. She wore red lipstick and nail polish to complement her outfit and honey complexion.

They were a beautiful couple, Jana thought silently, but she still thought the gift they'd given had been inappropriate.

"Jana, you look beautiful," Lela murmured. "You still have that newly-wed glow going on."

Lawrence wrapped an arm around his wife. "Hey! What about me? I should have something—at least a tan."

"You always look nice," Lela told him. "You got a li'l something going on."

Lawrence pulled her into his arms, holding her close.

They all laughed.

Ron took Lawrence to his office to discuss business, leaving Jana with Lela, who offered to give her a tour of the house.

"Your home is beautiful, Lela," Jana remarked as they went from room to room.

Lela tossed her long, flat-ironed hair over her shoulder and said, "Thank you. It's a work in progress, actually. I'm redoing the kitchen and my bedroom." In a low whisper, she added, "I've been after Ron to redecorate for two years now."

"How long have you two been married?" Jana inquired.

"Six years," Lela responded. "Six months after he divorced wife number two. We were together for two years before we got married. I've been with him since I was twenty-two."

"Oh." From what Lela had just told her, Jana could only assume that Lela was the reason Ron had divorced wife number two. Lela was a pretty girl, with long, dark hair, a flawless, deep honey complexion that didn't need much makeup, almond-shaped eyes, and perfect lips.

Although she was trying to be more discreet, Lela surveyed Jana from head to toe. "You're exactly the type of woman I knew Lawrence would marry."

"Meaning?" Jana asked.

"It's pretty clear that Lawrence is a breast man. He's attracted to the Marilyn Monroe body types. Those are the only types of women I've ever seen him date."

"His first wife was—".

Lela nodded. "She wasn't as well endowed as you are—those are real, aren't they?"

Jana recoiled in shock and Lela laughed. "I'm sorry. I shouldn't have said that."

Ron and Lawrence joined them as they settled down in the family room.

Lawrence gave a slight nod of approval when she glanced in his direction. He took a seat beside her.

Jana couldn't help noticing the way Ron kept watching her. It made her a little uncomfortable. "Man, I still can't see how you lucked out with a beautiful woman like Jana," he told Lawrence. "How did you manage that?"

Lawrence laughed, surprising her. She still hadn't decided if she simply disliked Ron, or if he just came on too strong.

"Yeah, she's definitely a beauty."

Jana stole a peek at Lela, who did not seem bothered at all by her husband's words. Jana knew that she wouldn't have been as comfortable if the shoe had been on the other foot.

During dinner, Lawrence brought up the subject of shopping. "My wife needs a new wardrobe. Lela, I hope you're able to go with her this week. We have some dinners coming up, and I want her to have everything she needs."

Beneath the table, Jana clenched and unclenched her fist. Lawrence could be so rude at times. She didn't want to rock the boat so soon in their marriage, but she couldn't let this continue. She wouldn't tolerate his treating her as if she were a child.

"What day is good for you, Jana?" Lela asked.

"I'll let you know," she managed tersely.

Lawrence sent her a look that showed his displeasure, but Jana ignored him.

It was a struggle to hide her true feelings. Jana was upset with Lawrence, but she tried to hide it from Ron and Lela.

"What's with the attitude?" Lawrence asked when they returned home two hours later. "Is something wrong? You seemed upset during dinner, and you hardly said two words to me in the car."

Jana's hand stroked the back of the wing chair in the living room. "Why didn't you tell me before we got married that you don't like the way I dress?"

"I told you that I wasn't a jeans person when we first started going out."

"But you never said you didn't like me wearing them," she responded. "It's pretty obvious that you think I can't dress and you don't trust my choices. Otherwise you wouldn't have asked Lela to take me shopping."

Lawrence remained infuriatingly calm. "Jana, I didn't have the right to say anything while we were dating. You're no longer my girlfriend—you're my wife. And yes, I'd like my wife to dress a certain way. Is anything wrong with that?"

"You didn't have to ask Lela to take me shopping in the first place, but then to blurt it out like that over dinner really offended me." Jana paused a moment before continuing. "Lawrence, I'm a grown woman. I can pick out my own clothes. You've made it abundantly clear that you think I dress too conservative. *I heard you.*"

Lawrence shrugged, as though the point was obvious. "I was only trying to help you, Jana. Besides, I thought it would be the perfect opportunity for you two to get to know each other. Lela has excellent taste when it comes to clothes."

Still irritated, Jana folded her arms across her chest. "So you don't think I have any taste?"

He looked like he was losing patience with her. "You're a very casual dresser. I've never really seen you dressed up other than our wedding and a couple of dinners, but even then you were dressed like somebody's mother."

His words stung.

Jana averted her eyes. "I see."

"Look, I'm not trying to hurt your feelings, Jana, I'm just telling you how I feel. I want you to dress more your age instead of like you're in your fifties. That's all."

Jana glared at him. The more he talked, the more he was digging himself into a hole.

His voice softened. "Honey, you have such a beautiful body. Don't be afraid to show it off. I'm not the jealous type—I want other men to admire you."

She didn't know how to respond to those words, so she remained silent. The last thing she wanted was the attention of other men. She'd had to deal with that all her life.

Smiling like a father, Lawrence pulled her into his arms. "I love you and I know that you love me too. I just thought you might want to dress nicely for me. I don't want to see you all covered up. Pleasing me should be your priority, sweetheart."

"Of course I want to please you, Lawrence. I just don't think I have to dress like a hooker to do it."

His smile disappeared. "I'm not asking you to dress like a hooker. Didn't you like what Lela was wearing?"

"It was nice," Jana admitted. Lela's dress had fit as if it had been made for her. "I really liked that dress."

"You would look stunning in something like that. That's all I'm trying to say, Jana."

She looked up, meeting his gaze. "I'm doing this for you. But when I'm here at home, I just want to be comfortable. I hope that's not a problem for you."

Lawrence kissed her gently on the lips. "I'm glad we were able to come to an agreement on this subject. It's late, and right now all I want to do is enjoy my beautiful wife."

HE NEXT MORNING, JANA woke up early. Her eyes traveled the length of the two-room, tastefully decorated master suite, with its mint green and chocolate theme. Lawrence had had the decorator work with Jana before the wedding because he wanted no traces of his former life with Gia to intrude upon his new life with her.

This is all mine.

High coved ceilings and archways, walnut floors, custom light fixtures, and wrought-iron details throughout completed the private oasis. She still couldn't get over the walk-in closet, which was as big as her last bedroom. Jana especially loved the spa tub with travertine tile accents. She had never lived in such luxury.

Jana snuggled close to Lawrence, who was sleeping. She sent up another prayer of thanksgiving. The last thing she remembered before falling asleep was how God had blessed her richly and that she couldn't thank Him enough.

She and Lawrence exercised together in their home gym before going their separate ways. He needed to run down to the office to pick up some paperwork for a client, and Jana decided she'd go to the grocery store for a few things.

She met up with her best friend for coffee first.

Graciela Ruiz strolled into Starbucks as if she owned the place, dressed in a deep lapis–colored shift dress by St. John, her waist-length, curly dark hair looking like a million dollars.

The two women embraced.

"You look beautiful as always," Jana complimented. "I love this shade of blue. It looks good on you."

"Naaw, look at you, *mi'ja*," Graciela murmured with a thick Puerto Rican accent. "You're glowing, Jana. Poppy must've put some good loving on you."

"Keep your voice down," Jana whispered as they stood in line to place their orders. "What's wrong with you?"

Graciela laughed. "Aww . . . you don't have to be all embarrassed. At least you're married and you waited until your wedding night. That's saying a lot. I *wanted* to wait, but when I saw Enrique . . . that just flew out the window along with my clothes. *I'm serious.* I would see him, and the clothes—they just fell to the floor. Just like that. I'm gonna tell the Lord that it was His fault for making that man so fine and sexy."

"I'd love to be a fly on the wall when you do that," Jana responded with a laugh. "I can see you now, getting drop-kicked out of Heaven."

Graciela laughed. "God loves me even though he knows I have issues. Look how he blessed me with a wonderful husband. Enrique's a good man and he loves me to death."

Jana agreed. She'd never seen a more loving couple, apart from Robyn and Daniel.

After they got their coffee, they found an empty table and sat down to talk.

"So, how is Lawrence Collins, Esquire?" Graciela asked.

Jana scanned her friend's long face, her lips turning downward. "Why don't you like him, Graciela?"

"Poppy doesn't care for me," she replied after taking a sip of her coffee. "I don't know why. I haven't done nothing to him."

"That's not true, Graciela," Jana said. "He's never said anything bad about you to me. Lawrence is very reserved, that's all."

Graciela shook her head. "Naaw . . . I think it's more than that. You know I have good instincts when it comes to people."

Jana was willing to concede that point, but it didn't help her. "He's my husband. Will you please give him a chance?"

"Of course," Graciela replied. "He's in the family. We're stuck with him now."

Jana sipped her vanilla frappuccino. "Graciela, once you really get to know Lawrence, you'll change your mind about him. He's been so sweet to me." She broke into a smile. "I feel like we're still on our honeymoon."

Graciela smiled. "That's exactly how it's supposed to be."

Jana pulled back, remembering the night before. "We already had our first disagreement. It was a tiny one, though," she confessed. "Lawrence wants one of his partner's wives to take me shopping for a new wardrobe. I can't help it, but I was insulted."

"So why does he want this chick to go with you to buy clothes?" Graciela said, puzzled. "You've worked in a clothing store since forever. You can pick out your own clothes. But even if you couldn't . . ." She spread her arms wide. "You have me, a true fashionista, if ever there was one."

"Apparently, Lawrence doesn't like the way I dress. Interestingly enough, he never said anything about it before we got married."

"I hope you told him where to go and to take his personal shopper with him," Graciela uttered. She picked up her BlackBerry to check her schedule.

"I told him that I could shop for myself."

Graciela's eyes grew large in surprise. "Jana, that wasn't strong enough. I hope you at least threw something at him, and I'm not talking about a pillow. I mean something like a vase or a plate."

Jana released a soft sigh. "I thought about it, believe me."

Graciela muttered a string of words in Spanish.

"He kept saying that I was taking it the wrong way," Jana said, trying to explain. "He doesn't want me dressing like I'm about to go to church or step into a courtroom."

"Well, you do dress more on the conservative side when you're not in jeans, but if you want to liven up your wardrobe, Jana, I'll go with you, *mi'ja*."

Jana nodded in agreement. "You're about the only person I'd take shopping with me. You know my taste."

"I know what will look stunning on you," Graciela confirmed. "Jana, I agree with Lawrence to a certain extent. You need to dress more your age. I've told you this before."

"You and Lawrence need to get off my choice of clothing." Flustered, Jana ran her fingers through her short hair. "If he wanted a fashion diva, then he should've married one. I actually like the way I dress."

Graciela shook her finger. "It's not about the way you dress, Jana. I think it's more that Poppy wants you to dress a certain way for *him*. He wants to show you off—that's a compliment."

Jana considered Graciela's words. "I know that. But Graciela, you know what I've been through. I grew up being groped by strangers in lines for the movies, in the lunchroom, and even at church that one time."

"I know, *mi'ja*. That's why you're always wearing clothes so loosely."

"Lawrence doesn't really know all I went through. I should probably apologize to him."

"I didn't go saying all that now."

Jana laughed.

They talked for another fifteen minutes. Before they had to leave, Jana said, "Let's do lunch sometime next week. I'm going to get all of my stuff unpacked and settle into my new home."

"I'll call you by Friday," Graciela stated. "I have two photo shoots scheduled this week, and I'm finishing up another campaign—it's a busy week for me."

Jana nodded in understanding. "The life of an art director."

"Speaking of which, tell Robyn it's a good idea to have some color cards prepared. The real fabric color cards—it'll give buyers something to touch and feel."

Jana agreed enthusiastically. "I love those. It's tedious to cut little square pieces of fabric and paste them on the card stock, but it's definitely worth the time."

"I checked, and the Lookbook is almost ready. She's going to love it."

"I hope so," Jana responded. "Robyn almost had a coronary when she saw the price quote. She kept saying that some of the most successful companies have never produced one and they're doing just fine."

"This is true. However," Graciela pointed out, "nice photos of the clothes on a model is clearly going to help your sister's designs sell better than a flat sketch would."

"I can't wait to see the finished product," Jana told her friend. "Thanks, Graciela."

The two women embraced.

"Good to have you back, Jana. I missed you."

"Our wedding pictures should be ready sometime this afternoon. Lawrence and I saw the proofs yesterday—they came out really nice. I'll email you the link and password so that you can see them."

Graciela broke into a smile. "I can't wait."

They walked out to their cars.

"So, what are your plans for the rest of the day, *mi'ja*?" Graciela asked.

Jana shrugged. "I'm going to run some errands, then invite my hubby to lunch so that I can apologize to him."

"Hmmmm . . ." Graciela tossed her long hair over her shoulder. "Maybe you should have him come home so that you can apologize properly."

Jana grinned, recalling last night. "I like the way that you think."

AWRENCE WALKED INTO THE house and found rose petals strewn on the floor and up the spiral staircase. His lips turned upward into a smile.

Upstairs, he found Jana wearing the lingerie that Ron and Lela had given them as a gift. He recovered quickly from his shock and grinned. "Wow!"

A small table had been set up in the master bedroom. It was covered with champagne, two plates laden with lobster salad, and rolls. Lawrence noted there was also a silver tray with chocolate-covered strawberries.

"What did I do to deserve this?" he asked with a smile.

"I wanted to say that I'm sorry for overreacting when you asked Lela to take me shopping."

Lawrence kissed her. "No apologies are needed, sweetheart. I went about this the wrong way. I figured women bonded over shopping. She is very much into fashion and you were a buyer—you two would have a lot to talk about."

"Well, it's over with now." She led him over to the table. "I hope you brought your appetite with you."

They sat down and enjoyed their lunch.

"This was delicious," Lawrence stated. He wiped his mouth with the end of his napkin. "I guess the chocolate-covered strawberries are dessert."

Jana shook her head. "Actually, I had something else in mind."

She stood up, walked to the center of the room, and began loosening the strings on her teddy.

T HE NEXT DAY, LAWRENCE decided to spend most of the morning working from home. He was in his home office at 6:00 a.m., but he took a break long enough to eat breakfast with Jana.

"You keep staring out that window," Lawrence stated. "What are you looking at?"

"Everything," she responded. "I was thinking what a beautiful picture God painted when he designed the landscape."

Lawrence followed her gaze. "It is nice. It's one of the reasons I bought this house."

"I love it here." Jana took a sip of her cranberry juice.

"I'm glad." Lawrence finished off his coffee. "I want you to be happy here."

"I don't think you ever have to worry about that, Lawrence." Jana took a bite of her toast, then scanned through the newspaper. She enjoyed reading the sports section. She was as big a basketball fan as Lawrence was. "The Lakers are on a roll."

"They're playing the Phoenix Suns tomorrow night," Lawrence announced. "Do you want to go?"

Grinning, Jana nodded. "You know I do."

He went back to his home office, while she went upstairs to take a shower.

The telephone rang a few minutes after she stepped out of the shower. Lawrence wasn't going to answer it, so Jana ran over to the nightstand and picked up the phone.

"That was Robyn," Jana stated when she walked into her husband's home office ten minutes later. "She invited us to have dinner with her and Daniel."

"What did you say?" Lawrence asked.

"I told her that we'd be happy to join them. We're meeting them at seven o'clock." She turned toward the door, saying, "I'm going back upstairs to get dressed."

"Why didn't you tell them that we were still on our honeymoon?" Lawrence grumbled.

Jana paused in the doorway, not letting the remark pass. "We've had dinner with your partners—why not my family? Besides, we were planning on eating out anyway." She folded her arms across her chest. "Why don't you like my sister and Daniel?"

"It's not that I don't like them, sweetheart. They're okay," Lawrence stated, leaning back in his chair. "Daniel's just a little too religious for me. He thinks that it's a sin to enjoy a glass of wine. I don't. I don't need someone frowning over everything I do or say."

"Daniel's not like that," Jana argued.

Lawrence grunted in protest. "He didn't want us to have a bar during the reception. Daniel didn't want people getting drunk or having a good time. Whatever it was, he gave us a fit about it, remember?"

She didn't deny it, because what Lawrence was saying was true. Her brother-in-law took his position as pastor and leader of his flock seriously. He diligently sought to avoid any place or situation that might cast a shadow on his ministry.

Playing with the pen on his desk, Lawrence eyed her. "I guess that if I refuse, it might cause a rift between us, huh?"

"It might," Jana shot back.

He released a soft sigh. "I'll be home in time for our dinner date."

"Thank you," Jana said. "Lawrence, I appreciate this. I'm very close to my family."

He pushed away from the desk to stand up. "They're my family now, so it's not like I can avoid them forever."

That remark rubbed her the wrong way. "You don't want to avoid them, right?"

"No, honey, I don't." Lawrence stuck some papers into his briefcase, then closed it. "I'm getting ready to head to the office. Come give me a proper good-bye."

Jana walked her husband to the front door. When he was gone, she went upstairs and slipped on a pair of jeans and a tank top.

She spent most of her day making notes of things she wanted to change and moving around furniture to suit her taste.

When Lawrence returned, Jana was in the master bedroom with a book of wallpaper samples.

"Honey, what do you think of these?" she asked, holding up two pieces of wallpaper.

He hardly glanced at them. "I'm fine with whatever you pick."

"Lawrence, are you sure?"

He nodded. "I'm jumping into the shower."

Jana finished curling her hair.

"Will you try to have a nice time tonight?" she asked when he joined her downstairs twenty minutes later.

"I'll be fine, but I'm telling you now—I'm ordering a glass of wine. I don't care what Daniel and Robyn think. I'm in the mood for wine."

"Lawrence, it's really not a big deal." Jana eyed her reflection in the hall mirror and adjusted a last curl. "If you want to order a shot of whiskey straight—do it." She turned around to face him. "You're a grown man. Daniel will be just fine."

Chapter 3

"DID YOU HAVE FUN last night, honey?" Jana asked after strolling out of the bathroom, toothbrush in hand.

"It was fine," Lawrence admitted. "Although Daniel looked like he wanted to lay hands and pray over me every time I ordered a drink."

"You're wrong for that, Lawrence."

He gave a short laugh. "It's the truth and you know it."

She nodded in agreement as she untied the belt on her silk robe. "Daniel does have very specific views on drinking, dancing, and playing cards. He would never let me play a card game on Sunday—said that it was gambling. I was just playing spades." She chuckled. "Ooh, he used to make me so mad over that."

"He really believes that you shouldn't touch anything with alcohol in it," Lawrence said, annoyed. "But I don't agree. I don't believe you should drink to the point that you're inebriated, but it's not a sin to drink sociably."

"I tend to agree with you there," Jana responded. "I do enjoy a glass of wine every now and then, but I respect my brother-in-law's beliefs. I'm not much of a drinker anyway."

She slipped on a pair of white shorts and a salmon Ralph Lauren knit top, then ran her fingers through her short, curly hair. "I need to get my hair cut—it's growing out so fast."

"Don't," Lawrence protested. "You'd be beautiful with long hair. Just let it grow out."

Jana glanced over and smiled. "Sure, if that's what you want, but I have to be honest with you. I love wearing my hair short."

He didn't respond, so Jana let the subject drop for the moment.

After they were dressed, Lawrence and Jana headed downstairs. They were on their way to the Beverly Hills Country Club.

"I have to warn you—I'm not very good at tennis." Jana smiled.

"Don't worry about it. I've signed you up for tennis lessons," Lawrence announced. "I'm going to play with Ron. Lela's taking the class with you."

Jana stopped in her tracks. "I assumed that we'd be playing together."

He shook his head. "Not this time."

She chewed on her bottom lip, a habit she had developed as a child. She only did it whenever she was nervous or frustrated.

"What's wrong?"

"Nothing," she responded.

Lawrence grabbed her by the hand. "Jana, we've been together long enough for me to tell when you're unhappy about something, so you might as well tell me what it is. I can't read minds."

"I just thought we were spending the day together," Jana confessed. "I didn't know that we would be joining your partner and his wife. Is this payback for my insisting that we have dinner with Robyn and Daniel?"

"I wouldn't be so childish," Lawrence responded.

"Then why are you just now mentioning that Ron and Lela would be joining us?" she demanded. "Why did you keep it a secret?"

Lawrence released an impatient sigh. "Jana, you don't have to overreact. I wasn't trying to keep any secrets from you. I'm sorry you took it that way."

Not convinced, she climbed into the SUV without another word. Lawrence closed the door behind her, then strolled around the car to the driver's side.

As he climbed in, Jana continued to stare out the window.

"I suppose you're mad at me now," he said.

She didn't respond.

"I see. Now you're not talking to me," Lawrence said wearily. "Jana, it's really not that serious, sweetheart."

She finally turned toward him. "When I wanted to spend time with my family, you wanted me to tell them we were still on our honeymoon. Yet when it comes to your partners . . . I'm sorry, but I'm missing something here."

"I'm just asking you to spend a couple of hours with Lela. I want you to get to know her and Ron. What's so wrong about that?"

Jana did not want to get into an argument. "Nothing. Nothing at all."

"We're just playing a couple of rounds of tennis with them," Lawrence said, trying to make nice. "Afterward, we'll have lunch with Ron and Lela, then we have the rest of the day to ourselves."

All Jana wanted to do was spend time with Lawrence. She wasn't in the mood to divide her time between her husband and his friends. But he was right—she didn't mind giving up some of their quality time to have dinner with her sister and Daniel.

I can't be selfish, she thought. *I really shouldn't be acting this way.*

"Will you please talk to me?" Lawrence questioned.

"It's fine," Jana informed him. "I'll play tennis with Lela, have a little girl talk, and then we'll see you and Ron for a delicious lunch. I don't have a problem with it."

Lawrence glanced over at her. "It sounds like you're still a little irritated over this."

"I'm not."

He reached over and took her hand in his. "We're going to have a great time."

Jana gave him a tiny smile. "You're probably right. I guess I'm being a little selfish, wanting to keep you to myself."

"Baby, we have forever."

Thirty minutes later, a valet at the Beverly Hills Country Club opened the door and assisted Jana out of the Mercedes.

Lawrence escorted Jana over to the beverage bar to enjoy a cup of tea while he ordered coffee for himself and read the newspaper. They had arrived earlier than expected.

Jana sipped on her tea as she quietly took in her surroundings. She had only been here once, for a church function. She'd always wondered what it would be like to be a member. Robyn and Daniel were not the country club types.

"Ron and Lela are here," Lawrence announced in a low voice. "Act as if you're happy to see them."

She met his gaze. "That sounded a little bit like an order."

"It wasn't."

Yes, it was, she thought. But then again, he might be nervous that she wouldn't like his law partner and his wife.

"Hello, Ron. Hi, Lela," Jana greeted the couple as they joined them at the breakfast bar. "I hear we're taking tennis lessons together this morning."

Lela chuckled. "Yeah, we are. I'm not much of a player. Ron hates playing with me."

Lawrence and Ron walked over to the service center to check them in.

"I'm not any better," Jana assured her. "I guess that's why Lawrence didn't want to play with me. I know he's very competitive."

"They both are," Lela confirmed. She waited until Ron and Lawrence walked away. Pointing back out at a table, she said, "Jana, we don't have to get out there and embarrass ourselves—we can just sit down and talk."

"Lawrence scheduled a tennis lesson for me," Jana said doubtfully, "so I guess I should probably go."

Lela nodded. "Of course, Jana, you're right. I guess I was hoping to get you to play hooky with me. The truth is that I'm not crazy about tennis and have no interest in learning how to play."

"I feel the same way," Jana confessed with a laugh. "But I'm going to try it. I'm doing it for Lawrence," she said, throwing up her hand dramatically to her forehead.

"I can see now that we're going to be great friends," Lela said. "I like you, Jana."

Their instructor was already on the court, awaiting their arrival. His bright smile reminded Jana of a chipmunk.

While he smoothly hit balls over the net, the two of them flailed away. Jana couldn't wait for her lesson to be over; she discovered she had no love for the sport.

"I'm so glad this is over," Lela whispered at the end of the class.

"Me too," Jana uttered. "I don't care for tennis. I'm more of a football or basketball girl."

"I like basketball too," Lela said. "Not crazy about football, though. It's probably because I was in a bad relationship with this football player right before I met Ron. I used to be a cheerleader for the Philadelphia Eagles."

Jana had already noticed how trim and athletic Lela was. "Did you enjoy it?"

She nodded. "I did. I had a great time except for the relationship. He hit me one night. I packed up my stuff the next day and just left Philly. I didn't stop until I arrived here in Los Angeles. I just wanted to get as far away as I could from that dude."

"Is he still playing?" Jana inquired.

"No. He's actually paralyzed from the neck down from a car accident he was in a couple of years ago."

"Oh, how sad." Jana knew exactly whom Lela was speaking of, but she didn't volunteer the name. She remembered reading about the troubled young man and his exploits. Just when he'd seemed on the verge of getting himself together, he'd been involved in an accident one night after leaving a party.

Lela could tell Jana had figured it out. "I feel bad about what happened to him, but I'm glad to have him out of my life. Jana, he was so mean to me. Life with him was horrible."

Jana and Lela joined their husbands on the patio of the country club for lunch.

"How did your lesson go?" Lawrence asked after planting a kiss on her lips.

Jana glanced over at Lela. The two women burst into laughter.

"Well . . . ," he prompted.

"I need more lessons," Jana replied dryly. "A lot more. I'm horrible at tennis. It's really not my sport."

Lawrence chuckled. "The more you play, the better you'll get, sweetheart."

"I don't know about that," Lela interjected. "I've been trying to improve my game for almost a year now. It's not happening for me."

Jana was quick to support her. "Lawrence, I don't know if you should waste your money on tennis lessons. I'm not really interested in playing."

"That's because you don't know how to play. You'll change your mind after your lessons."

Jana was about to disagree, but she stopped herself. They were around company.

Lawrence ordered the Mandarin steak salad for himself and the Greek shrimp salad for her. Ron and Lela both ordered the seared ahi tuna salad.

While they waited for their food to arrive, they made small talk and sipped glasses of wine. Jana found that she enjoyed talking with Lela. She was smart and well versed in American literature.

"Have you met Angie yet?" she asked Jana.

A cloudy image appeared in Jana's mind. "I think I met her at the wedding."

"She was there, so you probably did," Lela uttered. "Anyway, she sits on the board of a couple of charities, and I'm telling you now—she's going to try and recruit you for a committee. Fund-raising is her life, although you wouldn't know it." The men snickered, and Lela went on to explain.

"She's about five feet tall, blond hair, about a forty double D with a twenty-inch waist, and she wears clothing that looks like it's been painted on her. She's married to Lenny Nielson. He's a huge movie director—I'm sure you've heard of him. I heard that she was trying to be an actress until she hooked up with Lenny. Of course, Angie denies it. She tells everyone that they met at a charity ball for leukemia."

Jana vaguely remembered seeing someone fitting that description at the church. "Did she have on white at the wedding?"

Lela nodded. "That was her. Angie loves wearing white. It's her signature color."

"Oh," Jana murmured. She didn't have a signature color, and she hadn't ever really thought about it either.

"In our world, it's important to brand ourselves," Lela explained. "I wear bright, vivid colors all the time. You'll never see me in anything soft or pastel. That's my signature." She checked out Jana, assessing her. "We need to find your trademark color."

Jana wasn't sure she'd heard Lela correctly. "Excuse me?"

Lela waved airily in Lawrence's direction. "You're married to a very successful man, and he has to have the ideal wife. If she's not an asset to him, then he doesn't really need her."

Jana stiffened at these words, and Lela leaned toward her. "There are thousands of women dying to be in our shoes. Jana, if we want to keep our husbands, then we have to make sure that we become the women our husbands dream about. We have to make their fantasies come true."

Jana didn't know what to say. She had no idea what signature colors and branding had to do with being a good wife. She actually found the thought that she was like a Heinz ketchup bottle amusing, and she struggled to keep from laughing.

As for fantasies, she wanted to make Lawrence's fantasies come true, and she was sure they had nothing to do with branding or signature colors.

"I don't know about you, but I intend to keep my husband, Jana."

"I'm not worried about Lawrence leaving me," Jana responded, glancing at him. "Lela, I wouldn't have married him if I'd had those types of thoughts."

Ron had the nerve to laugh. "Jana, don't be naïve. That'll get you in trouble. Women are always trying to throw themselves at us."

"That's where prayer comes in," Jana stated. "And God. You can't just invite Him to the wedding. You have to invite Him into the marriage as well."

Lela shrank back, nonplussed by this idea.

Chapter 4

THE NEXT MORNING, LAWRENCE left home shortly after seven o'clock. When they'd woken up, he'd toyed with the idea of staying home, but he'd apparently changed his mind by the time she walked out of the bathroom.

Maybe I was getting on his nerves to the point that the poor man just wanted to get away from his nonbranded woman, she mused in silence.

Jana discarded the thought like an old rag. Lawrence loved her, but he had several high-profile cases waiting for him. He was a dedicated attorney and didn't want to get behind in his work.

The housekeeper arrived thirty minutes later.

Jana felt like she was in the way while Sofia cleaned, so she called Graciela and Robyn and asked them to meet her for lunch.

I might as well start spending some of my allowance money.

The first thing she intended to buy was a new Lakers sweatshirt. After their victory over the Suns last night, Jana decided to splurge on some more Lakers apparel. She was positive they were going to the NBA playoffs.

Jana met her sister and Graciela at Mako, a Beverly Hills restaurant situated on Beverly Drive, south of Wilshire Boulevard.

"Hey, what's up with this fancy restaurant, Jana, and this overpriced meal for me and Robyn? Have you and Lawrence run out of things to do already?" Graciela asked, perusing the room's contemporary design, which nevertheless gave the restaurant the feel of an informal cafe.

They sat inside, where the tables were pulled close together in the L-shaped room featuring a display kitchen at the back.

"You're hanging out with the girls," Graciela teased. "Don't tell me that the honeymoon's over already."

Jana chuckled, shaking her head. "The honeymoon is definitely not over. Lawrence changed his mind about going into the office today. Sofia was at the house cleaning, and I felt like I was in her way, so I left. Besides, I thought it would be nice if I treated my two favorite people in the world to a nice lunch."

"Who is Sofia?" Robyn asked before taking a long sip of ice water.

"She's the housekeeper."

"Well, of course," she said. "What was I thinking?"

Jana laughed. "Robyn, stop it. I know you didn't think Lawrence cleaned the house himself. Sofia's been with him for years."

Reaching for her chai tea, Graciela asked, "So, *mi'ja*, what are you gonna do all day long in that mansion now that you're not in school and not working at the boutique?"

"I don't have a clue," Jana confessed. "Lawrence suggested that I do some volunteer work for a charity. I like staying busy, so I've got to find a way to keep from being bored to death."

"I still don't get why he wanted you to quit college," Robyn said with a frown. "It's not like you don't have enough time to complete your studies. Getting your degree won't hurt—it can only help."

Jana loved her sister dearly, but Robyn's constant comments about withdrawing from Bible college were grating on Jana's nerves. She had done what her husband had asked of her—it was as simple as that. "Lawrence wanted me to be a full-time wife. I thought you understood that, Robyn."

"And do what?" Graciela inquired. "You don't have to clean the house—you have a maid for that. You guys will probably eat out a lot. Didn't you tell me that you're having dinner at somebody else's house every night this week?"

Jana nodded, trying to come up with a good answer. "We'll also be entertaining clients and having guests over at our house. I'll oversee that."

Graciela chuckled. "Robyn, did you hear your sister? She'll *oversee* the dinner parties. *La dee da . . .*"

Jana uncomfortably took a sip of her mocha latte. "You know what I mean."

Robyn checked her watch. "Ladies, I need to leave. I have to get back to the boutique to take care of the new inventory."

"Do you need any help?" Jana asked. "I was going to spend some more of this allowance money Lawrence allotted me, but I can help you instead."

Robyn and Graciela exchanged looks.

" 'Allowance money'?" Robyn repeated.

Jana tried to play it down. "He's giving me two grand a month—that doesn't include my clothing allowance or any household bills." She stopped short. "What am I supposed to do with two thousand dollars a month?"

Graciela held out her hand. "Help a sista out. I changed my mind. I like Poppy. I like him a lot."

"I didn't make that much when I was working," Jana said. "Don't get me wrong—I'm grateful, and I know I can come up with things to spend it on. It's just that I'm not like that."

"One thing you better do is have your checking account statements sent to Robyn's house and start putting aside some of that money every month," Graciela advised. "Don't transfer it. Take out cash and deposit it into your mad fund."

"Mad fund?"

"Yeah," Robyn agreed. "Have some backup for when he gets mad and acts a fool. I love me some Daniel, but I do have my mad fund."

Jana was appalled by the idea. "I didn't know that."

"I just put a little into it every month—I've never had to go into it, so I have a nice little nest egg saved. I was thinking about using some of it for a romantic getaway." Her eyes turned dreamy. "Daniel and I need a vacation, and we've always talked about taking a fourteen-day cruise to the Mediterranean. He's been working so hard."

"He needs to hire another assistant pastor," Jana stated. "I keep telling him that. But back to the secret savings account. I don't want to do anything behind Lawrence's back."

"Didn't you just tell us that the money is yours?" Graciela questioned. "Is he gonna want an accounting of it every month?"

Jana shook her head.

"So if you took out five hundred dollars cash once a week, it's not gonna bother him, right?"

"Right," Jana agreed.

"Then what's the problem?" Graciela finished her drink.

"I guess there really isn't one. I just don't want to start my marriage off with secrets."

Graciela met her gaze straight on. "Girl, you think Lawrence don't have his own secrets?"

LAWRENCE WOKE UP EARLY Sunday morning and announced that they would attend services at his church.

"I've been to a couple of nondenominational churches. What is yours like?" She had grown up in a Baptist environment steeped in tradition passed down from father to son. Daniel's father had built Jefferson Street Baptist.

"It's not like what you're used to, Jana," he told her. "We are a very nontraditional church, and that's what I like about New Vision Christian Center. We don't follow religious traditions," Lawrence said. "We follow the Bible."

"I like that," Jana replied uncertainly. When she and Lawrence had been dating, he had attended services with her most Sundays because she was a Sunday school teacher at her brother-in-law's church. They had discussed which church they would attend after their wedding, and Jana had decided to give his a chance before making a decision.

They arrived at church seconds before Ron and Lela Boykin. They all walked into the sanctuary together. Jana had on a sleek black pantsuit by Calvin Klein, while Lela wore a tangerine-colored dress with pleating around the bottom.

Several people came over to congratulate Lawrence and Jana on their marriage before taking their seats.

"Is everyone always so friendly?" she whispered.

Lawrence nodded. He led her up toward the front, where they sat down in the third row beside Lela and Ron.

Jana didn't know what it was, but she didn't really get into the service like she normally did when her brother-in-law preached. *Maybe I shouldn't compare this pastor to Daniel*, she thought.

Her mouth dropped open in shock when Pastor Laney stated, "The name Adam consists of two syllables—A-DAM—and means 'an obstruction.' I need you to hear me now. Adam signified the obstacle that the serpent would impose between man and his Creator. That obstacle was sin."

That's not correct, she wanted to shout. The Hebrew word for "earth" is *adama*. God formed man from the dust of the earth and that connection with earth was the basis for Adam's name.

Pastor Laney then moved on to discuss the blessings of Abraham.

"God doesn't want us to come to Him and ask for whatever we desire. Read Galatians 3, where it talks about the blessings of Abraham. Why would anyone want to be a Christian if we were walking around all bound up and broke?"

Jana glanced over at Lawrence, who was nodding his head in agreement.

This book was a reproof, warning the Galatians' church not to revert back to the law, for they were justified not by the law but by faith, which was the real blessing of Abraham. It had nothing to do with receiving material blessings. Pastor Laney was giving out incorrect information to his flock, but there was something more about Pastor Laney that bothered her. She studied the man in the pulpit, reading his body language. Jana just couldn't put her finger on it, but she knew that God would reveal whatever it was in time.

Maybe she could get Lawrence to reconsider attending Daniel's church. Jana was comfortable there, knew that her brother-in-law was diligent in his biblical studies. She didn't really feel led to leave.

"What was going on with you in service?" Lawrence asked when they were in the car and on the way to the country club for brunch.

"Pastor Laney twisted the scriptures, and it bothered me. That's what's wrong with a lot of the churches today: Congregations are being fed the wrong messages, and if you don't study for yourself—"

"Jana, I know you went to Bible college, but how do you know that what you've been taught is right? Unless you read the original documents, you have no choice but to trust your pastor. Laney knows the word of God. He has his doctorate and he's written a couple of nonfiction books."

"I'm not saying he did it deliberately. He was probably taught that same thing, but it is wrong. Galatians was not about naming it and claiming it in Jesus' name. It was showing that faith was the blessing of Abraham—not material wealth, as a lot of people imply."

"I'm sure there is more than one way to interpret a lot of the scripture," Lawrence responded.

Jana agreed. "But that's why we are to search the Bible for ourselves and ask God to rightly divine the word for us."

He released a sigh. "Jana, I know you would rather be at your brother-in-law's church, but I like my church, and this is where we're going to worship."

"I feel more comfortable at Daniel's church, and I thought you were enjoying it as well, since that's where we went while we were dating."

"I gave it a chance, and it's not where I want to worship, Jana. I didn't get much out of it. Daniel's preaching bored me. I'm sorry, but it's the truth."

Lawrence showed no signs of relenting, so Jana let the subject drop for the moment.

Chapter 5

LAWRENCE KEPT NAGGING JANA about scheduling a shopping date with Lela Boykin until she finally relented. Frankly, she was tired of hearing his mouth on the subject. He kept trying to convince her that it was just an opportunity for them to get to know each other, but Jana believed he really had a problem with the way she dressed. It whittled at her self-confidence if she thought about it long enough.

She walked out of her closet and made a phone call before making her way downstairs, where she walked into his home office and announced, "I just got off the phone with Lela. We're going to the mall to do some shopping before having lunch."

His head lifted and he turned with a broad smile. "I'm glad you finally decided to listen to me," he said. "Trust me; Lela has exquisite taste when it comes to fashion."

"Lawrence, I can shop for myself," Jana responded in a dry tone. "But I agreed to spend the day with Lela Boykin because I know it's something you want me to do."

"I think you two should get to really know each other. We are going to be spending a lot of time together."

Jana wasn't sure yet if she liked the idea. Running her fingers through her short hair, she said, "Oh, I thought it was because you pretty much said I need a stylist."

A shadow crossed his face and he shot back, "Don't be petty, Jana." He pushed away from his desk and stood up.

"I'm being honest," she said, not backing down. "I can't believe you actually want someone to dress me. Lawrence, do you know how that makes me feel? I've worked in my sister's boutique from the time I was sixteen years old. I went on my first buying trip at eighteen. Just because I prefer jeans and T-shirts doesn't mean that I have no fashion sense."

She followed Lawrence out of his office and into the kitchen.

"We've already been over this," Lawrence uttered, his lips puckered with annoyance. "I am not in the mood to rehash all this." He sat down at the table and picked up the newspaper. "What are we having for breakfast?"

Jana resisted the urge to toss the multicolored bowl on the breakfast bar at her husband's head.

"Did you hear me?" Lawrence asked. His stare drilled into her.

"You can fix a bowl of cereal," she answered pointedly. "I need to go upstairs and get ready for my date with Lela."

Jana half expected Lawrence to follow her and offer an apology, but he didn't come upstairs. Pushing away her disappointment, she slipped on a pair of jeans and a tank top.

She left the house fifteen minutes later.

"I'm so glad that you were able to join me for a day of pampering and shopping," Lela said when Jana drove up and parked beside her. "I hope Lawrence didn't have to push you too much."

"He didn't," Jana lied. She didn't want to risk hurting Lela's feelings.

Lela smiled. "Great. I really want us to become friends."

Jana admired the sleek black Mercedes S class parked beside her five-year-old Ford Explorer. Lawrence had a year-old BMW 528i sitting in the garage, and Jana wished for a moment that she had driven that automobile instead. It looked much better than her SUV, with its fading green color.

They strolled along the sidewalks of Rodeo Drive as they talked.

"Lela, what do you do with your time?" Jana asked out of curiosity.

Aside from complaining about the traffic, talking Hollywood gossip, and struggling to stay away from carbs, Lela didn't seem to have much to do.

"I shop."

Jana smiled. She knew that much was true. Like someone training for the Olympics, Lela was definitely dedicated. She had their shopping spree all mapped out.

Jana followed Lela into Bebe.

"I'm only kidding about the shopping," Lela informed her. "I volunteer with Habitat for Humanity—I'm the editor of their newsletter. I'm also on the board of a couple of charities. I try to stay busy."

"Did you go to college?" she inquired. "Please tell me if I'm being too nosy."

Lela dismissed her concern with a slight wave of her manicured hand. "Oh, you're fine. I went to Temple University, but never finished." She held up a striped banded-style dress in red and black. "Oh, Jana . . . this would look stunning on you."

Jana eyed the skimpy outfit in Lela's hand with horror. "Oh, I don't know about that, Lela, that's not really my style."

"I'm telling you—this is perfect for you," Lela insisted, holding it up to Jana. "At least try it on. Lawrence will love something like this on you."

Jana wrinkled up her face. There wasn't much to try on. "You really think so?"

Lela nodded. "Trust me, this was made for you."

Jana still wasn't convinced. "Maybe I should get it in a bigger size, though. I think this one might be a little too tight for me."

Shaking her head, Lela responded, "This dress was made to hug your curves. Jana, if I don't know anything else, I know fashion. This is the type of outfit Lawrence wants to see on his wife."

"I don't know about this, Lela." Jana chewed on her bottom lip. How could Lela really know what Lawrence liked or disliked?

"I'm going to pass on that one," she told Lela. "It's just not me."

After walking around and finding nothing to Jana's liking, they moved on to another store.

"So what did you think of Pastor Laney?" Lela asked when they entered La Perla. "I'm sure he's not exactly what you expected. Lawrence told me that your brother is a minister."

"Daniel's my brother-in-law," Jana corrected. She tried to think of something nice to say. "Pastor Laney is very forward-thinking, while Daniel is very traditional. They're very different people."

Lela smiled, though she kept her eyes hooded. "He's quite the liberal."

Jana agreed. "Lawrence told me he was a member of a progressive church, but I guess I'm so steeped in tradition that it's going to take some getting used to."

"Religious traditions have nothing to do with the word of God," Lela said a bit too forcefully. "I like NVC because it is a Bible-teaching church."

"How long have you and Ron been members of NVC?"

"For as long as we've been married," Lela answered. "Pastor Laney married us."

The thought brought back an unpleasant memory. "Lawrence wanted him to marry us as well, but I really wanted Daniel to do it." They'd had a big fight over her insistence that they marry at her brother-in-law's church.

Lela slowed her pace, pausing to check the price of a shirt on one of the clothing racks. "Lawrence really loves you, Jana. I hope you know that."

"I love him too."

Lela broke into a smile. "I can tell. You have the look of a woman in love. We're both very lucky women. Ron can work a nerve, but I do love him like crazy."

"I guess we can all say that about each other," Jana contributed. "I'm sure I've gotten on Lawrence's nerves since we've been married. It's part of getting to know each other and understanding what our love languages are."

Lela chuckled. "I read that book too. Ron and I are totally opposites of each other except for our love language." Almost as if speaking from the book, she said, "We both like gifts and words of affirmation."

"I'm into quality time," Jana stated. "Gifts are nice, but it's not really my love language. Lawrence's love language is words of affirmation."

Lela stopped at a rack of lingerie. "This is gorgeous," she exclaimed, lifting out a sheer peignoir.

It *was* nice, but definitely not something she would wear, Jana thought. "That can't be the right price," she uttered when she glimpsed the four-hundred-dollar price tag.

"It is," Lela confirmed. "I think I'm getting it. Ron is going to love it!"

"He should at that price for something so skimpy. That's not even a yard of fabric."

"Less is more," Lela said with a laugh.

"It is nice." Jana picked up another item from the Black Label collection. It had flocked polka dots that swamped the tulle base of an underwire bustier. "This is gorgeous."

Jana ran her finger across the delicate braiding and velvet trimmings. She noted the metal heart that read "Made with Love."

"You should get that top and wear it with these." Lela held up a pair of G-string panties. "I'm telling you, your husband will lose his mind when he sees you in something so sexy."

Her enthusiasm overcame Jana's doubts. "You really think so?"

"Lawrence is going to love it, Jana."

Jana examined the bustier, revolving it on its hanger. "I still have to wrap my head around the price. I've never paid more than fifteen dollars for a pair of underwear. That G-string is ninety-five dollars." Jana gave Lela a sidelong glance of utter disbelief. "Five hundred dollars for lingerie?"

"Welcome to your life as Mrs. Lawrence Maxwell Collins."

JANA EYED HER REFLECTION in her bedroom mirror.

Lela had talked her into getting a facial and a makeover after lunch. Jana had to admit she liked the new mineral makeup and the way it felt on her skin. She ran her hand down the side of her new form-fitting dress, loving the feel of the soft silk.

She was curvier than she'd realized—at least that's the way it looked in this dress. Jana hoped that Lawrence didn't think it was too fitting. It wasn't tight or anything; instead, the black-and-white garment hugged her curves lovingly.

"You look beautiful," Lawrence complimented from the doorway. "I love that dress."

Jana smiled, then turned around to face him. "I didn't know you were home."

"I just got here," Lawrence replied. "Perfect timing, I see."

"I'm glad you like the dress. For the record—I picked it out. Lela wanted me to buy another one, but this one looked more like me."

"You won't get a complaint from me. In fact, I can't wait to take you out tonight. I'm looking forward to showing you off." His eyes traveled from her face to her chest and downward.

"Lawrence, you don't need to show me off. I'm not dressing for anyone but you, honey."

He winked at her. "It pleases me when other men admire my beautiful wife. It thrills me when I see the look of envy on their faces."

"I guess I feel the same way whenever I see a woman watching you," Jana admitted. "There's that part of me that goes, Yes, he's fine and he's mine."

Lawrence chuckled, clapping his hands. "Let me take a quick shower and change. I'm taking you out for a romantic dinner."

"I cooked dinner," Jana called after him, "but it'll keep until tomorrow."

While Lawrence was in the bathroom, she studied her reflection once more. Jana was pleased to see how much he loved her dress. She'd have to find a few more similar in style.

Jana's mind traveled back to the day she'd met Lawrence. She'd been in her car, leaving Los Angeles Bible College in a hurry. She'd been on her cell phone and not paying attention. Jana had ended up in a fender bender when she'd hit Lawrence's Mercedes.

While she'd been near hysterics, he'd acted surprisingly calm and hadn't seemed angry over the accident. He'd been more concerned about her. They'd exchanged phone numbers.

A week later, Lawrence had called and asked Jana out to dinner. Six months after their first date, he'd asked her to marry him.

Lawrence was dressed and ready fifteen minutes later.

As they left the house, Jana inquired, "Where are we going?"

"You said that you've never tried Japanese food before, so I thought I'd take you to Koi Restaurant. You're going to love it."

Jana frowned. "I don't think I'm going to like sushi."

"You'll like it," he assured her. "If you don't mind, I'll order for you tonight."

"I trust you," Jana responded with a grin.

She felt safe with Lawrence. He was a wonderful husband despite the fact that he could be moody at times. Jana made a mental note not to take his mood swings personally. He loved her, and it showed in everything he did for her.

They drove to West Hollywood, where the restaurant was located. Jana didn't realize they had arrived until she saw the line of cars waiting for valet service and the paparazzi outside, hoping to catch Hollywood icons coming and going.

Inside the restaurant, Jana checked out the dimly lit surroundings and the romantic ambiance. Sushi chefs greeted them with a nod, and a member of the waitstaff seated them.

"How was your day?" Jana asked Lawrence while they waited for their beverages to arrive.

"Okay," Lawrence responded. "I'm in court all day tomorrow, so I prepared for that case."

"I'd like to come to court one day just to see you in action." Jana took a sip of water. "I know that you're a great attorney."

"I love my job," he replied. "I've always wanted to be a lawyer for as long as I can remember."

"I wanted to study law at one point," Jana said. "Then I considered going to school to be a doctor. I was interested in psychology, so that's what I studied at Cal-Poly. When I graduated, I was thinking about applying to law school, but then a couple of years ago, I decided to attend Los Angeles Bible College."

Lawrence met her gaze. "Do you regret dropping out?"

Jana shook her head. "I don't. Being your wife is my most important role at this moment."

The waiter arrived to take their orders.

Lawrence reached over and squeezed her hand. "You trust me?"

She nodded back at him without speaking.

"We will start with the baked crab rolls, the salmon skin roll, and the baked scallop on a California roll. For our entrees, my wife will have the seafood tempura, and I'll have the grilled lamb chops."

Jana smiled as the waiter walked away. "Everything sounds good. I can't wait to try it."

"You really look beautiful," Lawrence told her. He gazed all around. "Baby, the men in this room can't keep their eyes off you."

Her smile disappeared. "I don't want that kind of attention, Lawrence."

"Looks can't harm you."

Jana noticed that a man sitting at one of the tables beside them kept staring at her. She shifted uncomfortably in her chair. "Maybe I should've worn a jacket or something."

"Why?" Lawrence asked.

"That man keeps staring at me—at my chest."

He laughed. "Honey, he can look, but if he wants to keep his nose straight, he won't come near you." He fired a hostile look at the guy, who suddenly found his wife more interesting. "Jana, you can't stop people from looking at you. It's not against the law."

"I think it's disrespectful," she uttered.

"Jana, the man isn't doing anything—not really."

Their food arrived.

After saying a blessing, Jana sampled her entree.

"How do you like it?" Lawrence asked.

"It's delicious," Jana responded with true warmth. She wiped her mouth with the edge of her napkin. "How's yours?"

"Oh, it's good."

Jana and Lawrence continued to make small talk over dinner.

Lawrence couldn't stop commenting on her new dress. "You're beautiful, you have an incredible body, and you're a great cook," he exclaimed. "I hit the jackpot when I met you, baby."

"I'm pretty smart too," Jana stated with a smile.

He clearly wasn't amused. "I'm aware of that."

Jana reached over and covered his hand with her own. "Honey, you need to stop being so serious all the time. Lighten up, will you?"

Lawrence returned his attention to his plate.

Shrugging nonchalantly, Jana did the same. She told herself that he was probably exhausted from preparing for his new case. However, whatever it was, she hoped it would pass soon. Jana loved her husband dearly but did not care for his mood swings.

"Are you in the mood for dessert?" she asked.

The look he gave her had nothing to do with anything on the menu.

Jana broke into a smile. "I guess we should ask for the check."

"You read my mind," he whispered.

Lawrence quickly paid the check, and they were happily on their way home.

Jana couldn't stop smiling. This kind of attention she liked—her husband's attention. He was a wonderful and attentive husband.

Chapter 6

THE NEXT MORNING, JANA got up early because she wanted to run some errands before meeting up with Lela and Angie for an early lunch at the Beverly Hills Country Club. She didn't know Angie, but Lela had told her that she was married to a Hollywood movie producer, that she was petite and blond, and that her signature color was white. Jana still hadn't put any thought to her color. After last night, she supposed it was red, for passion.

Jana was the first to arrive.

Angie showed up within ten minutes. She was exactly as Lela had described. Jana admired the white sundress but thought it was a little too snug for a woman built like Angie.

I would never wear something so tight. The last thing I want to do is bring attention to these mounds of flesh on my chest.

Jana had wanted to have a breast reduction, but Lawrence had been adamantly against it. Lawrence felt she should be proud of her body, but she wasn't—she hated the fact that she was so well-endowed.

"How are you, darling?" Angie asked.

"Great," Jana responded. "It's good to see you again."

At that moment, Lela blew through the front doors of the restaurant. "I'm so sorry I'm late," she said. "Traffic was a nightmare."

Angie laughed. "We're in Los Angeles, hon. Traffic is always a nightmare."

Jana secretly surveyed Angie as they waited to be seated.

She looks like an aging porn star.

Her attention turned to Lela. "Lawrence loved the dress."

"Did he?" she asked, delighted. "That's wonderful."

"What dress?" Angie inquired. "What did I miss?"

"We went shopping yesterday and Jana found a dress and some sexy lingerie from La Perla that she thought Lawrence would like."

"Just one?" Angie wanted to know. "I can never leave a store with just one bag."

"Neither can I," Lela admitted. "But Jana's a much more disciplined shopper. I was impressed."

"I was the buyer for my sister's store, so I've learned to work well within a budget."

They sat down near a huge picture window.

Angie ordered a glass of white wine, then said, "So, Jana, tell me more about yourself. You mentioned that you were a store buyer."

Something about the woman's manner put Jana on guard. "Let's see . . . I'm not that much of a shopper, but it's because I never really had to be. My sister owns a boutique, so all of my clothes have come from her store and from vendors when I was on buying trips."

"What's the name of her boutique?"

"Robyn's," Jana responded. "That's her name."

"Oh, okay. I've been in there," Angie said, losing interest. "It's a beautiful store, but the clothing's not really my style."

"Her customers are mainly women who work in corporate America. Her clothing is designed for the more conservative."

"Well, that's certainly not me," Angie uttered with a chuckle.

The way Angie was staring at her made Jana pick up her menu.

Lela leaned forward and said, "I think I'm having the pecan-crusted salmon. It sounds like it'll be delicious."

"I'll have the same," Jana seconded. "It does sound wonderful."

Angie had two more glasses of wine before the waiter brought their meals to the table. Jana was concerned that she wouldn't be able to drive home, but she seemed to hold her alcohol well.

Angie dove into her Chinese chicken salad without a word of thanks-giving. Lela also was going to dive in, but she paused as Jana closed her eyes and said a silent prayer.

They made small talk while they ate.

"I called Ellen's people to see if we can get her to be our mistress of ceremonies," Angie said. "If I don't hear anything by the end of today, then I'll check to see if we can get Whoopi."

Jana sipped her iced tea as she listened.

"Have you gotten all of the door prizes yet?" Lela inquired.

Angie responded, "All but two of them. I'll have everything by the week's end."

Before they went their separate ways, Angie managed to enlist Jana's help on the upcoming charity fashion show and luncheon.

Lela grabbed Jana by the elbow. "What did I tell you? Didn't I say that she would do that?"

Jana smiled easily. "I don't mind. It's not like I have a job to go to."

At home, Jana changed clothes and decided to spend the rest of her day working outside. She had picked up some vividly hued roses to add more color to the garden.

Before going outside, however, she put a chicken into her Crock-Pot, prepared her vegetables, and took her homemade yeast rolls out of the freezer.

Her dinner taken care of, Jana strolled outdoors, humming softly.

She didn't know how much time passed as she planted her rose bushes. Hearing the garage door go up, Jana walked around to the front of the house. Lawrence was home, but to her dismay, he hadn't come home alone. He brought a couple of men with him.

He frowned as he scanned her from head to toe. "Why aren't you dressed?" he hissed in a low voice.

"Why didn't you tell me that you were bringing guests home for dinner?" Jana whispered. "Thank goodness I put a whole chicken in the Crock-Pot."

"Didn't you get my message? I called and left a voice mail for you. I said that I was bringing some clients home with me."

"You called on which phone? I had my cell with me outside."

"Why didn't you take the home phone out there too?" Lawrence wanted to know. "How can anyone reach you?"

"Keep your voice down," Jana said. "All you had to do was call me on my cell when I didn't answer the home phone." His face was implacable, and she shifted gears. "Lawrence, I'm sorry I didn't get the message, but instead of arguing with me, let me shower and change. The chicken is ready and the vegetables won't take that long. I've already made yeast rolls. It'll be okay."

"Do we have anything for dessert?"

Jana nodded. "I made a strawberry cake. We have some pound cake left too, if they don't eat strawberries."

Lawrence was clearly not happy. "I would've preferred salmon for dinner, but the chicken will have to do."

Jana glared at him. He was acting like a spoiled brat.

Lawrence took a step backward, saying, "I'm going to go attend to our guests. Please hurry."

Jana made her apologies and rushed inside the house. She ran up the stairs and jumped into the shower.

She was back downstairs inside of fifteen minutes. Thank goodness she'd prepared dinner before going outside.

Lawrence eased up behind her as she sliced up the chicken. "You look beautiful," he whispered.

Jana didn't respond to his compliment. She knew this was just his way of trying to make up with her, but it wasn't going to work this time. She still resented the way he'd talked to her. "I need to get this on the table so your guests can eat dinner."

His smile disappeared, but Jana was gone before he could open his mouth to comment.

She pasted on a smile and acted the loving wife all through dinner and dessert. Jana didn't want anyone to know that she and Lawrence were at odds with one another. She would never embarrass him that way.

If only he had given her the same respect.

After everyone left, Lawrence helped her clean up the kitchen.

"Everything was delicious."

"Thank you," she said shortly.

When they were finished, Lawrence tried to pull her into his arms.

"I'm sorry, Lawrence," Jana stated, stepping out of his reach. "I'm just not in the mood. You can't talk to me like I'm nothing in front of your clients and then expect me to make love afterward."

He sighed. "Why am I not surprised? I knew you still had an attitude. Jana, all I did was ask why you didn't take the phone outside with you."

"You treated me like I was your child and not your wife. Lawrence, I'm grown, and I won't allow you to talk to me any kind of way." She walked over to the door on her way to leave. "Sorry, but it's just not happening."

"I'm sorry," Lawrence said. "I don't want to argue with you. This is not how I would like to end the evening."

Jana met his gaze. "It's not what I had in mind either. I appreciate your apology, Lawrence, but I need you to understand that I'll not be disrespected. You really hurt me earlier."

"Now you're overreacting."

He always had to control the agenda. He wanted to make how she felt fit into how she was supposed to feel—according to Lawrence.

"This is exactly what I'm talking about." Jana shook her head sadly. "I'm going upstairs to change for bed. I can't deal with you right now."

Chapter 7

TROUBLED, JANA LEFT THE house shortly after Lawrence went to work.

She had spent most of the night tossing and turning. This morning her husband had readied himself for work without so much as a word to her. It was obvious that Lawrence was upset because she had refused to make love with him.

After he left, she picked up the phone to call him but changed her mind. Jana decided she needed to stand her ground. She wasn't the one who was wrong. Lawrence had no right to treat her like a child.

Jana drove to her sister's boutique. Robyn had received a new shipment and would need some extra hands getting it unpacked, steamed, and ticketed.

"What's wrong?" Robyn asked when she saw the troubled expression on her sister's face.

"Lawrence and I had a fight," Jana announced. "He got upset because he brought home some clients for dinner last night and I wasn't ready. Mind you, this is without telling me that we were having guests over. When they arrived, I had on some old jeans and a T-shirt. I'd been working in the yard and I wasn't expecting to have company."

"He didn't call to give you a heads-up?" Robyn asked.

"Lawrence called home but I was outside, I guess. I didn't bother to check voice mail." Her eyes flashed with irritation. "I figured if I didn't answer the home phone, he would just call me on my cell. I had it outside with me."

"I assume you explained all that to him."

She nodded. "I did, but Lawrence feels that I should've taken the house phone outside with me." Jana released a short sigh of frustration. "He can be so difficult at times. Then, after everyone left, he wanted to make love. There was no way I was doing that." Eyeing her sister, Jana asked, "Was I wrong?"

Robyn embraced her. "Jana, you two are still getting to know each other. It'll work itself out—just wait and see."

Jana walked over to a box and peered down at its opened top. "I just want him to lighten up. Sometimes Lawrence acts like he's my father instead of my spouse."

"I think you just need to tell Lawrence how he makes you feel."

"I know I should," Jana responded. "But I'm just trying to keep the peace. We haven't been married all that long and like you said—we're still getting used to each other. I don't want to be too critical of him."

"Bathe your words in love when you discuss this with Lawrence," Robyn advised. "Don't accuse him of anything—just share the way his words make you feel. He needs to know your love language and how best to communicate with you. You need to know the same of him."

Her sister had always been her mentor; Robyn was so sensible. "You're right." Jana gave her sister a hug. "Thanks for the advice."

She looked back down at the box. "I've been meaning to talk to you more about expanding the boutique. You could design, manufacture, and resell your own designs under the Robbi label."

"I don't have enough designs for a store, Jana."

Jana had heard this argument before. "It could be a one-stop shop that carries all accessories or items that complement any dress—from shoes and handbags to lingerie and beauty products. The new boutique would also carry labels such as Robert Rodriguez, Ingwa Melero, and Vanitas in addition to other independent designers like yourself—Sophia & Chloé, Shelley Beckett, and La Befana."

Robyn paused, intrigued by the idea. "If I did something like that, I'd want you to manage the store, Jana."

"If you definitely decide to do this, just let me know. I really feel in my spirit that this is the next step for you, Robyn. You have some wonderful designs. I even think you should consider doing a bridal line. I'm still getting compliments on my wedding gown."

Jana left the boutique and drove home. A smile tugged at her lips. A verse from the Bible had come to her, and she knew it was just right for what ailed her marriage.

WHEN JANA GOT HOME, she headed straight to the sunroom. She enjoyed sitting there, admiring the afternoon sunlight as she read her Bible.

She closed her eyes and said a quick prayer before reading the first chapter in the book of Esther.

Jana wrote down what she felt God was saying in the scriptures.

> King Ahasuerus was humiliated because he had gone to great expense showing off his wealth and power. Now he wanted to show off his most beautiful possession—his wife. When she refused, he felt like a common man who could not even get his wife to do a simple thing for him. His family structure was the example for the rest of his vast kingdom. He felt disrespected.

Jana read over what she had written, then added the following:

> There may have been cause for Queen Vashti to feel uncomfortable with her husband's request. In my opinion, to make such a public refusal would require a great deal of boldness and confidence.
>
> My first impression of Queen Vashti after reading the scripture was that of a rude and undisciplined woman. Now I'm beginning to think differently about this woman we know so little about and who

*basically fades to nothingness after the first chapter. What was the
real story? What was her reason for refusing the king?*

Jana sat there, letting her mind wander. Queen Vashti intrigued
her, prompting her to want to find out as much as she could about the
woman.

Lawrence sat down at the table to read the newspaper while she prepared their plates. Jana brought their food to the table.

"Thanks, babe," he muttered.

"I was reading about Queen Vashti this morning," Jana told him.
"What are your thoughts on her refusing her husband's request?"

Lawrence knew his verses. He preferred to do his Bible study in the
evenings, while she liked to get up early in the mornings. "She disrespected
him and he was right to divorce her," he said. "A wife is to submit to her
husband. If she doesn't, then why do you need someone like that in your
life?"

Jana didn't know why his words bothered her.

"WE'RE GOING TO LE Luxure Manoir tonight," Ron announced,
bursting into Lawrence's office. "You and Jana want to join us?"

"She's not ready," he answered as he watched Ron's face, analyzing his
reaction.

Ron displayed a flash of disappointment, but it disappeared as quickly
as it had come. "That's too bad." He leaned against the huge oak bookshelf.
"I was hoping we could have some fun tonight."

Lawrence agreed. "Jana is very naïve, so it's taking more time than I initially thought it would. It doesn't help that she's been brainwashed by that
closed-minded, religious-fanatic sister and brother-in-law of hers."

"Why don't you just tell her the truth? Or let Pastor Laney counsel
Jana?" Ron asked. "She does enjoy sex, right?"

"Ron, I can handle my own wife," Lawrence stated firmly. "I'll know when she's ready for the lifestyle. You saw what happened to Gia. I intend to be more careful this time. I love Jana, and I don't want to lose her."

Ron sat down in one of the visitor's chairs facing his desk. "Why don't you grab Rhoda and come out with us anyway?"

Lawrence considered his suggestion. He hadn't gone to the club since he'd gotten married, and he missed the excitement. He also enjoyed the attention of his secretary. They hadn't been together since he'd met Jana, although Rhoda had let him know that she was willing.

"I just might do that," he murmured. "I'll let you know by the end of the day."

Standing up, Ron said, "I need to head out of here. I have a deposition in an hour."

When he left, Lawrence picked up the telephone and called Jana. "Hey, babe."

"Hey, yourself," Jana responded. "I was just about to call you. I was thinking about making a roast for dinner tonight and wanted to know if you prefer mashed potatoes or rice."

"I'm working late this evening, so don't worry about it," Lawrence lied. He didn't like being dishonest, but he had desires that he'd pushed aside out of respect for his wife. He vowed that soon he would not have to keep secrets.

"Oh. Okay."

Lawrence heard the disappointment in her voice. "Have you started the roast already?" he asked.

Rhoda entered his office carrying a file. Her full breasts strained in protest against the tight knit shirt she was wearing, and when she bent in just the right way, he could tell she was wearing thong underwear.

Lawrence looked her over, smiling in appreciation, while he talked with Jana.

"I just pulled it out of the freezer to thaw. I was thinking we'd have a nice dinner tonight and spend some quality time together. That's all. It's not a big deal."

"Um . . . just save it for tomorrow unless you have a taste for it," Lawrence suggested, forcing his attention away from Rhoda. "I want to spend time with you too, but all that will have to wait until tomorrow. Just so that you know, babe, you don't have to cook for me every single night. I appreciate it, but there are times when I have to work late. It depends on the caseload."

Rhoda winked at him, then disappeared as quietly as she had come. Lawrence liked working with her because she was one of the few women who could actually separate business from pleasure. She had never once overstepped her boundaries or threatened to sue him for sexual harassment.

"I love cooking for you, Lawrence. I'll be fine," Jana was saying. "I'll just make a dinner salad for myself. We can have the roast tomorrow."

Lawrence coughed before he said, "Don't wait up for me."

"You're going to be *that* late?" Jana inquired.

"Yeah," he responded. "I'm working on a big case and I need to interview clients. There's still a lot that needs to be done."

"I guess that means that Rhoda will be working late as well," Jana said, concerned. "Don't work your secretary too late. Rhoda is still a single woman. She deserves to have a life outside of the office."

Amused by his wife's words, Lawrence broke into a smile. "She'll get a chance to enjoy her evening. I can promise you that."

He glanced up at the doorway and found Ron standing there, a big grin on his face. He gave Lawrence a thumbs-up sign.

"I have to go, babe. I have a client waiting. I'll see you later."

"Oh, okay. Well, don't work too hard," Jana said. "Wake me up when you get home, Lawrence."

"If it's not too late, I will."

"That's my man," Ron said when Lawrence hung up the phone. "We are going to have some fun tonight."

Chapter 8

T HE NEXT DAY WAS Friday. Lawrence came home that evening and announced that he was taking Jana on a date.

"Where are we going?" she asked.

"It's a surprise," was all that Lawrence would tell her, no matter how
much Jana pressed him. He seemed a little off. Maybe, she guessed, he was
feeling guilty for working so late. He hadn't gotten home until well after
midnight. She knew, because she'd awakened when he'd tried to ease into
the bedroom.

"Well, how should I dress?"

"To please me," was all that he would say. "Babe, you're not going to
get any more information than that."

Jana and Lela had gone to the Beverly Center earlier that day, so she
slipped on one of her new purchases, a fuchsia-colored dress that flattered
her curves in all the right places.

Lawrence beamed his approval as he checked her out from head to toe.
"That's perfect. Babe, you look beautiful."

"I'm glad you like it. When I saw it on the rack I knew that I needed to
buy it." Jana released a soft chuckle. "I guess it was screaming my name."

He took her to a beautiful restaurant with an ocean view in Marina Del
Rey. They decided to dine outside so that Jana could enjoy the picturesque
vista of the moonlight dancing on the water.

While they were waiting to be seated, a young woman who had been watching them from her stool in the bar suddenly got down and walked straight up to Lawrence.

"I haven't seen you in forever," she gushed, ignoring Jana. "Lawrence, where have you been hiding?"

She glanced over at Jana and pasted on a fake smile. "Hi, I'm Sherry."

Lawrence made the introduction. "This is my wife, Jana."

"I-I didn't know you'd remarried," Sherry stammered. "Congratulations."

Jana had never seen Lawrence look so uncomfortable. *What is wrong with him?* she wondered.

"How do you know her?" Jana questioned when Sherry strolled off to speak to someone else. She seemed to know quite a few customers dining in the restaurant.

Lawrence had recovered his usual face of stone. "She's an old client of mine."

Jana surveyed the scantily clad woman. "That's interesting. She doesn't look as if she can afford your services." *She looks more like a prostitute*, Jana thought.

"Looks can be deceiving."

She glanced up at her husband. "Meaning . . ."

He shrugged. "Just that. You can't judge a book by its cover. Sherry is a chemist."

Jana glanced over her shoulder. "Really? I never would've thought that by the way she's dressed. That dress looks like it was painted on her."

"Like I said, you can't judge a book by its cover."

Sherry sashayed over to their table and sat down without preamble. "I hope you two don't mind my joining you. It looks like my date is late or I've been stood up."

Lawrence didn't look at all pleased, and Jana couldn't help wondering if the sort of chemistry Sherry made wasn't cooked up in a lab.

"Your wife is beautiful, Lawrence," Sherry complimented. "We should get together soon."

"I don't think so." Jana eyed her husband in confusion. She couldn't understand why he was acting so annoyed. Maybe he didn't like mixing business with pleasure, but that didn't make much sense to Jana, as they usually spent a lot of time with his clients.

"Why don't you call your date to see if everything's okay?" he said rudely. "You never know—something could've happened to him."

"Lawrence . . . ," Jana cautioned.

"Hey, stuff happens all the time."

Sherry cut her eyes at Lawrence. "I guess I will go make that call." She rose to her feet. "It was nice meeting you, Jana. Hopefully I'll see you around."

"I hope you find your date," Lawrence told her.

He was making a valiant effort to hide his frustration, but Jana could hear it in his voice. "What's wrong with you, honey?" she asked after Sherry left their table. "Why do you have an attitude?"

He waved it off. "Sherry gets on my nerves. I don't want to deal with her any more than I have to," Lawrence said. Seeing her confusion, he let the tension in his voice soften. "Besides, tonight I just want to focus on you."

As they ate, she touched his arm. "I'm having a great time. These are the times that I cherish most. I love our time together."

"I'm glad."

Lawrence wore a bored expression on his face, which made Jana's smile disappear. "What's wrong?" she asked.

"Nothing, baby. I'm just sitting here watching you."

"You look bored to death, Lawrence."

"I'm not," he argued, then admitted, "I'm tired, Jana. I worked all day, but I wanted to spend some quality time with you."

"We can eat dessert at home, if you'd like," she told him. Jana didn't really want to leave, but her husband was tired. He'd been thoughtful enough to take her on this surprise date—she didn't want to make him regret it.

"You sure you won't mind?" Lawrence questioned.

"We can go."

On the way home, Lawrence glanced over at Jana. "I'm sorry, honey. I really wanted to make this evening special for you. I was going to take you out to a jazz club. I didn't realize how tired I was."

"It's fine," she responded. "I know how hard you've been working lately. I'll be glad when this case is over."

"Me too."

Lawrence went upstairs and showered as soon as they got home. Jana sat down on the edge of her bed to remove her shoes.

She picked up Lawrence's jacket and stood up to take it to his walk-in closet.

Something fell to the floor.

Jana bent down to retrieve it.

She frowned as she eyed the napkin, reading the words *Le Luxure Manoir*.

What is this? she wondered. Jana stuck it back in his pocket, deciding that it was probably somewhere he took his clients. Lawrence and his part-ners often entertained their VIP clients, as he called them.

Lawrence strolled out of the bathroom in his pajamas. He yawned be-fore crawling into bed.

"You look exhausted," Jana murmured.

"I am."

She considered asking him about the napkin, but as she noted the weary expression on his face, she decided it was something that could wait.

"WHAT ARE YOU DOING here?" Robyn asked when Jana strolled through the front door of the boutique Saturday morning around ten thirty. "Aren't you supposed to be at home living the life of a woman of leisure?"

"I didn't feel like sitting at home all day long so I figured I'd come and help out in the shop." She followed her sister to the back of the store.

Jana's eyes surveyed the stacks of boxes that had come in the day be-fore. "You got in a pretty big shipment."

"This is the newest Ana Riel suit collection."

Jana carefully opened one of the boxes. "Oooh, Robyn . . . I love this suit," she murmured. "This is why I love helping out when you get new shipments. I get first pick."

Robyn laughed. "You're like a kid in a candy store. Seriously, I really appreciate your helping me out. I need to hire another employee—just haven't gotten around to it. We've been pretty busy." She indicated the back door. Behind it was a small studio where she did some of her drawing. "I'm designing some bridesmaid gowns for one of my customers. Another customer wants me to design a wedding suit for her. This is her second marriage and she doesn't want to go all out with a wedding dress."

"I guess I can understand that," Jana said as she removed another suit from the carton. "These are so nice. . . ."

She worked most of the afternoon unpacking and steaming the inventory. Finally, Jana checked the clock and told Robyn, "I need to get going. I want to have dinner all warmed up and ready by the time Lawrence gets home from the office. He went in today to clear some of the cases on his desk." Jana smiled. "I'm trying to be a good wife."

"You are," Robyn confirmed. "Thanks so much for your help."

"Call me if you need me to come by here on Monday. It's not like I have anything pressing to do. I can cancel my tennis lesson." The sisters exchanged a glance and started laughing.

Jana gave Robyn a hug, then left the boutique.

"Where were you?" Lawrence demanded when she got back home.

"I was at the shop with Robyn," Jana responded. "When the new inventory arrives, I go over and help her out. I thought I would be back before you came home. Lawrence, what's wrong?"

"I expected you to be home."

She could tell he was in one of his moods. "Dinner's ready—I just need to warm it up," Jana said. "What in the world is your problem?"

"I don't have a problem," he snapped. "Just an expectation that my wife will be home waiting for me. It's not like you need the money. I give you an allowance."

"She isn't paying me, Lawrence. I just went to help my sister with her store." Seeing his aggrieved look, Jana folded her arms across her chest. "Look, I don't want to fight with you. You said you didn't mind if I volunteered my time—well, that's what I did."

"I don't want Robyn taking advantage of you."

"She's not," Jana argued. "She wouldn't do that, and besides, Robyn didn't even know I was going to be there."

She marched off, and he went to his home office.

Irked, Jana went through the stack of mail that Sofia had left on the sofa table in the foyer. She opened an envelope bearing her name written in a feminine handwriting. This was perfect, she thought. It was time for Lawrence to do some bending.

"Graciela's throwing her husband a surprise birthday party," Jana announced as she entered his office. "It's next Saturday."

"I suppose you'd like to attend."

She kept her voice light. "Of course I would. They're my friends. Don't you want to go?"

"Like you said, they're *your* friends, sweetheart."

Why was she not surprised by his attitude? "They would be hurt if we didn't come to the party, Lawrence. They are like family to me."

"I didn't say that we wouldn't attend, sweetheart. You asked if I *wanted* to go, and I was just being honest. Our relationship is built on honesty, right?"

"We're going to have a lot of fun," she said, chuckling, trying to lighten the mood. "Graciela really knows how to throw a party."

Lawrence gave her a tight smile.

Jana decided to let the matter drop for the moment. She held out a stack of mail to him. "These are all for you."

He took the envelopes out of her hand. "Thanks, babe." He perused the stack quickly, flipping through the addresses. "You know that we don't have to have the same friends," he noted. "You can hang out with your friends without me."

"I know that," Jana replied. "But this is a party. I want you to be there with me, as it will be mostly couples in attendance."

Lawrence laid the mail down on the desk. She could tell by his face that he was giving in. "I don't want to talk about Graciela or her husband anymore. I just want to focus on you. Jana, I know I haven't been the easiest person to live with lately. I'm sorry about that, but I appreciate your patience."

"I'm your wife, Lawrence. It's my job to be patient and understanding."

"It's not your job to take abuse. I'm aware that I've been a little snappish, but I'm going to try and work on that. You didn't deserve being talked to that way."

She wrapped her arms around him. "Taking ownership for your actions is the first step," Jana said. "Lawrence, I love you so much more for this. I know that we're going to have our ups and downs, but as long as we talk to each other"—she turned her head to look him in the eye—"we're going to be fine."

Chapter 9

J ANA WALKED OUT OF Graciela's house when Lawrence pulled into the driveway and parked beside her SUV. She was wearing the salmon-colored strapless dress he'd bought her last week, with silver accessories. "I'm glad you're finally here," she told him. "I was beginning to wonder if you were going to show up. Robyn and Daniel were just asking about you."

Lawrence planted a kiss on her lips. "Has Enrique already arrived?"

"Yeah," she responded sourly. "You missed the big surprise."

Jana took Lawrence by the hand and led him up the steps to Graciela's front door. The guests were a melting pot of various ethnicities—Native American, Hispanic, African American—friends of various races. People were talking, laughing, and dancing. Everyone seemed to be having a great time.

Lawrence glanced around, his eyes taking in everything. "Jana, how many people did she invite to this party? This house isn't big enough for all these people."

She sent a sharp look his way. "Be nice."

"I'm just saying that this house is way too small to try to have a big party like this."

"Graciela knows how many people her house can hold. Besides, it's a nice-sized home."

Lawrence glanced down the street at all the small brightly painted houses. "Can't we just wish her husband a happy birthday, give him this gift, and leave? I have a pile of work I need to do."

"These are my friends, Lawrence."

He didn't respond, but Jana could tell by the tightness around his mouth that he was in a mood.

Jana stopped to speak to a couple of guests while Lawrence propped himself against one of the walls in the dining room.

Graciela soon came over to Jana. "Hey, what's up with Poppy?" she asked. "Why is he acting all stuck-up?"

"He's not being that way," Jana replied, trying to sound casual about it. "Lawrence had a hard day at work, and he's just a little tired."

Graciela wasn't buying that excuse. "Then why didn't he just stay home? We don't need a party pooper here. I want Enrique to enjoy his birthday celebration."

"Lawrence isn't going to ruin anything," Jana said tiredly. "I know you don't like my husband, but give him a break." She was feeling a little irritated over Graciela's attitude.

Their gazes met and held.

After a moment, Graciela said, "I need to check on the food."

She walked away before Jana could respond.

Still, Jana thought Lawrence could make an effort. She strode over to where he was holding up a wall. "Are you feeling any better?"

"I don't suppose you're ready to leave this so-called party yet."

Jana glanced over her shoulder. "Can you please keep your voice down?" She turned her glare, boring a hole through him. "Lawrence, we haven't been here that long. Graciela and I have been friends for a very long time. I'm not just going to walk out in the middle of her party. *It's rude.*"

Lawrence shrugged in nonchalance. "You can stay if you'd like, but I'm leaving, Jana. I've had a long day and I'm just not in the mood for partying."

He was talking too loudly. Jana took him by the hand and led him outside on the porch. She didn't want the other guests overhearing them. She especially didn't want Graciela to know what was happening between them.

"Lawrence, I know that you're tired, but can you at least stay until after we eat? Can you do that for me?"

"I don't like Mexican food."

"We're not eating Mexican food, Lawrence. Graciela prepared lobster, scallops, shrimp, and a couple of types of fish. Enrique loves seafood. And FYI . . . they're not Mexican."

His mouth tightened. "I'm exhausted, Jana."

She folded her arms across her chest. "How is it that you're never tired when we're hanging with your friends but whenever we're around Robyn, Daniel, or Graciela, you're suddenly exhausted. *Why is that?*"

The fire in her eyes finally caused him to concede the point. "I will stay until after dinner, and then I'm out of here. That's the best I can offer, Jana. I'm tired and I'm sure you're aware that I'm not in the best of moods right now."

"Fine," Jana muttered. She was glad that she'd driven her own car over. She had arrived early to help Graciela with decorations and the food.

She went back inside the house and navigated to the kitchen. "What can I do to help?" she asked Graciela.

"I have everything under control, *mi'ja*," Graciela responded, her tone cool and brisk.

"Are you mad at me?"

Graciela shook her head. "Jana, I really don't have any interest in being angry. This is my man's night and I'm going to make it special for him." She jabbed her thumb at the counter. "If you want to grab that tray for me, I'd appreciate it."

Jana helped her lay out the food.

Sulking, Lawrence didn't say much to anyone. He prepared a plate for himself and sat down. Jana held her tongue when she joined him at the table. She tried a couple of times to make conversation with him, but it was clear that Lawrence wanted out.

True to his word, he left right after dinner without even bothering to tell her good-bye. She didn't realize he was gone until Enrique mentioned it.

Graciela gave Jana a sympathetic glance but didn't comment on Lawrence's disappearance.

Jana felt a strange sense of relief when he left. She could now relax and just enjoy the party.

After the crowd started getting loud and rowdy, Robyn made her way over to where she was standing. "Where's Lawrence? I don't think I've seen him around."

"He's gone," Jana responded. "He was really tired."

"Oh." Robyn sipped her glass of iced tea.

Jana felt the need to explain further. "Lawrence has been working so hard on this case. He needed to go home to finish writing his closing argument."

"Sweetie, you don't have to explain anything to me," Robyn told her.

Jana knew that wasn't true. "I know. It's just that everyone thinks Lawrence is rude and stuck up, but he's not really." She eyed her sister. "You think so too, don't you?"

Robyn cocked her head to the side. "Lawrence is very standoffish, Jana."

"I don't think it's intentional," she lied.

"You know him better than we do," Robyn said. "We're trying to get to know Lawrence, but we can't if he keeps running away."

"I know," Jana responded. "Robyn, I don't know what it is. Lawrence just isn't much of a people person. He has his friends and he's fine with them."

"Maybe we make him uncomfortable."

Jana sighed. "I guess. I so want all of us to be close."

Robyn embraced her sister. "Just give him space. He'll come around."

"I don't want you and Daniel to think badly of him. Lawrence really is a good person."

"We believe that," Robyn stated. "He's a good man with some issues with certain people."

They walked across the room to join Graciela.

"I see Lawrence left," she said to Jana. Her cheeks were flushed with excitement. "I guess the party was too much for him. He was afraid of having too much of a good time, huh?"

"Graciela, it's not like that."

"Really? Then tell me how it is," Graciela said with a harder edge. "Because from where I'm standing, it looks like your husband thinks he's too good to party with people like us."

"Lawrence . . ." Jana paused, and then began again. "He's not really sociable at times. He's working on another high-profile case, and I guess the pressure's getting to him."

"Whatever," Graciela muttered. "He may have you fooled, but not me. Lawrence is rude."

"You know what?" Jana shot back, covering her irritation. "This is a party, so let's have a good time."

Robyn grinned. "As a matter of fact, I need to find Daniel. That's our song playing."

Jana poured herself another glass of lemonade while she watched her sister and brother-in-law dance. They fit together so easily.

Graciela was across the room with Enrique. Jana felt a pang of regret. She didn't want Lawrence to come between her and Graciela. They had been friends a long time and were close as sisters.

"Lawrence, how can you be so rude?" she whispered to herself.

Each time she tried to speak with Graciela, her friend pretended to be busy. Jana even offered to help clean up after the party.

"You should probably get home," Graciela told her frostily. "I don't want to cause any problems for you and Lawrence."

"You won't be," Jana responded.

"I have everything under control. Just go on home to your husband."

"Graciela . . ."

"We'll talk later. Go on home."

Lawrence was either asleep or was pretending to be asleep when she entered the bedroom.

Jana undressed as quietly as she could, then joined her husband in the king-size bed. She lay there for almost two hours before falling into a troubled sleep.

How could Lawrence treat my friends like this? I've had to put up with his leering friend Ron and his other snobby partners. I've put on ten pounds from all the lunching Lela and the other wives do, and he couldn't survive one birthday party for me.

"WHAT IS YOUR PROBLEM?" Lawrence demanded. "Did you wake up on the wrong side of the bed this morning?" She had been ignoring him all morning.

"I don't like the way you treated my friends last night."

"I thought we'd already fought about that."

"It's far from over, Lawrence." Jana paused for a heartbeat before adding, "We've been fighting a lot lately over stupid stuff. I'm tired of this."

"So am I," he admitted.

"Maybe we got married too soon," Jana suggested. "Maybe we should've taken more time to get to know each other."

"Do you love me?" Lawrence asked.

She met his gaze with her own. "You know that I do. I love you more than anything—I can't see my life without you."

He tried to be reasonable. "We're not going to agree on everything. Even if we'd dated seven years, we'd still come up with something to argue about, I'm sure."

"Graciela and Enrique are my friends, Lawrence. They are actually more than that—they're family. I thought you understood that."

"Jana, I'm sorry." He scowled and turned away. "I never meant to be rude, but Graciela—I have to be honest. There's just something about her that rubs me the wrong way. However, because she means so much to you, I will try and build a relationship with her and Enrique."

Jana broke into a smile. "Thank you. That's all that I'm asking."

Lawrence reached out for her. "I really do love you."

"I love you too."

Jana knew that Lawrence hadn't scored any points with Graciela. She would have to do some damage control. She wanted her husband and her friends to like one another. She didn't expect them to be close or anything. She just didn't want to feel she had to choose between them.

Chapter 10

A S JANA DROVE TO Beverly Hills, her thoughts drifted to Robyn and Graciela. She felt like they were starting to drift apart. They hadn't been spending much time together lately, and their phone calls to each other were less and less frequent.

Jana supposed it was because she and Lela were building a friendship as they spent their days shopping, or participating in a book club and doing charity work. These days, they seemed to have more in common than Jana had with Graciela and Robyn.

Jana noted that she and Graciela seemed to be at odds with each other more often. Graciela had actually accused Jana of being so caught up in her new life with Lawrence that she was forgetting where she'd come from. Graciela talked about how much Jana had changed.

Jana felt like Graciela was a little jealous over her relationship with Lela and that jealousy was behind the problems they were having.

Angie and Lela were already inside the restaurant when Jana walked in wearing a blue-and-white halter dress with red sandals and matching purse.

"You don't even look like the same woman Lawrence married three months ago," Angie stated. "I love the makeover. Now you're truly one of us."

Jana chewed on her bottom lip. Angie's words brought back to mind something Graciela had said to her during their last conversation.

It was true that she'd changed a lot over the course of a few short months. Her hair had grown out considerably, to the point that Lawrence insisted it was long enough to have extensions put in. He wanted Jana to have shoulder-length hair even if he had to pay for it.

Jana's style of clothing had changed as well, although she still wasn't quite comfortable with the way Lawrence wanted her to dress.

That point was brought home to her later, when Robyn called and asked if she could stop by. She'd delivered some clothing to a customer that lived in the neighborhood.

"Sure. I'm home."

Robyn arrived a few minutes later.

"Jana, what in the world are you wearing?" Robyn asked when she entered the house. She looked totally disgusted.

"It's called a dress."

Robyn twisted her face into a frown. "It looks like a tube of stretchy fabric."

"Lawrence picked it out, and he wanted me to have it on when he gets here," Jana said defensively. "You design clothes, Robyn. I'm surprised by the way you're carrying on. *It's a dress.*"

Robyn was very relieved. "Oh, he wants you to wear it for him. *Thank you, Jesus!* I thought that maybe Lawrence expected you to wear it out in public."

Jana was getting irritated. "There's nothing wrong with this dress. I'm covered up, Robyn."

"It doesn't leave a whole lot to the imagination," her sister countered. "You can't even wear a pair of panties underneath. I can still see the thong you're wearing." Jana repositioned her legs as she was called out by her sister. "I don't see how something that resembles a slingshot can be comfortable."

"It's not that tight, Robyn. Besides, I'm a grown woman and I'm married. You need to stop being so old-fashioned."

"Excuse me?"

"I'm not out in the streets, Robyn. I'm home and I dress for my husband. Isn't that what you do for Daniel?"

Robyn pressed a hand to her chest. "I would never wear a dress like that. Daniel wouldn't want me in something like that unless I was coming to bed."

"Well, I'm not you, and Robyn, you're not me."

Her sister glanced all around the richly appointed house. "You're right about that."

"Robyn—"

"I'm meeting Daniel in half an hour," she announced. "I need to be going." Robyn walked briskly to the front door.

"I'll call you tomorrow," Jana said.

"Bye," Robyn uttered without a glance in Jana's direction.

Jana was left shaken by the argument. She and Robyn rarely argued. She was still upset when Lawrence came home.

"What's wrong with you?" he wanted to know. "Did something happen?"

"I had an argument with Robyn. She doesn't like my taste in clothing," she grumbled. "Everyone seems to have an opinion of how I should dress."

"Well, you're my wife and I love the way that you dress now that I've got you out of those jeans and T-shirts." He gave her a penetrating look. "It doesn't matter what she thinks. My feelings are the only ones that should count."

"Robyn and I don't argue."

"Everybody argues," Lawrence replied. "It's a part of life. It's not a big deal, Jana, so you don't have to fall apart."

Her body stiffened. She didn't like being patronized. "I don't like fighting with my sister. It *is* a big deal to me. I owe her so much for what she's done for me."

"You don't owe her anything, Jana. That's part of your problem. You are still trying to please her and Daniel. Yes, they raised you, but it was their choice—you could've gone to other relatives. They wanted you and they did a great job, but you're a grown woman now and you have a husband. Right now I should be the most important person in your life."

Jana considered his words. They were married, after all.

"What are we having for dinner tonight?" Lawrence asked.

"I made spaghetti."

He smiled, pleased. For all his fancy ways, he liked down-home meals. "I'm going up to shower and change. When I come down, I expect my very sexy wife to look happy." He came close enough to give her a few playful pokes to her tummy. "I want to see that pretty smile of yours. Forget about Robyn and that I'm-so-saved attitude of hers."

"I wish it were that easy," Jana said, trying not to be tickled.

"It is," Lawrence answered. "Just focus on me. The man who loves you more than his own life and who will stop at nothing to give you the world."

She closed the distance and kissed him. "I'm a very lucky woman."

"Remember that when I come back downstairs."

While Lawrence was upstairs, Jana picked up the phone and called Graciela. They had not talked since the party. She missed her best friend and wanted to clear the air between them. She also wanted Graciela's opinion on her new way of dressing.

"Hey, it's me," she said when Graciela answered her phone.

"Who's me?"

Jana settled back in her chair, disappointed. "C'mon, Graciela . . ."

"I'm sorry, who is this? I don't recognize the voice."

"You could've called me, you know," Jana said. "Graciela. I'm so sorry for the tension between us."

Graciela's voice softened as well. "Jana, we have been friends forever, and I just don't want anyone to come between us. Including our husbands."

"Graciela, I know that Lawrence is not the friendliest person around, but his heart is good. Please just get to know him and accept him as he is—that's all I'm asking."

"You're right," she responded after a moment. "I'd want you to do the same. I'm sorry for bashing your husband the way that I did. I shouldn't have done that."

Jana invited Graciela for a girls' night out. Lawrence had planned to get together with his partners after work, so she decided to spend some quality time with her friend.

"I look forward to seeing you," Graciela said before they ended the call.

T HEY PLANNED TO MEET at Southern Style Restaurant around seven thirty.

"Look at you," Graciela exclaimed when Jana got out of her car. "Girl, I don't think I've ever seen your legs before—didn't even know you had any."

Jana laughed, glad she wasn't offended. "You are so wrong. I hope you know that."

"I don't know what Poppy's doing to you, but he's definitely got you coming out of your shell."

Her hands on her hips, Jana released a soft sigh. "By the way, will you stop calling my husband Poppy? His name is Lawrence."

"I know the man's name, *mi'ja*, but Lawrence sounds so stuffy." She lifted her nose with her finger until Jana laughed. "Now what's up with this dress? It's gorgeous, but when did you start dressing like this?"

"Lawrence bought it for me," Jana informed her. "He likes me wearing stuff like this. Does it look okay?"

"You look good," Graciela responded with a sly smile. "I just never thought I'd see you in a dress that's two inches above the knee and doesn't fit you like a sack."

Jana laughed. "C'mon, was I really that bad?"

Graciela nodded. "Pretty bad . . ."

"I still have to get used to how much it shows my shape, you know."

"You have beautiful curves, Jana. I've been telling you for years that you shouldn't be afraid to show them off."

"Robyn thinks that I'm showing more than I should. We had a big argument about it yesterday. She looked at me as if I were dressed like a prostitute."

Graciela took a sip of her white wine. "That's because Robyn dresses like she's a hundred years old."

Jana gave her friend a playful pinch. "Leave my sister alone. Robyn is very conservative."

Graciela waved off Jana's comment. "Call it what you want to—Robyn dresses way too old for her age. She needs to let me take her shopping. Daniel would lose his mind if I did a makeover on his wife."

"I think that my brother-in-law loves Robyn just the way she is," Jana responded with a chuckle.

"He doesn't want her to change a thing?"

Jana picked up her menu. "I'm in the mood for seafood . . ."

"*Mi'ja*, you are always in the mood for seafood. Me, I think I'm going to have chicken," Graciela said. "Maybe the smothered chicken."

Jana ordered the blackened catfish, while Graciela decided to have meat loaf. They both selected macaroni and cheese and collards, along with cornbread.

Jana made another plea. "Graciela, I really want you to understand the type of man that Lawrence is—he's private, and he isn't much for parties. He loves to play golf and he has a very small circle of friends."

The animation left Graciela's face. "I'm not trying to be his BFF, but he's married to you and you are like a sister to me," she responded.

"Enrique is very outgoing," Jana pointed out. "I really wish my husband were more like that, but he's not. That's just not who Lawrence is. I just hope that you can accept that."

"I do," Graciela said, willing to leave it at that. "Now that we know, we won't expect him to kick it with us. It's cool."

Their food arrived and Graciela blessed their meal.

"Lawrence will come around once he really gets to know everyone. You'll see." Jana sliced off a piece of her catfish and stuck it in her mouth.

She looked up to see Graciela giving her a shrewd look. "Are you really happy, *mi'ja*?"

Jana stopped eating. "What made you ask that?"

"Because you're my girl. I'm just making sure that Poppy is treating you all right."

"I'm very happy," Jana told Graciela confidently.

"I'm glad," she said. "He'll have to answer to me if he starts acting stupid."

Jana smiled. "Thanks for having my back."

Soon, Graciela finished off her macaroni and cheese. "I'm glad we did this. I really missed you."

"I can't believe we acted so childish. My husband is different—I need to just face that fact."

Graciela laughed. "He might be a little different, but one thing I know—he loves you. I believe that, and I know how much you adore him. Poppy just needs to lighten up some. You need to teach him how to have fun. Let his hair down. . . . Hey! That's the problem, *mi'ja*. He's bald. Tell Poppy to grow an Afro or something."

"You so wrong," Jana said with a laugh.

Chapter 11

JANA CAUGHT A WHIFF of a sweet fragrance even before she saw Lawrence enter the room with his arms laden with three dozen red roses.

"Oh, my goodness!" she exclaimed. "Lawrence, they're stunning. They smell so good."

"I know how much you love flowers, so I thought I'd get you a dozen for each month that we've been married."

She had forgotten about their three-month milestone but only because they'd celebrated the Fourth of July by hosting a huge barbeque for the law firm employees at a park in Marina del Rey.

Jana took the flowers from him and laid them on a nearby table. "You are such a sweetheart." She rose up on tiptoe to plant a kiss on her husband's lips.

"Happy three-month anniversary, babe." He wrapped his arms around her midriff, his hands exploring the hollows of her back.

Jana grinned. "Same to you."

She edged out of his arms and walked over to the table. She gathered up the roses, holding them to her nose, inhaling their combined scent ranging from musky to lemony.

"They smell so good." She sniffed the fragrant bouquet again, wanting to savor another whiff. "I need to put them in a vase or two."

He laughed. "I'll help you."

Lawrence followed her closely into the kitchen. He reached up and retrieved two tall crystal vases. Jana arranged the flowers and set the vases on the counter. She then turned her attention back to her husband.

Putting his hand on her waist, Lawrence drew her to him. "Babe, I want you to know that you've made me a very happy man. I love you more and more each day."

He seemed oddly eager, like he was holding back a surprise. Jana chalked it up to the anniversary. "You've made me the happiest woman alive, Lawrence. I couldn't ask for a better husband—especially one who remembers that he married me on this date three months ago."

"I know how sentimental you are," he said huskily, pressing his lips to hers, caressing her mouth more than kissing it.

They pulled apart slowly.

"Dinner's almost ready," Jana told him, slightly out of breath. "Why don't you go upstairs and get comfortable? When you come down, I'll have everything on the table."

While Jana finished cooking, Lawrence went upstairs to shower and change.

The telephone rang. It was Robyn, but Jana wasn't in the mood to talk to her sister. She wanted to enjoy her evening with Lawrence without any more distractions, so she turned off the ringer.

They had dinner, and Jana surprised her husband with his favorite dessert—a chocolate mousse cake.

When they were done, Lawrence offered to clean up, while Jana went upstairs to change into something more comfortable.

She came down wearing a lavender nightgown with yards of lace.

Lawrence whistled, his eyes raking boldly over her.

Jana smiled and struck a sexy pose.

Slowly, his gaze slid downward. "Babe, you look hot!"

She felt a ripple of excitement, wrapped in invisible warmth.

"Come here," Lawrence said.

She was very happy to oblige her husband.

"I hope that I've made you happy these past three months," he whispered. "It's my goal to make you happy for the rest of your life."

"I'm exceedingly happy." Wrapping her arms around his waist, Jana asked, "Do you know what would make me happier?"

"What?"

"A baby."

She had been thinking more and more about getting pregnant since going to the doctor to get her birth-control dosage lowered. She had been having breakthrough bleeding between cycles, and she suffered too many headaches.

Lawrence's expression changed. "A what?"

"A child. Ours."

He gave her a pensive look. "Jana, I do want children, but not right now. We've only been married three months."

She tried to hide her disappointment.

He planted a kiss on her lips. "We will have a baby, but not this soon. I want at least two beautiful children with you." Taking her hand in his, he led her down to the media room. "Let's watch a movie."

Jana smiled. "That's fine." She sensed a mood shift and assumed that mentioning the word "baby" had put a damper on his desire.

He pulled a DVD out of a case lying on the shelf and slipped it into the player.

The lights in the media room were dimmed, giving the room a soft glow.

Jana curled her body against Lawrence and lay back, enjoying what hinted to be a romantic story, but a few minutes into the movie, everyone on-screen began shedding their clothes. Jana turned and asked, "Lawrence, what in the world are we watching?"

He laughed, a burr deep in his throat. "Sssh . . . babe, it's just a movie."

She shook her head. "This is porn."

"Yeah," he said lightly. "Don't tell me that you've never seen a pornographic movie."

"I haven't," Jana admitted. "Although some of the movies today aren't too far from it, I guess." She watched a secretary pucker her wide lips. "Lawrence, why are we watching this?"

He wrapped an arm around her. "Honey, it really gets me in the mood."

"I'm not enough to get you in the mood?"

Lawrence chuckled. "Jana, there is no reason for you to feel insecure. I enjoy watching other people have sex, but it has nothing to do with my love for you. Don't you see? It just adds more excitement to our love life."

Jana had been a virgin on her wedding night, so she couldn't help but wonder if she pleased Lawrence. He always said that she did, but if so, then why did he need to watch a pornographic movie?

She tried to suffer through the movie in silence but could not. Jana found the film disgusting. "Lawrence, I'm sorry, but I can't—"

He held up his hand to quiet her. "I really don't want to debate this with you right now, Jana. Just sit back and be quiet so that we can enjoy ourselves."

"*Enjoy* . . . I'm not enjoying watching this mess!"

"Then shut up and let me enjoy it in peace," Lawrence demanded.

"Don't you ever tell me to shut up again," she told him. "I don't disrespect you, and I won't let you disrespect me." Folding her arms across her chest and drawing the folds of her silk robe closer together, she mumbled, "I just don't see why you would want to watch something like this."

"Jana, it's a movie," Lawrence said. "A very sexy movie—there's nothing wrong with it. We're at home and I'm trying to have a romantic evening with my wife."

"But why do we need to bring pornography into our marriage?" Jana took a deep breath and released it slowly. "Honey, a Christian who is truly filled with the Holy Spirit would not want to watch porn."

Lawrence sighed in frustration. "Here we go . . ."

"I'm sorry, but I believe that it just opens the door to other things. I've read that porn affects men more adversely than women. Besides, what woman really wants her husband looking at another woman who might have a better body or doing things she might be uncomfortable doing? It might cause him to go and commit adultery."

"What's wrong with adding some spice to our sex life?"

Jana was confused. "We just got married, Lawrence." The painful thought occurred to her that she didn't please Lawrence in bed. "Is our sex life already so boring that we need to add spice?"

He rolled his eyes in disbelief. "Your sister and brother-in-law have really got you brainwashed, don't they?"

Jana shook her head. "This has nothing to do with them. Lawrence, the Bible tells us that God condemns the lust of the flesh and the lust of the eyes. Well, that's exactly what pornography does," she argued. "It appeals to the lust of the flesh and the lust of the eyes."

"You really know how to ruin a romantic evening."

She pulled fully apart from him. "Lawrence, I'm not trying to ruin anything—I just didn't realize you needed to watch a dirty movie before you can make love to me."

"I hate when you start acting childish," he said wearily.

She stood up. "Then why don't I just excuse myself," she told him. "I'm suddenly not in the mood for anything other than sleep. Happy three-month anniversary, and thanks again for the roses."

Jana left the media room in a huff.

When she woke up the next morning, she saw that his side of the bed had not been disturbed. She slipped on her robe and left to go find him.

Lawrence was down in his home office, asleep on the leather couch, partially covered with a chenille throw.

Jana woke him up. "Why did you sleep in here?"

Lawrence blearily glanced down at the pile of folders on the floor. "I came in here to do some work, and I must have fallen asleep."

"I thought that you were upset with me, and that's why you didn't come to bed," Jana confessed.

He pulled her down into his lap. "I'm not angry with you, babe. We had a disagreement, but I have a feeling that we'll find some common ground." Lawrence checked the clock. "Why don't you run and get dressed? Let's go to the country club this morning. I'm in the mood for a game of tennis and then lunch. The chef is great."

"I don't enjoy tennis."

"You'll learn, babe." Lawrence kissed her, then said, "Go on up and get ready."

Jana rose to her feet. "Are we okay?"

"We're fine."

She bent down and planted a kiss on his forehead before rushing off.

Jana hoped that Lawrence wouldn't try to bring pornography back into their marriage. She'd never be comfortable with it. Porn had no place in a Christian marriage.

When Lawrence came into the bedroom, she said, "I hope that we can agree to keep pornography out of our home. It leads to other stuff."

"Jana, I enjoy watching porn. It's not a sin, so I don't understand why you have such a problem with it. We're all adults—there are adults on-screen. Don't make a big deal about this," Lawrence advised.

"You won't even consider my feelings?" she asked.

"Have you considered mine?" Lawrence countered.

Jana sighed in frustration. "Do whatever you want, I don't care."

"Now you're lying," Lawrence said. "If you didn't care, you wouldn't be saying that."

"Watch porn if you want to," she responded. "I just won't be watching it with you."

His brow lowered. "Not even if I asked you to do it for me?"

"I can't," Jana replied. "It goes against everything that I believe."

He seemed stymied, not knowing how to win her over. "There is nothing wrong with watching a blue movie every now and then."

"You may not think so, but it can become an addiction, Lawrence. Do you visit sex sites on the Internet too?"

"Sometimes," he admitted. "But not a lot. You're wrong if you think that I'm addicted. I'm not."

Jana cradled her head in her trembling hands. When she looked up, she said, "I just don't get it, Lawrence. Why do you watch it? Do you imagine that it's you on the screen? Do you fantasize about being with other women?"

"I had no idea you were so insecure," Lawrence protested. "It's just a movie, babe. I'm not so weak-minded that I'll become addicted."

Jana couldn't believe what she was hearing. Had she been so mistaken in thinking that he had enjoyed making love as she had? She noticed the roses on her bureau. All of a sudden it felt like they had ushered in a living nightmare.

Chapter 12

"JANA, ARE YOU OKAY?" Lela asked when they met for lunch in the country club dining room after their tennis lesson. "You're not your usual bubbly self."

Angie agreed, and Jana knew why. Halfway through, she had stopped even pretending the idiotic yellow balls would hit her racket.

"Lawrence and I had an argument last night," Jana said in a low whisper. "He wanted to watch . . ." She glanced over her shoulder before continuing. "You know, a . . ."

"A pornographic movie," Angie filled in with a chuckle. "Hon, it's not a big deal. My husband loves porn movies. We watch them all the time."

"Doesn't it make you uncomfortable to watch movies like that?" Jana asked, trying to keep the surprise out of her voice. Maybe Lawrence was right—she'd grown up too sheltered.

Angie shook her head. "Jana, it's harmless, hon. Think of it this way. You would rather your man watch porn at home with you than scouring the streets after some tramp." She tapped the table with a long fingernail for emphasis. "You know, we have to do whatever our men want in order to keep a happy marriage. Men will find a woman to do whatever his wife won't do—just remember that."

Jana wasn't buying it. "I believe in pleasing my husband, but there are limits to what I'm willing to do. Watching porn is just not something I intend to indulge in. I don't care for moaning, groaning naked bodies all over my television screen." She swallowed deeply. "I don't want that mess in my spirit."

Angie smiled tolerantly. "So what does Lawrence have to say about that? He really enjoys watching blue movies."

"Then he'll have to do it without me," Jana announced, nettled. How did Angie know what her husband liked?

Tossing her blond hair over her shoulders, Angie said, "I told Lela that you were different."

Jana eyed her, wondering if she should be offended or not. "What do you mean by that?"

"Just that you're not like us." Angie shifted her Chanel handbag from one side to the other. "We don't mind if our hubbies watch a little porn or flirt. We're not threatened by other women."

Jana released a short laugh. "You think I'm jealous or that I feel threatened? I'm not jealous, and I don't feel threatened at all. I just feel that watching porn is wrong."

Angie was mildly amused. "Weren't you attending a Bible college before you married Lawrence?"

"Yeah," Jana responded, feeling a bit defensive. "What about it?"

"Honey, that's probably why you think the way you do," Angie explained. "God created sex, and there's nothing in the Bible that says you can't enhance your marriage in the way of your choosing. I used to think the same way that you do because I grew up in a Baptist church. However, since joining NVC, I've come to realize that I no longer have to hide or be afraid of my own strong sexuality." A strange gleam had come into her eyes. "I love God more than anything, and the freedom He gives us is intense. Jesus gave us the most important commandment, to love God and love others as ourselves. So I don't feel like a sinner just because I watch porn or . . ." Her voice died when she glanced over at Lela.

"I don't hesitate to tell anyone what Jesus has done for me," Lela quickly added. "And I know that God created sex to be a positive influence in our lives."

"I agree with that," Jana stated. "But—"

Angie cut her off by saying, "Sex has exploded from a private matter into our movie and TV screens, so it's not like we can push it back behind closed doors. God is concerned about all areas of our life, and since He created sex, He is not ashamed of our sexual needs or how we fulfill them—especially if we're married." She leaned in closer. "What He is ashamed of is our lack of expressing kindness and goodness to other human beings."

Jana looked at the woman as if she'd lost her mind. Lela put in, "I don't need anybody to tell me what I should be doing in the privacy of my bedroom. What Ron and I do is our business."

Lela sounded mighty defensive. Jana wasn't trying to turn them to her way of thinking, but she wasn't going to agree with something she didn't believe, either.

Angie gave a tiny smile. "I agree with Lela."

Jana chewed her bottom lip for a moment before saying, "All I can say is let the Lord lead you. That's what I intend to do."

"Don't get caught up in religiosity, Jana," Angie warned her.

"I'm not," she defended. "I don't try to interpret what God's word is saying. Instead, I take it the way it's written. You don't need to add or take away from the scripture. It can stand alone."

"Now, you have to admit that some of the scriptures are not to be taken literally." Angie ran a hand through her blond curls. "A lot of the scriptures are symbolic. I'm an educated person, and I know that I have a good understanding of the Bible."

Jana didn't care much for Angie. Something about her didn't ring quite true. Too often she found the woman staring at her. At one point during the lesson, Jana had caught Angie eyeing her breasts.

What's up with that? Maybe she's just wondering if mine are real. Lela had already spilled the beans about the enhancement surgeries Angie had gone through to get the perfect body her husband desired. But the reason didn't matter—Jana just wanted Angie to focus her attention on anything but her.

Creepy.

• • •

ROBYN CALLED JANA SHORTLY after she arrived home.

"I guess you're still mad at me," she said when Jana answered the phone. "I'm sorry if I offended you."

In fact, Jana was extremely happy she'd called. She could trust her sister. "I've been really busy. I meant to call you back, Robyn."

"I mean it. I'm sorry."

"Robyn, we're okay," Jana assured her. "You don't have to apologize about anything. I think it was just a bad day for both of us. Anyway, enough of that. How are things at the boutique?"

"Good. I finally hired another employee, so that's helping a lot. I have my dresses ready for the wedding."

"You might need to hire another seamstress too."

Robyn chuckled. "I have. I hired one yesterday. I'm thinking about getting one more but just part-time. I'm getting more requests for my designs."

"Sounds like the boutique is about to really take off," Jana stated. "But I still think it's better to have a second store for your couture fashions and just sell ready-to-wear in the other."

"Daniel said the same thing, so we're praying about it. But if we did that, I'd want you to run one of the stores for me."

"You know I'd love to do it, but I have to see how Lawrence feels about it."

"I know," Robyn stated. "I know he doesn't want you working, but it's always been a longtime dream of mine to have you as my partner. We built Robyn's together."

"Robyn, I'd love to be your partner. Let me talk to him. I really don't see him saying no when he sees how much this means to me. Lawrence is always talking about how much he wants to make me happy. Going into business with you would thrill me."

"Well, talk to him and let me know what you two decide."

After they hung up, Jana paced the floor waiting for Lawrence to come home. She wanted to talk to him about going into business with her sister.

The more Jana thought about it, the more she wanted to do it. She had always wanted her own couture boutique. Robyn was a wonderful designer, but not for the current store. Robyn's catered to the businesswoman, and it was a favorite among the wives of pastors. Only a few special customers commissioned Robyn to design certain outfits for them.

Lawrence walked into the house through the garage.

Jana greeted him with a kiss. "I'm glad you're home."

She gave him time to relax and eat before broaching the subject. "There's something I want to discuss with you."

"Okay."

"Robyn and I had a talk today about the boutique," Jana began. "She's thinking about expanding her business."

His expression became guarded. "She wants me to invest, right?"

"No," Jana responded. "She wants me to be her partner."

"She wants you to invest, which means that she wants me to invest. Don't be so naïve, babe."

"This has nothing to do with money. Robyn and I have been talking about this for years."

"And now you have the means—"

"My sister doesn't want your money, Lawrence," she said, exasperated. "She's not like that. Besides, she and Daniel are doing quite well. They've made a lot of money from investments, her business is doing great, and the church pays Daniel a nice salary. They don't need your money."

"So she'll make you a partner without you investing a dime? That's what you're telling me?"

"She would," Jana confirmed. "But I won't do that. I would rather invest in the business. I wouldn't feel right otherwise."

He went back to eating. "So it still comes down to money."

She had given that angle too little thought. "I have some money saved. Maybe I can get a loan or something—I don't know."

"You don't have a job, Jana," Lawrence pointed out. "Let me think about this, okay? I'm not saying no, but I want you to understand something—I would prefer that you be home. I don't want my wife working. Even if we decide this partnership is a good deal, you will be a silent partner."

"That's not what I want to do," Jana said. "I really enjoy working in retail. Lawrence, I'm bored to death being home all day long."

He shook his head, as though that was of no significance. "You can volunteer somewhere. I just don't want you having to punch a time clock. If I want to pick up and go somewhere I don't want to have to check your work schedule. I had enough of that when we were dating."

Jana chewed on her bottom lip.

"You look upset," he noted.

"I feel strongly about this, Lawrence. I want to work with my sister. It's been a dream of ours for a long time. I'm positive that I can handle being your wife and a businesswoman too."

Lawrence leaned back in his chair. "I'm not saying you can't handle wearing both hats. That's not the point, Jana."

"Then what is the point?" she demanded. Jana was not going to give in this time around. She wanted to work with Robyn, and while she loved her husband, she wanted control over her own life.

Lawrence met her gaze. "The point is that I want you home, Jana."

"What if I agree to make sure that I'm home every day to make dinner and spend time with you? I don't have to work in the evenings unless there's an emergency."

"I'm pretty sure there will always be an emergency of some sort," Lawrence grumbled. "What if it's a night we're supposed to entertain clients?"

"Then Robyn will have to handle it," Jana said. "Trust me, honey. I won't let this business come before you or our marriage. I promise."

Lawrence didn't look convinced.

Chapter 13

AFTER CHURCH, THEY JOINED the others at the Beverly Hills Country Club for Sunday brunch.

"Are you okay?" Lawrence whispered.

Jana nodded as she picked up the tongs to retrieve a slice of bacon. "Uh-huh, I'm fine. Why?" She handed them to Lawrence, who did the same.

"Angie Nielson was trying to make conversation with you a few minutes ago, but you brushed her off. Is there something going on I should know about?"

"Something's not right about her," Jana stated in a low voice.

Lawrence frowned. "What do you mean by that?"

Jana stole a peek over her shoulder before shrugging. "I can't really put a name to it yet, but all I know is that I don't really feel comfortable around her." Jana checked around again before adding, "Lawrence, I caught her staring at my chest."

He burst out laughing.

"I don't think it's funny."

With his free arm, Lawrence hugged her. "Do you think she has the hots for you?"

Jana pulled away from him, frowning. "Hey! That's definitely not funny. I don't know what her issue is, but it's her problem—not mine."

"You don't have to worry about anything," Lawrence said with a chuckle. "Your precious virtue is safe."

"Do you think she's bisexual?" Jana asked. She stole a peek to make sure the others weren't able to overhear them. She felt sorry for Lenny. They had been married for over ten years, and he seemed to adore Angie. "If she is, does her husband know?"

"She might be," Lawrence responded. "If she is, then I'm pretty sure that Lenny knows and it doesn't bother him. Babe, Angie's not going to bother you unless you're okay with it."

Jana grunted. "Humph. That will never happen." She gazed up at her husband. "How do you know? She is, isn't she?"

Lawrence chuckled. "You should see the expression on your face. Babe, she's not going to touch you."

"She'd better not," Jana warned. "I'm not so Christian that I won't give her an old-fashioned beat-down. To tell the truth, I've had enough of your friends eyeing me like I'm a piece of meat."

His smile disappeared. "What are you talking about?"

Jana pinned her husband in her sights. "I don't like the way Ron looks at me. I've mentioned this to you before, but you always tell me that I'm making more of it than I should. Now Angie's tripping."

"Ron doesn't mean any harm, babe. I've known him for a very long time. He loves women, and he appreciates beauty. Lela understands that. She's very secure in her marriage because she knows that he'll look but he's not going to touch." His hand reached out to cup her face. "You can't stop people from looking at you. Jana, you can wear a paper bag and you would still get all eyes on you. You're gorgeous, babe."

She shrugged in resignation. "You're right, there's nothing I can do to stop people from looking at me, but I don't have to like it."

Lawrence wrapped an arm around her. "No, you don't, but why worry about who's looking at you? Nobody has come to you in the wrong way, right?"

"No, they haven't," Jana admitted.

"Then just let it go. My friends don't mean any harm."

"But it's disrespectful, Lawrence. To you."

"Jana, I can admire the beauty of another woman. It doesn't mean that

I'm going to jump into bed with her. It doesn't mean that I even want to sleep with her."

Jana had a feeling that she wasn't going to win this argument. Lawrence viewed life differently than she did—that much was clear.

As she followed Lawrence back over to their table, Jana pasted a smile on her face. She sat down beside Lela and pretended she was enjoying the camaraderie as much as everyone else was.

Deep down, she was miserable.

THE WEEK PASSED BY in a blur.

Lawrence spent the time working a trial. A couple of evenings, he went out late when his wife thought he was working. He liked that Jana never asked any questions. She had a very trusting heart, a quality that he loved. Jana wasn't insecure and clingy. She generously allowed him his space.

He got up early Saturday morning to play golf with his friends.

As he selected his favorite club, the one that always brought him luck, he joked to his partners, "Jana told me that she caught Angie staring at her breasts."

Ron threw back his head and laughed. "What did you say?"

"There wasn't really anything to say. Angie's always eyeing our women. She's into girls—what can I say?" The two men shared a smile. "Lenny doesn't complain. Jana asked if she was bisexual, but I could tell she didn't really want to know the truth."

"You lied to her?"

Lawrence shook his head. "I just said that I didn't know, but if she was, then her virtue was safe because Angie wouldn't try to convert her."

Ron wasn't satisfied with that answer. "The lifestyle is about honesty, Lawrence. You're gonna have to come clean with your wife and soon."

"I know. I just don't want to push her too soon. Look at Gia."

Ron nodded in understanding. "Well, if you can't get your wife into the lifestyle, are you prepared to give it up? I know how much you love Jana."

"It shouldn't be a choice of one over the other."

"No, it shouldn't, but Jana may force you to choose," Ron responded. "Gia did."

"And she lost me," Lawrence said defensively.

J ANA SAT WITH HER sister and Graciela at the Crystal Charity Fashion Show and Luncheon held at Neiman Marcus. This was Angie's fifth year chairing the event, and she'd arranged to have Oscar de la Renta in attendance.

Her face void of emotion, Robyn surveyed Jana's outfit. Jana knew Robyn well enough to know that she didn't like the dress. It was probably too short in her opinion and too form-fitting, but it was designed by Oscar de la Renta, which was why Jana had decided to wear it.

Graciela looked stunning in the black-and-white pantsuit she had on, while Robyn wore what Jana called a "First Lady" outfit.

"I just heard that lady say that she paid two thousand dollars for her ticket to the fashion show," Graciela whispered. "Please tell me that I heard wrong."

"The tickets started at five hundred," Jana whispered back.

Robyn shook her head. "I guess that's why I've never come to this event in the past."

Graciela glanced around. "Everything looks nice. Your friend did a great job. This doesn't even look like a department store."

"Angie told me that Neiman transforms the store every year for the fashion show and luncheon. The Crystal Charity Foundation has benefited children's organizations all over Los Angeles—it's her baby. She started this charity after her son was diagnosed as autistic."

"I remember hearing her talking about it on TV a while back," Graciela said. "She wrote a book about it too."

Jana nodded.

"Her dress could stand to be a little looser," Robyn commented. "And

I'm so sure she's going to throw her back out having to lug those huge melons she bought and paid for."

Graciela and Jana laughed.

"How do you know they're not real?" Jana questioned.

"They sit way too high for a woman her age, and they are much too perfect. If those things are natural, then I need to find out the brand of bra she's wearing."

Jana was grateful to have Robyn and Graciela with her at the event. She couldn't believe how snobby some of the women were. She felt out of place despite the fact that Lawrence was a very wealthy man.

Graciela leaned over and whispered, "Jana, these are some uppity folks in here. I don't know how you can stand it."

"I'm up to the challenge," she whispered back with a confidence she didn't feel. Jana didn't have a whole lot in common with most of the women there.

As Lawrence liked to remind her, this was her life now, so Jana was determined to fit in her new world. Her only concern was how to let go of the old one.

Why do I have to? Jana wondered. There had to be some way to merge the two.

Angie bounced over to their table. "Jana, is this your sister?" she asked, referring to Robyn.

"Yes, and this is my friend Graciela," Jana said. "She's like a sister to me as well."

Angie smiled. "It's so nice of you two to join us this year. I hope that we'll be seeing you again." Her eyes traveled to Jana and stayed there. "Jana helped us this year, and she did a fantastic job."

Her gaze slid downward to Jana's chest for a brief second. "Well, I have a few more rounds to make, so we'll talk later."

When she left their table, Graciela leaned toward Jana and asked, "Did I just catch her looking at your breasts?"

Robyn's eyes grew big as saucers. "What did you just say, Graciela? Surely I didn't hear what I thought I heard."

Jana felt thoroughly humiliated. "Graciela, no," she responded.

"I know when someone is checking me out, and so do you. Now what's really up with that chick?"

Jana lowered her voice to a whisper. "I think she's bisexual."

"And you're hanging out with people like that?" Robyn asked.

Jana eyed her sister. "It's not our place to judge, remember? Let's just enjoy the luncheon, okay?"

Robyn didn't respond.

They sat in tense silence until Graciela tried to lighten up the mood by sharing a story about her niece.

Jana could feel Robyn's eyes on her, but she refused to look in her sister's direction. She had never thought her judgmental until now.

Chapter 14

J ANA PREPARED ALL WEEK for her first major dinner party.

She wanted everything to be perfect—the meal, her dress, the jewelry, her hair and makeup. Lawrence liked her makeup applied with a light hand. She loved him so much and wanted to please him.

Before going upstairs to change, she checked twice with the chef Lawrence had hired. "The Cornish hens look delicious," she told him. "There aren't any peanuts in the stuffing, right? Mr. Collins was very specific about that. One of our guests is allergic to peanuts."

Jana rushed off to her bedroom. Her dress lay on the bed, along with her accessories. She walked to the shower and turned on the water, then stuck a shower cap on her head to keep from messing up her hair.

Jana was a bundle of nerves. The hot water felt soothing on her skin.

Lawrence had invited some of his clients and close friends. She had invited her family, Graciela, and Enrique. She needed some moral support while her husband entertained her friends.

After her shower, she sat down and added more curls to her hair, then applied the mineral makeup.

There was a knock on the bedroom door.

"It's me, Mrs. Collins."

Jana laid down the foundation brush. "Come in, Sofia."

"Everything is ready, Mrs. Collins. I've set the table, and the place cards are just as you wanted them."

"Thank you so much for helping me like this. I know this isn't your job, but I really appreciate it."

"Mrs. Collins, I'm grateful for the chance to make more money. My nieces are here to help with the serving. I've given them uniforms, and they're getting dressed now. They will do a good job."

Jana picked up an envelope. "Lawrence wanted me to give you this, Sofia. He knows it's been hard on you since your husband passed away. We love you, and with your daughter going to college in the fall—this is a token of our appreciation. We also know that tomorrow is your birthday. By the way, we don't want to see you here. Enjoy your day with your family."

Sofia's eyes filled with tears. "God bless you, Mrs. Collins. You and your husband." She wiped her face with the tissue Jana handed her. "I better go check on my nieces. I want to make sure everything is perfect for your dinner party."

Jana smiled. "Thank you. I'll be down in a few minutes."

She glanced over at the clock on the nightstand. Their guests would start arriving within the hour.

Jana stood up and removed her robe. It was time she got dressed.

Lawrence would be arriving home any minute now, and she wanted him to find her fully dressed. He was just as excited about the dinner party and had already called five times to check on everything.

Jana had assured him nothing would go wrong, and she intended to keep her word.

The telephone rang. Grinning, she answered it. "Lawrence, everything is fine. The only thing missing is you."

He chuckled. "I know that I've been bugging you, but this time I wanted to let you know that I'm just down the street. I wanted to make sure I didn't need to stop at the store for anything."

"Come home so that you can shower and change, honey."

"I'll see you in a few."

Jana hung up the phone, a smile on her face.

• • •

"WHAT ARE THEY DOING here?" Lawrence demanded when he strode into the kitchen. "Did you invite your sister and brother-in-law?"

Jana could hear a thread of anger in his voice. "Robyn and Daniel are my family," she told him. "And Graciela is my best friend. You invited your friends, so I figured I could invite a couple of my friends and family."

"This was supposed to be a business dinner."

Jana released a long sigh. "You never said that, Lawrence. You told me that you wanted me to plan a nice dinner party and invite our friends. That's what I did."

The doorbell rang.

He glared at her. "We'll discuss this later."

Lawrence walked off, leaving her standing there, perplexed.

"Is everything okay between you and Lawrence?" Robyn asked in a low whisper when she joined Jana. "Lawrence didn't look all that happy when he walked past me just now."

Jana nodded. "Yes, of course. Everything's fine."

"You sure?"

"Robyn, we're fine." Jana waved at a couple who had just arrived, glad for the excuse to escape. "I need to check on the main course. I'll be right back."

Sofia and her nieces circulated the room carrying trays of mini crab cakes, shrimp California rolls, and raw vegetables.

Graciela strolled into the kitchen. "I love this kitchen, *mi'ja*. Need any help?"

Jana shook her head. "I'm not about to put you to work. You're my guest, so just enjoy yourself."

When she walked out with Graciela, Lawrence was standing a few feet away with Daniel and two other men Jana had met briefly. She couldn't remember their names but knew that they were associated with one of the movie studios.

Ron and Lela Boykin arrived.

She went over to greet them. "I'm glad you were able to join us."

Ron embraced her tightly. "You look stunning, Jana."

"Thank you," she muttered as she backed away from him. Jana didn't feel comfortable with the way he eyed her or how he held her so close.

Lela agreed with her husband. "You look beautiful."

"So do you," she said.

Lawrence came over to join them.

"I'll talk to you later," Jana said to Lela. "I need to check on our dinner." She had nothing to say to her husband.

Jana made the rounds, making sure that she spoke to all of her guests.

Sofia ushered everyone onto the patio, where tables had been set up and they served the first course of dinner.

Jana observed everyone at the tables, laughing, talking, and having a good time. She was still upset with Lawrence.

Graciela leaned over and whispered, "Everything is going well. Relax."

Jana did her best to mask the tension between her and Lawrence until the last guest left, which was shortly after midnight.

"I'm sorry," Lawrence said when he came upstairs, where Jana was getting dressed for bed. "This time I overreacted."

"I didn't know it was a business dinner," Jana replied, tying the belt on her silk robe. "I just assumed we were inviting friends and family over."

He shrugged away the problem. "It was my fault for not making it clear, but I think everything worked out for the best."

"It did," Jana confirmed with a smile. "For the most part, the dinner was a success."

Lawrence sat down on the edge of the bed to remove his shoes. "The food was delicious. The house looks great. You did a great job, babe."

"Thank you. I was nervous. I think that I drove Chef Bernard crazy. Robyn came over and helped me with the flowers and the candles. I wasn't sure where to put all of them."

"I'll send her some flowers tomorrow to say thank you," Lawrence offered.

"She'd like that." She kissed him. "I love you. I love my family too. I'm very close to Robyn and Daniel."

"I know that. That's why I invited Daniel to play golf with us on Saturday."

Jana was surprised. "You did?"

Lawrence nodded. "I figured it would be a good chance for us to get to know each other."

She clapped her hands in excitement. "Oh my goodness, Daniel is going to love that. He loves playing golf. Thank you."

"I'd do anything for you, Jana. I hope that I can say the same about you."

His words gave her pause for thought. Was he referring to the porn flicks? Or did he have something else in mind?

"ONELY AND LOVELY," LAWRENCE stated. "Can you believe that's how this place has been described?"

He had planned a romantic trip to Mendocino, a town perched on a cliff facing the Pacific Ocean.

They were staying at a beautiful Victorian bed-and-breakfast located in the heart of the historic coastal village.

"The clerk told me that we are just a short stroll to the shops, galleries, and restaurants," Lawrence said. "And we can walk to the beach."

"Sounds great," Jana replied. "I've never been here before. I want to see everything."

"We can take a tour of the wineries, if you want."

Jana nodded. She glanced over at the bed. "I can't wait to try out the feather bed."

Lawrence began unbuttoning his shirt. "You don't have to wait another minute."

She laughed. "C'mon, there's too much to see. We have all night to make love."

Jana crossed the room to admire the fireplace. She imagined herself and

Lawrence cuddled in front of a crackling fire, drinking champagne and eating chocolate-covered strawberries.

They spent the afternoon checking out the shops and galleries nearby, then went to dinner. Afterward, they walked along the edge of the ocean, enjoying the moonlit evening.

When they returned to the room, Jana broke into a smile.

There were roses everywhere. In the middle of the room, a table had been set up with an ice bucket containing a bottle of champagne and a plate of chocolate-covered strawberries.

"How did you know?" she asked Lawrence.

"I saw the look on your face earlier," he explained. "I am going to make this an evening to remember."

Her heart overflowed with love for her husband; Lawrence was always trying to find ways to please her. Jana's smile disappeared when she saw what lay on the bed.

"Why is there a vibrator on our bed?"

"Jana, you can't be that naïve."

She glanced up at Lawrence. "I know what it is. What I want to know is why is it here? And what is that other thing?"

"It's a silicone G-spot vibrator. I was told that it's a favorite for women."

She was shaking her head from side to side. "I don't understand. Lawrence, we don't need this stuff. You're really making me feel as if I'm not pleasing you."

Her eyes watered, and she wiped away her tears.

Lawrence came up from behind and embraced her. "I don't want you to feel insecure when it comes to making love," he stated. "You please me greatly, Jana. I wish I could make you understand that."

She turned in his arms. "Then why am I not enough for you? Why did you bring all this stuff into our bed? I don't need sex toys."

"I just thought it might add to your enjoyment."

She dried her eyes. "What we have together works for me, honey. Trust me . . . it works."

He laughed. "I keep forgetting that you and I were raised very differently. My parents were very liberal people. My mother and father had what I would consider an open marriage. They had other relationships on the side, but they were truly committed to each other."

Why is he bringing this up? "How did you know this?" Jana asked. "Did they do all this in front of you?"

"No, they were very discreet. I used to hear some of my mother's conversations with her sister after my father died." He explained, "I didn't understand much of it until I got older."

After hearing him out, Jana had a better understanding of why Lawrence had such a casual attitude about sex.

She herself had been sheltered. "Robyn and I didn't talk a lot about sex until I started to complain about some of the comments boys in our church were making. I developed early."

"And the boys went crazy," Lawrence interjected.

She nodded. "Even some of the girls made me feel weird about it. I was embarrassed. Robyn even tried to tie down my chest, and I started wearing baggy clothing."

He caressed her lightly in the shoulders. "I understand why you feel the way you do about your body."

"I just don't like all that attention. I have a brain—I don't want people focusing on my physical attributes."

Lawrence laughed. "Babe, it's not easy, because you're so fine. You shouldn't be ashamed of how you look. You're gorgeous, Jana."

She gave him a grateful smile. "I'm glad you think so."

"Jana, I want to please you in every way. Can you understand that?" Lawrence asked. His voice became firmer as he came back to his original point. "What we do in our bedroom is just between us, babe. God created sex for married couples. He didn't put any rules on it except for committing adultery, right? He left the enhancement of our pleasure up to us."

She glanced over her shoulder to the bed. "So all of this stuff is for my pleasure."

"Yes," Lawrence almost shouted. "You keep thinking that there is something lacking in you. Babe, that's not the case at all."

She considered what he was saying, then smiled. "I think I get it now. Is it because I'm twelve years younger than you? Lawrence, are you worried that you won't be able to please me?"

"I *am* much older than you."

Jana wrapped her arms around him. "I don't think that's it at all."

"Then what is it?" Lawrence asked with a grin plastered on his face.

"You're just a freak."

He threw back his head and laughed. "You found me out."

"C'mon, honey . . ." Jana took his hand and led him back to the bed. "Let's see what you've got over here."

Chapter 15

"WHY DON'T WE GO to my old church this morning?" Jana suggested the following Sunday. Jana could not shed the guilt that had clothed her since that night. She had gone on the Internet the next day in search of articles and found that most of them stated what she knew herself—that sexual toys and porn have no place in the believer's sex life. Most stated that the practice of using sex toys and porn to enhance eroticism was dangerous, as more and more couples were becoming addicted to pornographic stimulation.

"Daniel is preaching and I'd like to hear him," Jana said. "Lawrence, he's such a good teacher, don't you think? I always take away some little nugget from his sermons. Besides, he and Robyn want us to have dinner with them."

"We're going to *our* church," Lawrence stated flatly. "Jana, I know how much you love your family, but you need to stop looking backward. We're married now and you need to cut ties with your sister and brother-in-law."

"What do you mean by cutting ties?" she demanded, folding her arms across her chest. "Robyn and Daniel are my family, and I'm not about to cut them out of my life. I thought you were trying to get closer to them. You and Daniel have been playing golf on the weekends and I'm going to be Robyn's partner. What is all that about?"

"I don't mean cut ties in that way, Jana," Lawrence clarified. "I'm just saying that you need to forge a life with me—your husband—right now.

Stop trying to be the little girl your sister raised. Let them live their lives and we'll live ours. We can still go over there for dinner if that's what you want to do, but we don't have to attend their church service."

Jana chewed on her bottom lip. She thought about her study on Queen Vashti and wondered if she was being disrespectful to her husband. "That's fine. I'll call her and tell her that we'll be there for dinner." She frowned. "I just don't know what it would hurt to fellowship with them this one time."

"I have a church that I enjoy and that's where I'd like to attend," Lawrence said. "Is this going to be a problem for us?"

"No," she responded quietly.

"Good," he stated. "Because I would rather not start off the day by arguing."

The results of Queen Vashti's actions came back to mind. Lawrence was the head of her household and she knew that a house divided would not stand. He was happy at NVC, while she preferred to attend the church she grew up in. So what was she supposed to do?

Jana pasted on a smile when she and Lawrence entered the sanctuary half an hour later. They sat down in their usual spot, the first two seats in the second row.

Ron and Lela joined them a few minutes later. Angie and her husband found their way to the row behind them. As Jana turned and greeted them, she could feel the heat of Ron's gaze on her. Jana glanced in his direction and awarded him a quick smile. Lawrence reached over and took her hand in his.

Jana listened intently during the sermon but still couldn't get past the fact that she just couldn't connect with Pastor Laney.

After the service, they left the church and headed over to the country club for brunch.

Jana caught Ron staring at her again. She gave him a tiny smile and turned away, but she could still feel him watching her. She got up, walked over to the tables laden with food, and picked up a plate.

"I apologize for staring, but you look so beautiful."

Jana turned around to find Ron standing there. She looked around the room, searching for Lawrence.

"It's just a compliment, Jana. Lighten up."

He walked away, leaving her unnerved. Did Ron use sex toys too? Did he think she was a sex toy?

When she spotted Lawrence, Jana rushed over to him. "Honey, why don't we go home? I'll make us some omelets and fruit—we can kick back and just talk."

"We're already here, Jana," Lawrence protested. "We come here every Sunday after church. What's wrong?"

"I'm not feeling that great," she said, which wasn't much of a lie. "I'd really like to go home now."

Lawrence eyed her for a moment, then said, "Let's say our good-byes."

Jana sent up a silent prayer of thanks.

Lela stopped her before they could make their getaway. "Are you coming to the Decadent Delight party that Angie's hosting Tuesday night? You did get your invitation, right?"

"I don't know," she responded. "I need to check my schedu—"

Lawrence interrupted her and announced, "She'll be there."

Her arms folded across her chest, Jana faced her husband square on. "I'm ready to leave if you are."

"You're leaving?" Lela asked, looking at Lawrence.

He nodded. "Jana's not feeling very well."

"Why did you lie to her?" she asked him when they were in the car.

"I didn't want to tell Lela that you didn't want to be around any of them."

"Lawrence, you can't be offended after the way you've treated my friends and family."

"So this is payback, I guess," he growled, staring straight ahead through the windshield. "Jana, I can't believe you are acting so childish."

Jana cut her eyes at him. "My wanting to spend some time with just my husband is being childish? Lawrence, you have two sets of standards here. It's okay for you to snub my friends, but it's a cardinal sin if I don't want to be around yours all the time. We do this every single Sunday. Daniel and Robyn have invited us over after church, and I'm constantly making excuses."

"You don't have to tell them anything except the truth—that we have other plans."

Jana sighed in resignation. She placed her face in her hands. "I'm so tired of this."

"So am I," he muttered.

They rode the rest of the way home in silence.

"HELLO, ANGIE," JANA GREETED when she walked into the house. "Thanks for inviting me to the party. I've never been to a Decadent Delight party before, and I'm not sure what to expect."

"You're going to have a great time. I promise. Larina brought all of her top sellers with her."

Jana walked over to where Lela was sitting and dropped into the empty seat beside her. "There are a lot of women here," she whispered. "I guess these parties are something, huh?"

Lela's eyes rose in surprise. "You've never been to a Decadent Delight party? None of your friends ever hosted one?"

Jana shook her head no. "It's sexy lingerie, right? My friend Graciela was given some at her bridal shower."

"That's part of it," Lela answered with a grin. "But there's much more to it. There's lingerie, movies, books, and toys."

This time Jana was the one in shock. "*You mean sex toys?*" What was with this crowd? she wondered. Did they all use toys?

Lela nodded. "Yeah, girl. This company has some great stuff." She lowered her voice to a whisper. "I have the vibrating panties, and I love them. I wear them sometimes when Ron and I are out on the town. He has this little remote control, so I never know when he's going to light me up, so to speak."

Jana was so repulsed that she didn't know what to say.

They were joined by another woman who sat down beside Jana. "I hope they still have the jelly egg. I—"

Rising to her feet, Jana interrupted the woman. "Please excuse me."

Jana didn't even want to hear what a jelly egg was and what it was used for. *Dear Lord, what am I doing here?* she thought as she stopped near a table laden with books on various sexual positions, DVDs, and other paraphernalia.

"Hey, are you okay?" Lela asked from behind her.

Jana turned around and gulped deeply. "I'm fine."

Smiling, Lela took her by the arm. "I was a little embarrassed when I came to my first party, but it's not like we're doing anything wrong," she explained. "We're married. And one of the other girls has a Christian sex toy business. She won't sell to anyone who isn't married."

"Christian sex toys," Jana repeated. She thought about the stuff Lawrence had taken with them to Mendocino. He'd probably purchased them from her. She said, "Those three words don't even belong together."

"There's nothing wrong with enhancing your pleasure," Lela responded. "You and Lawrence should attend one of the marriage retreats sponsored by our church. One of the facilitators last year even encouraged pole dancing for your husband."

"I see."

She didn't want Lela or Angie to think she was a prude, so she followed Lela back over to their seats. Jana did like some of the lingerie, and she decided that if she bought anything, it would be lingerie. She didn't have the stomach to purchase anything else. From the looks of it, Lawrence had already purchased a lot of what Larina was selling. He was definitely into sex toys, while she wanted nothing to do with them.

Jana was flabbergasted as she listened to these women openly discuss their sex lives. They talked about which items their husbands loved and their level of pleasure—things that should have been kept private between a husband and a wife. She sat there with her mouth open in shock at some of the things she heard. Maybe she really was a prude when it came to physical intimacy.

Lela glanced over at her. "That's how I was a few years ago."

"I'm sorry; I just think that some things should be left private."

"In a few months you'll be in here sharing just like the rest of us. You just have to get used to being around the girls." In a low voice, she added, "You can't tell everybody your business, though."

Jana was seeing another side to Lela, one she didn't like. She couldn't wait until it was time to leave.

"Did you enjoy yourself?" Lawrence asked when Jana walked into the house three hours later.

"It was interesting."

"Did you buy anything?"

Smiling, Jana held up the bag in her hand. "Yeah, I bought a little something. I'll let you see it later tonight."

They talked for a while before she went upstairs to change.

"That's all you purchased?" Lawrence asked when she returned.

Jana glanced down at the flimsy teddy she was wearing. "You don't like it?"

"Babe, I love it, but I'm a little surprised that you didn't buy anything else."

She shook her head. "I didn't want any of that other stuff."

Lawrence wisely changed the subject, but it was clear to Jana that he had expected her to come home with one of the little gadgets.

Not in this lifetime.

"GRACIELA, YOU WOULDN'T BELIEVE the stuff they had at that party," Jana told her friend the next day when they got together for lunch. "I can't believe people actually use those things. Some of the lingerie was really nice, so I bought a couple of items I knew Lawrence would like."

"Decadent Delight does carry some nice lingerie," Graciela stated. "I own a few pieces. Hey, I'm not gonna lie to you, *mi'ja.*" She pushed a curling tendril out of her face. "I've been known to use a handcuff or two in my day." Jana was about to protest, but Graciela held up her hand. "I stayed away from the gadgets that require batteries, AC power—that kind of thing. With my luck, I'd be trying to get my groove on and get electrocuted." With a sly smile, she bit into her turkey sandwich.

Jana cracked up with laughter. "I'm with you on that. Seriously, though, I just don't think I need equipment to spice up my sex life. Lawrence and I are great together."

"You might not, Jana, but there are some couples who may need the extra stimuli. The greatest sex organ is between our ears. I believe that you and your partner can please each other however you want, as long as the marriage bed isn't defiled or it goes against the Word of God."

"So you don't have a problem with sex toys?"

Graciela waggled her hand—yes and no. "I don't think there's anything wrong with using them. Personally, I don't care much for them . . . well, except for the handcuffs and whipped cream—"

"TMI," Jana interjected. "I guess I'm not as liberal as you, Graciela. I just don't believe that sexual toys and porn have a place in a believer's sex life. I looked up some articles on the Internet, and they line up with what I feel in my spirit. Using sex toys and porn to enhance eroticism is just not my idea of romance. It's good for having sex but not when it comes to making love."

"So for you, it's not romantic if you bring in accessories."

Jana turned serious. "I've heard over and over again about the increasing numbers of individuals of both sexes who have become seriously addicted to pornographic stimulation. I think that this tends to erode the gift of marital intimacy; it creates mistrust and a sense of betrayal, and I believe it leads to a broader exploration of sex—including even extramarital affairs."

"I can see your point," Graciela agreed.

"I want to honor God in everything, and that includes how I make love to my husband. I'm not saying that it's wrong if you use a sex toy with your spouse. It's just not for me or how I want to honor the Lord. Lawrence just doesn't see it that way, though." Jana stuck a French fry in her mouth.

Graciela wiped her mouth on the end of her paper napkin. "I'll say this to you, Jana. Just let the Lord guide and lead you as you work through what it means to have a Christian marriage. Your concern about sexual practices is an important one, but only part of the bigger marriage picture. Make it your goal to learn to love both God and your husband as completely as you can—and everything else will fall into place. You need to relax and stop try-ing to analyze every nuance of your marriage." Graciela broke into a smile. "And as your best friend, I'll add this: You better get your freak on."

The two exchanged a broad smile. "What am I going to do with you, Graciela?"

"You're married now, Jana. Enjoy being married and stop trying to fit your marriage into some type of box. Don't let your relationship with Poppy be defined by sexual dos and don'ts."

"So you're saying that I should be a little more adventurous, then?" Jana sipped her lemonade.

Graciela nodded. "I'm not saying you need to go out and buy any vibrating anything. I'm scared of those things, but that's because I have issues. Just do what feels right between you and your husband—your sex life is your business. Don't be afraid to try something new. That's all I'm saying."

"You're right," Jana stated. "Lawrence tells me the same thing."

They finished off their food and left the corner deli.

Graciela hugged her. "You're such a newlywed, wanting everything to be perfect. Honey, marriage is hard work, and it's a lot of compromise and never-ending forgiveness, but I wouldn't trade it for anything else. I love being married. Enrique and I have so much fun."

"We're not talking about sex anymore, Graciela," Jana commented. "We've moved on."

"Oh," she uttered with a chuckle. "Well, Enrique and I have fun out-side the bedroom too. He's my best friend. But Jana, that man keeps a smile on my face . . ."

Jana paused by her car. "You are too much, Graciela, but I love you."

"*Te quiero también,*" she responded.

Chapter 16

LAWRENCE COULD SMELL THE roast chicken as soon as he entered the house.

"You're home much earlier than I expected," Jana said when he entered the kitchen. She walked over to greet him properly. "How was your day?" she asked after kissing him on the lips.

"Pretty good," he responded. "How about yours?"

"Let's see . . . I had lunch with Graciela. I went grocery shopping, went to the shop to visit my sister, did some laundry, and spent the rest of the day slaving in this kitchen to make sure you have a delicious meal to come home to."

He embraced her. "Thank you," he whispered. "Don't think that I don't know just how lucky I am. Baby, I know."

They sat down to dinner.

"Jana, I know how much you want to go into business with Robyn, but I won't apologize for being selfish and wanting you home."

"I'm disappointed, Lawrence." She picked up her fork and began eating.

"You're her silent partner. That's not enough for you?"

"Lawrence, we're not going to agree on this subject, so let's just table it until another time," Jana suggested, trying to keep her mood light.

"What would you like to discuss?" he asked.

She smiled. "How about you tell me exactly how your day went? I know you had to go to court, because I called you around ten."

"Your day was probably more exciting than mine," he said. "You did a great job with dinner as always. This chicken is delicious."

"I wonder if you're going to be this attentive and complimentary after we've been married ten years."

He chuckled. "I plan to make every attempt to always be this way with you, I just hope I won't be too old for you ten years from now."

"You're my husband for better or for worse," she teased. "I'm stuck with you whether you're young or old."

"Remember that comment about me being young or old?" he asked her later that evening. When Jana nodded, Lawrence picked her up and carried her upstairs to their bedroom.

"What are you doing?"

"I'm showing you that I'm not too old to carry my wife up the stairs."

Cradled in his arms, Jana secretly wondered if Lawrence had sex toys scattered all over the bed like before. She still didn't like the idea of using them, but Lawrence could be very persuasive at times.

She released a sigh of relief when she saw that there were no gadgets on the bed. He gently put her down and began undressing her. Jana assisted Lawrence with removing his shirt, then ventured over to the bed and climbed in.

Her husband's eyes never left her face, except for the times they roamed all over her body. "Jana . . . ," he muttered huskily.

She smiled and held her arms out to him.

Lawrence didn't move. He stood there, wanting to savor his wife's physical beauty a moment longer.

"Touch yourself," he told her.

Their romantic evening came to a screeching halt when Jana blurted, "You want me to do what?"

"Honey, it's just you and me," he said, trying to be patient. "There is nobody in this bedroom but two people who love each other very much."

Shaking her head, she said, "Lawrence, I can't . . ."

"Jana, don't tell me that you've never—"

She cut him off by saying, "No, Lawrence. I never did anything like that."

"So what did you do when you were turned on?" he asked, his eyes narrowing. "And don't tell me you've never had any sexual urges—I know I didn't marry a robot."

"I'm human and yes, I've had desires, but I went to the Lord and prayed for Him to keep me, Lawrence. I wanted to keep my vow of purity. I'm not saying it was easy for me, but I made it through."

"So what is the deal with you now, Jana?" Lawrence couldn't keep the frustration out of his voice. "We're married. You don't have to act like a saint in the bedroom."

She was offended by his remark. "I wasn't aware that was the way I've been acting. Look, Lawrence, I'm doing my best here." Jana swung her legs outward and got out of bed, reaching for her robe. "This is all very new to me, so can you please bear with me?"

Lawrence's expression grew tender. "I'm sorry." He pulled her into his arms, holding her close to him. He kissed her, then his lips seared a path down her neck.

Jana moaned softly.

He began whispering in her ear, stopping every now and then to nibble her earlobe. Gently he eased her down onto the bed.

He repeated his earlier request.

Jana shot up. "Lawrence, you want me to touch myself while you watch—even if it makes me uncomfortable?"

He threw up his hands. "I wish I'd known you were such a prude before we got married."

Jana stiffened. They had been making love constantly since they were married. "I can't believe you just said that to me. Lawrence, you don't have to be cruel."

"I don't mean to be, but I have to be honest. This is very frustrating for me."

Her eyes filled with tears. "I'm sorry."

"Babe, just listen to me for a moment. We should celebrate our bodies and our sexual nature, and rejoice in the pleasure and satisfaction that they can bring us."

She wasn't convinced, and he warmed to the subject. "If you want, we can say a prayer of gratitude to thank the Lord for our bodies, for sexual pleasure, and for masturbation as a means of experiencing the bliss of orgasm. It's a gift from God."

"Are you serious?" she asked him. "Because I'm having a little trouble believing what I'm hearing come out of your mouth."

Lawrence was at the end of his patience. "Will you grow up, Jana? There is nothing wrong with what I'm asking you to do." His voice softened. "Just try it . . . do it for me. You can stop whenever you want to, babe. Trust me."

J ANA HUNG HER HEAD in shame. She'd never felt so humiliated. Deep down, she experienced a wretchedness she'd never known before. She lay in bed curled in a fetal position.

Lawrence inched closer to her, but Jana edged away. She just wanted to be left alone.

"Babe, what's wrong now? All I want to do is hold you in my arms."

"I'm tired," she responded after a moment. "I'm really tired and I just want to go to sleep."

"I want to hold you. You usually like when I do that. I'm just going to hold you in my arms."

Jana's body stiffened when she felt Lawrence's arm fall across her midsection. A lone tear slid from her eye. She closed her eyes in an effort to block out all memory of what had transpired.

"I love you, Jana."

His declaration was met with silence.

Jana woke up every hour on the hour. Lawrence was in a dead sleep and snoring softly in a steady rhythm.

Finally, at dawn, Jana eased out of bed, slipped on her robe, and went downstairs so that she wouldn't disturb her husband. She sat outside on the patio, her mind filled with confusion.

Jana closed her eyes in earnest prayer, embarrassed over her behavior.

It wasn't so much the request that Lawrence had made of her but the fact that she'd been such a baby about it.

Looking back, it hadn't been that much of a big deal. In truth, it had made their lovemaking better.

So why am I so troubled by this?

The question nagged at her.

She got up and went inside to grab her Bible, her journal, and a throw.

Jana returned to the patio and sat down in the lounger. She made herself comfortable, then began her daily study.

She searched through the scriptures looking for answers. Finally, after an exhaustive search, she wrote down her reflective thoughts:

> *I know that I'm not the only person who has had this question on her heart. If you're married and your spouse wants to use sex toys or masturbation to enhance your sexual relationship—is it a sin?*
>
> *I looked through the Bible and didn't find anywhere that gave the answer, but after much prayer, I've come up with this conclusion. This is what I would say if I ever had to counsel a married couple with these concerns:*
>
> *If you feel guilty, then it's possible that the Spirit of God in you is telling you that it is wrong. We are not sinless, even when we strive to sin less. However, it should be our goal to not fall into sin willfully. When we sin we should not make excuses for it but repent and ask God to forgive us.*
>
> *We are to glorify God in everything that we do, and we should make certain that what we do is according to His commandments. I am not referring to the Ten Commandments, but how He intended us to use our body. Sex is a God-given pleasure, but it must be within God's guidelines. Anything else is sin.*
>
> *I believe that your conscience is God's way of speaking to us and a great indicator of what is right and wrong.*

• • •

ANA CLOSED HER JOURNAL and sprang to her feet. Her husband would be getting up soon. Despite everything else, she was his wife. She made her way to the kitchen and retrieved a frying pan from the bottom shelf where she kept the cooking utensils.

She dropped a couple of beef sausage links in the pan, then took out eggs from the refrigerator. Jana also pulled out an onion and a bell pepper.

"Did you get any sleep last night?" Lawrence asked when he entered the kitchen and saw Jana preparing breakfast. "You tossed and turned for hours."

"Good morning to you too," she responded dryly.

He hugged her. "Morning, babe."

"I made scrambled eggs and sausages. I hope that's all right with you. Do you want toast or a bagel?" She deftly moved out of his arms.

"Everything smells delicious."

Lawrence reached for her, but Jana avoided his embrace. "What? No kiss for your husband?"

"I'm trying to cook breakfast," she said without looking up at him. "You know how clumsy I can be at times. I don't want to add another grease burn to the collection I already have."

He eyed her for a moment before asking, "Jana, are you upset about something?"

"Now, why would you think that, Lawrence?"

He released a long sigh. "Jana, I enjoyed last night and I had hoped you would too."

She didn't say anything.

Lawrence walked over to the breakfast counter and sat down on one of the stools. "I have to tell you that I don't want this, Jana. This attitude of yours."

She met his gaze straight on. "Lawrence, I did what you asked last night, and I don't want to talk about it. I just want to have a nice breakfast with you and forget what happened."

"If you would relax and let yourself enjoy—"

"I just said that I don't want to talk about it anymore," she snapped, losing it. "Just leave me alone and let me cook. I've done enough for you, don't you think?"

Lawrence wasn't fazed one bit by her outburst. "Jana, this is exactly why I don't want to go to Daniel's church. He is a part of that group of Christians who believe that sex is just for procreation only. That you're not supposed to enjoy it. They have set up all these rules that are not biblical. That's why so many men cheat."

She looked at him over her shoulder. "That's not true. Men cheat because they want to—they are not satisfied with one woman."

"It might as well be," Lawrence argued. "Unfortunately, the views of most people regarding sex are heavily tied to religion. Sweetheart, these religion-based views are not based in reality and consequently not in the best interest of human beings here on earth. You shouldn't feel bad about anything that we do in our sex life."

Jana put Lawrence's plate on the breakfast counter while she ate her bagel on the other side in the kitchen.

"Sex is God's gift to us. Since you're always reading that Bible of yours, you should know that it doesn't say anything about what a couple can or can't do in the bedroom."

Jana disagreed. "Lawrence, skinheads and the KKK also refer to themselves as Christians, and they believe that it's God's will for the white race to rule over the others. That just goes to show that you can twist the scriptures to mean anything you want it to—provided you begin with a certain goal in mind."

She took a sip of her cranberry juice. "You can try to justify this however you want, Lawrence, and attempt to convince others of your position, but I am willing to bet that you are dead wrong."

His gaze met hers. "But what if I'm right, Jana?"

"You're not," she replied.

"Why?" Lawrence wanted to know. "Because the Bible says so? Didn't you just say that people can twist the scriptures to mean whatever you want them to mean?"

Jana stood her ground. "My goal is to honor God in all that I do. What you're talking about is pure sexual gratification. It has nothing to do with honoring the Lord."

"God intended for us to enjoy intimacy. Do you agree with that theory?"

"I agree," Jana stated. "But he didn't intend for us to make it perverted."

"So you think I'm a pervert because I wanted to watch you pl—"

Jana interrupted him. "Let's just drop it, Lawrence. We're never going to agree on this subject. I can see that now." She pointed at his plate. "Eat your food while it's still hot. I know how much you detest cold eggs."

Lawrence suddenly got up and walked around the counter and into the kitchen. He pulled Jana into his arms. His mouth covered hers hungrily; his lips were more persuasive than she cared to admit.

His kiss sent the pit of her stomach into a wild swirl.

"Does this feel wrong?" Lawrence asked her. "Does it feel perverted?"

Jana moaned in response.

Reluctantly, her lips parted a few inches.

"What we have between us can't be put into words, babe. When we express our love for each other, there is no right or wrong when it comes to our passion."

"Your food is cold," Jana said after finding her voice.

"I don't want anything but you."

Lawrence picked her up and carried her upstairs to their bedroom. This time he got straight to business.

Chapter 17

JANA MET HER SISTER for lunch. She was glad to get out of the house for a little while. Sofia was there changing all the bed linens and doing laundry. Jana preferred to wash her own intimate garments and had done so before the housekeeper had arrived.

The two sisters embraced outside the restaurant.

"I'm so glad you were able to meet me today," Jana stated. "I know you just got back from a buying trip."

Robyn pulled back, but she still held Jana by both arms. "I was thrilled that you called, Jana. I was in the mood to eat out but didn't want to go by myself."

Jana laughed. "Lawrence works long days, so I have a lot of time on my hands during the day. I just needed to get out of that house for a little while."

The hostess guided them to their table, and their waiter came over to introduce himself and take their drink order.

Robyn surveyed her sister's face. "Jana, what's got you so quiet?"

Jana wasn't sure what to say. She wanted to confide in her sister, but she didn't want Robyn thinking badly about Lawrence. She also didn't want to involve her family in such personal matters.

"Jana . . ." Robyn prompted. "Sweetie, what's going on? I can tell by looking at you that something's wrong."

I need to talk to someone.

"I need to know something," Jana admitted before she lost her nerve. "In your opinion, what are the rules for sex when it comes to a Christian marriage? I know that the scriptures tell us that the joyous sexual expression of love between husband and wife is God's plan, but I need more than that. What can you do and not do?"

Robyn looked at her askance, then responded, "I'd really like to create such a list that could settle once and forever any doubts about sexual practices. But unfortunately that's not possible, Jana. So, since we aren't likely to find a definitive answer, the best we can do is find the principles God has given us and apply them to our lives." She reached over and took her sister's hand. "Jana, I can tell you this. God wants you to enjoy the gift of your sexuality to the fullest."

Jana felt comforted by those words. "I know that the Bible is not a manual on sexual technique," she replied. "When I was in school, there was a debate that Song of Solomon describes acceptable sexual positions and behavior. Others in the class, including me, saw it as a poetic love song that embraced the joy of sex. We didn't agree with the others that it was an attempt to outline any specific sexual practices."

"I agree with you," Robyn stated. "It's not a description of sexual positions."

"It's not the positions I'm concerned about," Jana responded. "It's more about, you know . . . the other stuff." She was too embarrassed to say anything more.

Robyn didn't press her. "Well, we know that there are some specific sexual behaviors forbidden in the scriptures. Having sex with another person's spouse or having a partner other than your own spouse is a sin."

"Yeah," Jana said. "Adultery is a sin. In the Sermon on the Mount, Jesus speaks of the importance of marital faithfulness and the prohibition of a lustful thought life. The Bible is clear about fornication, homosexuality, bestiality, and incest. I just want to know about sexual rules within the confines of marriage."

Robyn pulled back in alarm. "Jana, why don't you tell me what is really going on? You know that you can tell me anything."

"Robyn, you can't say anything about this," Jana hissed. "Especially not to Daniel."

"I won't."

Jana took a deep breath and exhaled softly. "I can't believe I'm about to say this to you, but I need to talk to someone. Robyn, please don't judge."

"Sweetie, I won't. You know that."

"Lawrence likes watching porn, and he wants me to watch it with him. It gets him excited. *Really excited.*"

Robyn tried to control her distaste. "How does it make you feel?"

"Very uncomfortable," Jana admitted. "I don't enjoy it because it just doesn't feel right. Besides, I can't help wondering if Lawrence is thinking about the women he sees on video when he's with me and if he's imagining himself with them."

"Have you tried to discuss your feelings with him?"

Jana nodded. "I have, but we usually end up arguing."

Robyn asked, more quietly, "Do you think he's addicted to porn?"

Jana shrugged. "I don't know, Robyn. Maybe."

Robyn suddenly looked very uncomfortable. She leaned forward, saying, "I hate asking you this, but I have to do it. Is that the only way he can . . . make love to you?"

Jana laughed and shook her head. "No, that is not a problem for us at all. Lawrence is always in the mood, but he just really likes to be . . . adventurous, I guess you can call it."

Robyn laughed as well, relieved. "Daniel's been known to be a little adventurous himself, but he's never suggested watching pornography, thank goodness."

"I guess this is the downfall to being a virgin on your wedding night," Jana said. "You have absolutely no clue what your spouse likes and dislikes."

"Unless you marry a virgin," Robyn contributed with a chuckle.

"I was probably the oldest virgin alive," Jana said. "Finding a male virgin . . . good luck with that one."

The waiter returned with their drinks.

"Are you ready to order?" Jana inquired.

Robyn nodded. "I'll have the tilapia and wild rice with grilled vegetables."

When it was Jana's turn, she said, "I want the grilled chicken Caesar salad and a bowl of your lobster bisque."

"That's all you're having?"

She nodded. "I'm not real hungry today."

When the waiter left with their orders, Jana continued, "I'm not saying that Lawrence does this all the time, because he doesn't. Actually, that was the first time. It was our three-month anniversary."

"Have you seen any other movies like that in the house?"

"No, I haven't," Jana responded. "But then I don't go into the media room much. We usually watch TV in the family room unless there's a game on or we have guests over."

Robyn took a sip of her water. "You have a right to be concerned, Jana. Porn is destructive."

"I've been praying about this since it happened. I don't want to say the wrong thing to Lawrence. I don't want him to feel that he's got to sneak around and watch it, but I don't think I handled the situation well at all. I think I came off too self-righteous."

"Continue to pray, and I'll be praying with you," Robyn suggested. "God can deliver anyone who wants it. If Lawrence doesn't want it right now, pray for him to get that desire."

Jana solemnly nodded in agreement.

Their food arrived, and Robyn said a prayer over their meal.

They talked about Robyn's buying trip while they ate.

Afterward, Jana walked her sister to her car. "It was good seeing you, Robyn. I appreciate being able to confide in you about this. It was really bothering me."

"Everything will work out between you and Lawrence," Robyn assured her. "He's not trying to do anything behind your back, so that's a good thing. Just remember to talk to him without judgment, sweetie."

"I already blew that, I think, but you're right."

"You can always go home and fix it—that's the good news."

Jana and Robyn hugged.

"I meant to tell you earlier about this," Robyn said. "I've been looking at locations for the new store."

"That's great," Jana declared.

"I guess Lawrence is still against your managing the new store."

Jana nodded. "I'm not totally giving up on the idea of it, Robyn." She really wanted to be more involved, but Lawrence was adamant about her remaining a silent partner.

"I can't see the business without you," Robyn admitted. "It's always been *our* dream, not just *mine*."

"I'm going to discuss this with Lawrence again. I don't see giving up something I've wanted to do for a long time. I don't want to miss this chance."

They hugged again.

"Oh, Lawrence wanted me to invite you and Daniel over for dinner on Sunday," Jana told her. "Can you make it?"

"Sure. We don't have any plans, but let me confirm with Daniel and give you a call."

Jana left Robyn at her car, then navigated over to where she'd parked the BMW. She got in and followed her sister out of the parking lot, then turned in the opposite direction.

Graciela called her while she was driving. Jana placed the call on speakerphone.

"Where are you?" Graciela asked.

"Just about to get on the freeway. I just had lunch with Robyn. What's up?"

"I have to attend an art showing this evening and Enrique just bailed on me. Would you please be a sweetheart and go with me?"

"Sure. Just let me call Lawrence and let him know."

"Okay." Graciela gave her the details.

When Jana got off the phone with her friend, she made a quick call to Lawrence.

"Hey, babe."

"Honey, Graciela just invited me to attend an art showing with her tonight. Her husband can't make it and she didn't want to go alone."

"That's fine," he said. "If you're going to be out, I can stay here a little longer to finish up a brief I've been working on. I have to go over to the courthouse this afternoon, so I'm going to be out for at least a couple of hours. Don't worry about dinner. I'll order something and have it delivered here to the office."

"I won't be out late," Jana told him.

"Call me when you're about to leave and I'll head home," Lawrence said. "Have fun with your friend."

"Enjoy the rest of your day, honey." There was so much more that Jana wanted to say to him, but this was not the right time or place. "We'll talk more when I see you tonight."

They said their good-byes and ended the call.

GRACIELA WAS WAITING OUTSIDE the art gallery when Jana arrived. The two women embraced, then ventured inside.

"I'm probably going to regret this, but I'm going to ask you anyway," Jana began as they strolled through the gallery. "Graciela, I know how you feel about sex toys, but how do you feel about sex and the Christian marriage?"

"Sex is a beautiful gift from the Lord." Hands up, she looked upward and said, "Thank you, Father, for this wonderful gift of sex."

Laughing, Jana shook her head.

"Okay, I'll be serious," Graciela continued. "I was serious about thanking God for sex, though—I appreciate that gift. It's a wonderful thing."

"Graciela . . ."

"Okay okay . . . you know, when you mention sex and marriage— that's a powerful combination." She took a deep breath, then exhaled slowly.

"Okay, I got my mind right. Sex and marriage . . . the becoming of one flesh with your spouse."

"That's what I believe as well," Jana agreed. "I want to make love to my husband—not have sex for sport."

Graciela turned sharply. "What's going on, *mi'ja*?"

"Lawrence wants me to watch porn with him."

Graciela frowned and shook her head. "Personally, I can't get my groove on with all that noise in the background. That stuff don't do anything for me, but Enrique—he likes to watch them every now and then."

"I keep telling Lawrence that it doesn't turn me on. Graciela, he even put a movie on when we had his friends and their wives over. I was never so embarrassed."

"How did the other women feel?" Graciela asked.

Jana gave a slight shudder, remembering how blasé they'd acted. "They didn't seem bothered by it. In fact, one couple looked like they were ready to tear each other's clothes off. I left the room, I was so disgusted."

Graciela was amused. "Jana, you got some freaky folk all around you, huh? You better watch out. Those friends of his might be into group sex or something."

Jana recoiled at the suggestion. "Well, I'm pretty sure Lawrence would draw the line at that. Thank you, Jesus!"

They were silent for a few minutes before Graciela said, "Can I be honest with you, *mi'ja*?"

When Jana nodded, Graciela continued. "I really don't think you have anything to worry about. Your husband has sexual fantasies, and the movies probably allow him to live out those fantasies visually."

"So then I should just let him watch them?"

"Jana, I don't think you can stop him," Graciela stated. "Lawrence is a grown man, and if you nag him enough, he might not watch them in front of you, but he'll end up going behind your back. I don't think you want that."

"So what do you suggest I do?"

"*Mi'ja*, this is about fantasy. Lawrence has them. You have them. Help him play them out in your bedroom. Make love to him in new ways. Seduce him. Love him. Most of all, understand that just because he is a Christian doesn't mean he only likes sex missionary style. I've told you this before—get your freak on. *Enjoy!*"

Jana smiled at all the Latin passion. "Only you, Graciela . . . only you."

"Now, you know I'll be real with you."

L AWRENCE WAS DOWN IN the media room when she arrived home shortly after nine. He cut off whatever he was watching as soon as she walked into the room.

"What were you watching?"

"I don't think that you really want to know," Lawrence responded guiltily.

Porn.

She sat down in the reclining chair beside him. "Why did you cut it off?"

"I know how you feel about it. Lord knows, you've made it clear over and over again."

"Lawrence, I apologize if I came off like I was judging you."

He accepted her gesture and returned it. "Jana, I know how sheltered you were raised. I called Pastor Laney and set up an appointment for us. I think we should talk about this issue. We're meeting him tomorrow at one o'clock."

"Really? Why did you do that?" She was surprised that her husband was willing to open up to their pastor, especially being the private man that he was.

"Because I really feel that we need an objective perspective," Lawrence explained. "I don't want this issue to have an adverse effect on our marriage."

Jana smiled. "Neither do I, Lawrence. Spiritual counseling is probably the best solution for us."

• • •

"PASTOR LANEY, I APPRECIATE you taking this time to meet with us," Lawrence said when they entered the office the next day. "My wife and I are having some issues in regards to exploring sexuality." He reached over and grabbed Jana by the hand.

Pastor Laney nodded in understanding. "It's important to understand that you should never feel ashamed of your body or any of its natural functions. You shouldn't feel embarrassed when other people see your naked body."

Jana glanced over at Lawrence, then turned her attention back to the pastor.

"Curiosity about our bodies is natural and innocent. Pleasuring yourself sexually is innocent. I always tell people to pleasure yourself whenever you feel like it." Pastor Laney gave a slight shrug. "It's not a sin to pleasure yourself or to watch other people pleasuring themselves. Many of my members have asked me about pornography and whether or not it's acceptable for Christians to view adult entertainment."

Jana couldn't believe the words coming out of the pastor's mouth.

"Depending on the circumstances, the act of intercourse can be either a defilement of the body and soul through lust and indulgence of the senses, or it can be a celebration of God-given sexuality that uplifts the bodies and spirits of both partners. Let's consider the Song of Solomon—a deeply sensual and erotic book of the Bible, which describes in lyrical detail the sexual and romantic relationship between a bride and bridegroom. There is little, if any, adult entertainment currently on the market that reflects these values and would be a good choice for Christians."

Jana nodded vigorously in agreement.

"That leads us to call for a new kind of porn—porn made to be viewed by Christians and tailored to their unique needs. We challenge Christians in the adult industry to step up and truly walk their walk and live their faith by producing pornography that men and women of God can view without compromising their relationship with their Savior, or their relationship with their spouse."

"E-excuse me," Jana sputtered. Her head was whirling. "I need to make sure I understand this. Pastor Laney, do you actually believe that there should be triple-X movies for Christians? Is that what you're saying?"

He nodded sagely. "Christians have so many questions about sexuality: what is acceptable or not, how to express sexual desires to their husband or wife, how to have a more fulfilling sex life, and much more. Unfortunately, few in the church are willing to talk openly and in detail about these matters. Believers need sexual resources that are unafraid to actually demonstrate and show them what healthy sexuality in a Christian marriage looks like."

Jana stood up quickly. Her heart was racing, and she felt as if she couldn't breathe. "I'm afraid I can't finish this conversation. I need to get out of here."

Lawrence grabbed her by the hand. "You're being rude."

"You're being misled and you need to leave with me." Jana snatched her hand away and glanced over at Pastor Laney. "You are in leadership over this church. I don't mean to be rude, but I don't agree one bit with your way of thinking. Have you actually studied the Word of God?"

He smiled. "That's fine if you don't agree, Jana. Everything I say is based on scripture. We don't teach religion here."

Jana held her tongue, but she wanted to say, *I'm not sure what you're teaching, but whatever it is it certainly isn't biblical.*

Pastor Laney looked as if he could read her thoughts. "I assure you that I've studied the Bible thoroughly."

"I've studied the Word for myself, and I assure you, we're never going to agree on this subject."

Pastor Laney gave her another indulgent smile. "We can agree to disagree."

Jana glanced her husband's way. "Let's get out of here, Lawrence." She headed to the door without waiting for his response.

Inside the car, Lawrence gave her an angry look. "I can't believe you disrespected Pastor Laney like that."

"Lawrence, don't start," Jana warned. "I'm not buying that crap your pastor spews from his lips."

"Search the Bible for yourself, then."

"Oh, I intend to do that," Jana said. "I know how you feel about us worshiping at the same church, but I can't go back there. I'm going back to Daniel's church."

"Jana . . ."

She shook her head. "I don't want to hear it, Lawrence. I'm not going to that church. If that's where you want to go—do it, but don't expect me to be with you."

"When we got married, we became one, or did you forget that part?"

Jana cut her eyes at him. "Don't go there, Lawrence."

"I am the head of our home, and I won't be disrespected."

"Neither will I," she responded. "I won't let you disrespect me either. Lawrence, you can't force me to go somewhere I don't want to go. Sorry, but it's not happening."

"While you're reading through the Bible, make sure you read the part about wives submitting to husbands."

Jana was ready for that. "Where do I find it? Tell me exactly where to find it."

When Lawrence didn't respond, she muttered, "Uh-huh. I didn't think you knew."

They rode the rest of the way home in silence.

THOUGHTS OF BECOMING AN active partner in Robyn's business and running the second boutique consumed Jana with a burning passion.

I've wanted this my whole life, and as much as I love Lawrence, I'm not sure I can just abandon my dream.

Jana went to see her sister.

"Hey," Robyn greeted. "I didn't expect to see you today."

"Robyn, I really need to talk to you."

"Let's go to my office," Robyn suggested. "Let me know if you need some help," she said to her employee as she and Jana walked to the back of the shop.

Jana settled down on the sofa while Robyn closed the door before join-ing her.

"What's wrong?" Robyn asked.

"There's nothing wrong, Robyn," Jana answered. "I've been think-ing more and more about being an active partner, and I know that it's my desire. I'm just not sure how to make Lawrence understand. I like that he wants me home, and I want to be there when he walks through the door. I love spending time with my husband, and I have to put him first."

Robyn agreed. "We will hire enough staff to cover the evening shifts, and I think Beth will make an excellent night manager—she's in class dur-ing the day, so this would be perfect for her."

"She's been with you for almost four years," Jana said. "She's a good worker and loyal. Maybe if I show Lawrence we have all of our bases cov-ered, he'll change his mind. However, I can't promise him that there won't be times I'll have to work late at the store. He wants a guarantee."

Robyn smiled. "There are no guarantees in retail. Things happen."

"But it's the same with him. There are times Lawrence will call me and say that he's working late. I understand and don't give him attitude. I feel like he should treat me the same way."

"Jana, have you told Lawrence that you'd rather work than stay home?" Robyn asked pointedly.

"I've mentioned it."

"See, that's where you're going wrong. You need to be straight with him. Say what you mean and mean what you say."

"I know that you're right," Jana said. "He's so good to me, Robyn. I want to make Lawrence as happy as he makes me, but staying home all day . . . it's just not me."

"Then you need to tell him exactly how you feel."

Jana considered her sister's words and agreed. "I'll talk to him to-night."

Robyn broke into a grin. "Good. I'll keep my fingers crossed."

"Since when do you believe in crossing your fingers?" Jana laughed. "You've been hanging around Graciela too much."

"I just want this so bad," Robyn confessed. "But I don't want it if it's going to cause problems between you and Lawrence."

Jana rose to her feet. "I just have to convince my husband that working with you will make me very happy."

Robyn escorted her through the store and outside to her car.

"I'm going home to make a nice romantic dinner, and then I'm going to seduce my husband into letting me go back to work." Jana chuckled. "That makes me sound manipulative, doesn't it?"

"There's good manipulation and bad manipulation as far as I'm concerned," Robyn said. "I pray your evening goes the way you want it."

Jana glanced upward. "Me too."

They embraced before Jana got into her car and left.

On the way home, Lawrence called.

"Hi, honey," she said. "I was just on my way to the store to pick up some groceries. I'm making a very special dinner for you tonight."

"That's why I'm calling," Lawrence interjected. "We're going out tonight, so don't worry about cooking."

He was ruining her plans for the evening. "Do we really have to go out?" Jana asked. "I'd really like for us to stay home tonight."

"We're going out with Ron and Lela. I already told them that we'd be joining them."

Jana frowned. "You can't back out just this once?"

"I don't want to back out," Lawrence said. "What's up, Jana?"

"Outside of wanting to spend some alone time with you—nothing," she responded. "Lawrence, I wanted this evening to be just about us."

"I'll make it up to you, baby. Besides, I think you're really going to enjoy yourself tonight."

"Fine," Jana uttered. "But I fully expect you to make it up to me. I want you to come home, and tomorrow night will just be about us."

"I give you my word," he told her. "All I want is you to be happy, Jana."

That's what she was counting on.

Chapter 18

JANA READ THE SIGNAGE. "Le Luxure Manoir . . . I've never heard of this club, but then my clubbing days ended after I graduated from college."

"I'm pretty sure this one isn't like any of the ones you used to frequent."

"Lawrence, I never figured you for a party animal. It was hard enough to get you on the dance floor at our reception."

The bouncer at the door greeted them. "Good to see you, Mr. Collins."

Surprised, Jana glanced over at her husband. "He knows you?"

Lawrence held up a gold card. "I'm a member here."

"You have a VIP membership to this place?" Jana asked, staring at the card in her husband's hand. She was shocked, because Lawrence had never mentioned the club to her. He'd never brought her there when they'd been dating. "You must come here often."

"I used to come here all the time," he responded without meeting her eye. "I haven't been as much since we got together."

The way Lawrence avoided eye contact made Jana question the truthfulness of his response.

He guided her through the heavy double doors. Jana glanced around the club, checking out her surroundings. Loud music played in the background, and there were people on the dance floor dancing. It looked like a normal club until she noticed all the scantily clad or completely nude couples in the dim lighting.

The hair on the back of Jana's neck stood up. "Lawrence, tell me exactly what kind of place you've brought me to."

He put a comforting hand on the back of her neck. "Just relax, sweetheart."

Her gaze continued to travel around the room. Jana noticed a woman standing near the bar without a stitch of clothing. She looked bored, and she wasn't the only one. Several other patrons seemed to be staring aimlessly into space.

"Where are we going?" she asked.

"To the VIP room," Lawrence responded.

Jana continued taking in her surroundings. When Lawrence led her past a group of beds lined up in a room, she asked, "Why are there beds in that room?"

"That's the Red Room. If you want to have sex, you just go in there. There is another room over there. It's the Blue Room."

She stopped in her tracks. The shock of what she was seeing hit Jana full force.

She glanced up at him, her mouth wide open. "OHMIGOSH!" she uttered after finding her voice. "Lawrence, there are people having sex in there."

Lawrence grabbed her by her shoulders. "Babe, get a grip, will you? We're all adults here."

Backing away from him, Jana shook her head. "Lawrence, I can't stay here. This is so wrong on so many levels." She turned to leave.

He reached out, grabbing her right hand. "You can and *you will*."

Jana tried to snatch her hand away, but Lawrence's grip was too strong. "How could you bring me to a club like this?" she asked, outraged. "What in the world are you thinking?"

"I can't believe you're that naïve, sweetheart." Her eyes bored into his in answer. "Look, I've tried to be patient with you. You're my wife and I've given you everything you can imagine. Now it's time for you to stop living in that tiny little world your sister and Daniel created. It's not real, Jana."

Jana snatched her hand out of his. "What are you talking about?"

"God created us as very sexual beings. Why would He do that if explor-ing our fantasies is wrong?"

She glared at him. "How dare you mention God in a place like this?" She retreated a step in the event God was about to pour His wrath down on her husband.

Lawrence chuckled. "You are quite the holy one, aren't you? I guess you think you're defending God's honor."

"God doesn't need me to defend Him," Jana responded hotly. "But if I were you, I'd be trying to get this right." She glanced around. "I'd also be trying to get out of Sodom and Gomorrah."

Lawrence's expression turned nasty. "I don't need you to try to save me. Jana, you need to really have a better understanding of God's word before you attempt to correct someone."

"Keep your voice down," Jana uttered. "I'm not the one who's mis-guided, Lawrence. You are."

"We will discuss this later," he said in a tone that brooked no argument. "Ron and Lela just walked in, and I expect you to be pleasant. Do you understand?"

A thread of embarrassment slid down Jana's spine. "I can't believe you brought me to a place like this. I can't imagine what Lela must think."

"They've been coming to this club for years. We all have."

A soft gasp escaped her.

"Hi, Jana," Lela greeted. "It's so good to see you."

"H-hello," she managed. Jana wondered why her supposed friend had never once mentioned coming to a place like this.

Before she could ask, Lela said, "I'm sure this is a bit of a shock to you, but everyone's really nice here. Why don't we find a table and sit down for a minute?"

"I can see how friendly they are," Jana muttered. "Lela, I have no inten-tion of staying here."

"We don't have to stay down here," Lela said, starting to look guiltier. "There's a couples-only area on the second floor, a group room and private rooms."

Jana wanted to ask, *Why are you telling me this?* but she decided to keep her mouth shut. Deep down, she feared that she already knew the answer.

Her chest constricted, and she felt like she couldn't catch her breath.

Lela reached over and took her hand. "Are you okay?"

"I just want to get out of here," Jana said. "I can't believe you're so comfortable in this place."

"Jana, it's going to be okay. We're just sitting up there talking. This club has strict rules and bouncers as big as sumo wrestlers, in case you haven't noticed. Nobody has to do anything."

Jana rose to her feet. "I'm sorry, Lela. This goes against everything I believe in. I'm leaving."

"Please wait until Lawrence and Ron come back," Lela pleaded.

Jana shook her head. "I can't take another second in this place."

She grabbed her purse and rushed off, heading straight toward the nearest exit. Outside, Jana hailed a taxi to drive her home.

Her cell phone rang. It was Lawrence. Knowing how furious he would be with her, she didn't bother to answer. She would deal with him later.

Jana went straight up to her bedroom as soon as she arrived home. Lawrence was still trying to reach her on her cell, so she turned it off.

He began calling the number to the house, and she ignored those calls as well.

She took off her clothes and showered, yet no amount of scrubbing could wipe away the sleazy images that popped into her head.

Afterward, Jana slipped on a pair of cotton pajamas—the pair that Lawrence hated most.

She climbed into bed and burst into tears.

LAWRENCE CAME HOME A couple of hours later.

Jana could tell that he was angry by the way he blew through the doors of their bedroom.

"How dare you embarrass me like that," he shouted. "I have been nothing less than a good husband to you."

"Why would you take me to a place like that?" Jana demanded. "What kind of woman do you think I am?"

"You're supposed to be my wife. Most of the couples in the club are married."

Jana shook her head in disgust. What was wrong with her husband? Why would he think she would want to go to a place like that?

"All I wanted to do was show you that it's okay to explore your sexuality."

Jana wasn't buying that line anymore. "I don't have a problem with my sexuality, Lawrence. But apparently you have a problem with it."

Seeing how determined she was, he groaned. "Will you please stop thinking so negatively? I don't have a problem with you in bed, Jana. I've said over and over again that we are great together. All I want is for you to be more open-minded."

Jana wanted to ask why Ron and Lela Boykin had been at the club, but deep down, she already knew. They had come to meet her and Lawrence. She briefly wondered if Lela enjoyed watching other couples in the throes of passion. She must, because she hadn't had any qualms about being there; Jana had been the only one freaking out.

Dear Lord, what is wrong with these people?

"Jana, I have to be honest with you about this," Lawrence said, exasperated. "You're going to have to get it together or we're not going to make it. All I'm asking you to do is have an open mind. Instead, you've been nothing but judgmental."

His words pierced her spirit. He had made absolutely no attempt to listen to her feelings.

"I'm trying to share my world with you, but Jana, you're making it harder and harder on me."

Jana wiped away her tears with the back of her hand.

Lawrence dropped down on the edge of the bed. "I don't know what else to do. I don't want to lie to you or keep secrets from you, but what choice are you giving me?"

"Lawrence, I'm sorry, but I'm not comfortable with what's going on. I don't like watching other people being intimate."

"How do you know?" Lawrence asked. "According to you, you hadn't done it before you married me. You can't dislike something without at least trying it out."

Jana wanted to bang her head against the wall. It was useless. They were never going to agree on this subject.

Grumbling, Lawrence changed into a pair of sweats. He glanced over at Jana, then, shaking his head, walked out of the bedroom, slamming the door behind him.

She spent most of the night trying to figure out what to do. She loved Lawrence, but she was confused.

By the time the clock struck six thirty, Jana had made a decision.

JANA GOT UP AND packed an overnight bag.

"Where are you going?" Lawrence asked from the doorway. "Are you leaving me?"

"I need a couple of days to myself," she responded without looking at him. Jana couldn't bear to see the look of hurt on Lawrence's face. "I'm checking into a hotel."

He walked inside and stopped in the middle of the room. "Jana, you don't have to leave. I can go to a hotel. Look, I have to go to San Francisco for a conference," he offered. "I wasn't planning to go originally, but with this stuff between us . . . it might be a good idea."

"Are you sure that's what you want?"

Lawrence nodded. "Maybe we both need a break. I won't be gone that long, but it will give us some time to think about things. I don't want to fight anymore."

"We haven't been married for very long and we already need a break from each other." She felt sick inside. "This is such a shame."

"I don't see we have a choice," Lawrence replied. "You're not happy, and neither am I, Jana. Something has to change."

You have to change, she thought, but she didn't say it. "When do you leave for San Francisco?"

"I'll have my secretary call you with my itinerary." Lawrence headed toward the bathroom. "I need to take a shower and get ready for work."

"Where did you sleep last night?" Jana asked. "I didn't sleep well because you weren't here with me."

"I slept in the guest room right down the hall." He gave her a tiny smile. "My night was just as miserable."

Jana reached out and took him by the hand. "Lawrence, I don't want you to leave. Maybe there is another solution."

"You need some time to think, and so do I," Lawrence insisted. "I'll only be gone for three days, babe. Once I get back, we'll sit down and try to figure this thing out once and for all."

"I really want us to get back on track."

"And we will," Lawrence promised. "I can't see my life without you. I know that I've given you a really hard time. I've said some not-so-nice things to you."

That reminder made her pull back slightly. "I guess we do need this time apart," she uttered. "I pray that when you come back, we'll be able to find a compromise."

"Let God lead you, babe. Remove all of the religious stuff from your mind."

"I'd like for you to do the same, Lawrence. Forget about what Pastor Laney has told you—read the word of the Lord for yourself."

Yet in his eyes she saw that would never happen. He had chosen Pastor Laney because he said the words Lawrence wanted to hear. She would have to find another way—through his heart.

Chapter 19

JANA MISSED HER HUSBAND.

Lawrence had been gone for only one night, but she missed him like crazy. Last night, when he'd called to check on her, they'd stayed on the phone for almost two hours.

She made herself comfortable in the middle of her bed with her Bible and her journal. Jana liked to write down her thoughts and any revelations revealed to her during her study.

Jesus told us that a house divided against itself will fall. Ephesians 5:22 tells us: "Wives, submit yourselves unto your own husbands, as unto the Lord."

Wives are to submit to their husbands just as they submit to the Lord! I believe that any woman not submitting to her husband cannot be in total submission to Christ. Instead, she is rebelling against the very Word of God. But in my heart I have a question, and that is, what is the husband's responsibility in all of this submission business?

Ephesians 5:25–32 says: "Husbands, love your wives, even as Christ also loved the church, and gave himself for it; That he might sanctify and cleanse it with the washing of water by the word, That he might present it to himself a glorious church, not having spot, or wrinkle, or any such thing; but that it should be holy and without blemish. So ought men to love their wives as their own bodies. He that loves his wife loves himself. For no man ever yet hated his own flesh; but nourished and cherished it, even as the Lord the church: For we are members of his body, of his flesh, and of his bones. For this cause shall a man leave his father and mother, and shall be joined unto his wife, and they two shall be one flesh. This is a great mystery: but I speak concerning Christ and the church."

Jana meditated on the scriptures for a moment, then picked up her pen to write down her thoughts.

This is an awesome calling for men. To love their wives as Christ loved the Church and gave up His life out of that love. I have to consider what my husband does for me. He gives up most of his day working a job to feed, shelter, and clothe me. Just as Christ nourishes and cherishes the Church, Lawrence nourishes and cherishes me.

Although I don't agree with most of Pastor Laney's beliefs, he was right when he said that women are merely called to be in submission, while men are commanded to love, cherish, nourish, and give their lives for their mate. Submitting to your husband in marriage isn't hard if you marry the right kind of man.

You have to trust that your husband has your best interests in mind and lays aside his own needs to love you the way Christ loved the Church. Why would you not submit to him?

God's truth for me: Lawrence and I have to be committed to putting the other one first in love. I have to think of his needs first, even when his love is not so perfect. Love covers a multitude of sins, and I have to remember that some days it may be Lawrence loving his not-so-grateful wife.

• • •

HE DIVA OF SHOPPING was at it again, and she commanded Jana to join her for another round. Lela was on the quest for the perfect gown, because she and Ron were attending an upcoming awards gala. Since Lawrence had a meeting at the firm, Jana didn't have to make dinner, leaving her free to join Lela at the store.

"I like your hair," Lela complimented.

"I just got it done this morning," Jana stated. "I'm missing my short hairstyle, but Lawrence wants me to let it grow out, so I'm dealing with this weave."

"Well, it looks like the real deal. I love the layers." Lela touched her own long, curly locks. "I need to have something done to this stuff on my head."

"You have beautiful hair, Lela. Or do you have extensions?"

She shook her head no. "This is all mine—I just want to do something different with it. It's all one length, which doesn't give me a lot of styling options. I'm thinking about wearing it up for the gala. That's if I can find the right gown."

"I need to ask you something, Lela."

"What is it?"

"Why do you allow Ron to take you to clubs like that?" Jana asked. "Do you enjoy being there?"

"It's what he likes to do, and he's not trying to hide anything. I appreciate his honesty."

"Lela, do you enjoy watching other people have sex?"

"Not really," she responded. "But I want to please Ron and I don't want him to start sneaking around on me."

"Do you really think that's what will happen? That Ron will start lying to you about where he's going?"

Lela eyed her. "You don't think Lawrence will do the same? Jana, I may not like some of the stuff my husband does, but I love him more than my own life and I don't want to lose him." Lela turned and picked up a gown. "Now this is what you call ugly. I wouldn't wear this to my own funeral."

Jana put on a tight smile. She knew that Lela didn't want to discuss the club any longer.

They went from store to store, but nothing spoke to Lela.

Angie called while they were out. She wanted to meet for dinner since they were all on their own for the evening. Jana discussed the time and location with her, while Lela tried on nearly a dozen dresses.

"This is awful," Lela complained. "I don't have time to have something designed—all of the designers are busy with their fall collections. What am I going to do?"

"Maybe you should meet with my sister," Jana suggested. "If you have an idea of what you want, Robyn can create it."

"Will she have time to do it?"

"I can call her," Jana offered.

A few minutes later, they were on their way to meet with Robyn.

Within an hour, Lela left the boutique singing Robyn's praises.

"She is so talented, Jana. I'm telling you, Robyn's designs should be on the runway during Fashion Week."

Jana agreed. She checked her watch. "We need to get going. Angie is expecting us to meet her at eight."

They were about ten minutes late.

"I'm sorry we're just getting here," Jana said.

"We were at Robyn's Boutique," Lela chimed in. "She's designing my gown for the gala."

"How wonderful," Angie murmured. "I hope you don't end up looking like you're at church."

Jana bit back a retort. It was pretty clear that Angie had already had more than one drink, and she had just ordered another glass of white wine. Lela ordered an apple martini.

Lela asked, "Would you like to try my drink?"

"No, thank you," Jana responded as she scanned the menu. "I'm not much of a drinker."

"You are such a Goody Two-shoes," Angie uttered. "How can you stand being so good all the time?"

Jana exchanged glances with Lela, who said, "She's kidding."

"Oh, honey, I'm just having a li'l fun. I didn't mean any harm."

"No harm done," Jana stated. "I enjoy a glass of wine every now and then, but I don't bother with anything else."

"I bet the boys are having themselves a ball," Angie blurted. "We probably need to go over there and pull them out of the club."

Jana glanced over at Lela and asked, "What is she talking about? What club?"

"Angie, I think you've had too much wine. Ron and Lawrence had a business meeting."

Angie frowned. "Are you sure? I thought my husband told me that they were going to the club. Maybe he just said that to get out of the house." She laughed. "He can be such a bad boy at times."

"What is she talking about?" Jana asked a second time.

"Nothing," Lela uttered. "She's a little drunk, I think. Just excuse whatever comes out of her mouth."

"Maybe we should call a taxi for her?" Jana suggested.

"I'll take her home. She's not too far from me."

"I can drive home," Angie stated. "Or Jana, you can take me home. Don't you want to come over to my house?"

Jana frowned.

Why does she want me to take her home? I don't live anywhere near her.

"Angie, let's go." Lela rose to her feet and pulled Angie up.

"What's wrong, sugah? You jealous? You don't have to be jealous . . . you're the one who doesn't want to—"

"Now I know it's time to go," Lela said angrily, cutting her off. "You get crazy when you drink like this." She grabbed Angie roughly by the arm and rushed her out of the restaurant.

Confused by the sudden turn of events, Jana followed them outside.

Paparazzi began snapping photos of Angie escorted by Lela. Jana walked briskly to her car, grateful that they didn't seem interested in her.

She drove home and settled down in the family room.

Jana didn't want to spend another night alone in her home, so she invited Graciela and Robyn to a sleepover.

• • •

"
HAVEN'T DONE THIS IN a long time," her sister said happily as she pol-
ished the nails on her right foot. "We should have big-girl sleepovers
more often. I haven't pampered myself this much in so long."

Graciela agreed. "Enrique is in Dallas, so I'm glad I didn't have to be
home alone another night." She held up her hands to admire her handi-
work.

"Hey, do you have a signature color?" Jana inquired.

Graciela looked at her funny. "If I did, I guess it would be hot pink. I
love that color."

"Signature color," Robyn repeated. "I don't have one of those. Do you
have one, Jana?"

"No. Angie and Lela do, though. When I first met them, they told me
that I needed to brand myself as Lawrence's wife."

"I guess the wives of rich men are now a business," Graciela said sarcastically. "I sure didn't get the memo on that one."

"Jana, you've done that," Robyn pointed out. "Look how you've
changed your look and the way you dress. Lawrence wanted a sexy vixen,
and now he's got one."

"He sure does," Graciela contributed.

Jana didn't like the two-on-one attack at all. "When did you say that
Enrique would be back?" Jana inquired, trying to change the subject. "Lawrence won't be home until Thursday." She held up a bottle of spice orange
nail polish. "I think I'm going to try this color. I want something bright."

"He'll be back tomorrow, and don't think we don't know what you
doing. You trying to be slick." Graciela picked up a carton of shrimp fried
rice and spooned some on her plate. "I can't wait to see my man, though. I
miss my boo."

Robyn took a sip of her sparkling water. "Daniel's right here in town
and I'm missing him. Jana, don't be offended if I decide to go home tonight.
I don't like to be away from my man."

"It's just one night, Robyn. What do you do when Daniel has to
travel?"

"He's not traveling as much as he used to," she replied. "I try to go with him most of the time, but when I don't, it's no more than a night or two. I have no choice when that happens, but this I can control."

"Robyn, it's getting late," Jana said. "Please, just stay with me tonight. If you want, call Daniel and tell him to come over, but he'll have to stay upstairs or in the media room. It's our night. I really need my girls right now."

Robyn appeared to be considering Jana's suggestion.

Graciela laughed. "C'mon, Robyn . . . you can do this. You don't need your man babysitting us."

"Oh, the peer pressure," Robyn moaned. "Both Enrique and Lawrence are out of town. Daniel's home."

"He'll be fine," Jana pleaded. "Call him."

Robyn picked up her cell phone and dialed Daniel's number. "Hey, sweetie. You missing me yet?"

"Your sister is so funny," Graciela whispered. "I can't believe she's trying to go home like that."

"She loves herself some Daniel," Jana responded. "I know the feeling. I really miss Lawrence."

"Daniel, if you want me to come home, I will," Robyn said.

They both cracked up at her next reply: "You must not be missing me too much if you're telling me to stay over here."

Robyn sent them a sharp look.

"Let Daniel have some alone time," Jana whispered.

Robyn talked a few minutes more and hung up the phone. "I can't believe him. He actually told me that he thought I should stay here."

"Daniel's right," Jana seconded. "I need you."

The three women laughed and talked until they fell asleep in the family room. Jana took the floor, surrounded by a stack of oversized pillows with a cashmere throw covering her body. Graciela took one leather sofa, while Robyn had the other.

Jana was the first to wake up.

She sat up slowly, her gaze traveling the room. She broke into a smile when she glimpsed Graciela sleeping with her mouth wide open. Robyn was on the other side, snoring softly.

Jana stifled a yawn and pulled herself off the floor. She tiptoed to the kitchen and started a pot of coffee as quietly as she could.

Robyn stirred first. She sat up and glanced around the room.

"Good morning," Jana said from the kitchen.

Graciela woke up as well. She sat up and ran her fingers through her hair. "Morning, ladies."

"I just put on the coffee," Jana announced. "It should be ready shortly. I don't have any chai tea, but I do have some orange spice."

Graciela nodded. "That'll do."

Over breakfast, Jana said, "I really appreciate you both staying here with me. Especially you, Robyn. I know that you really wanted to be home with Daniel."

"I had fun with you and Graciela." Robyn took a sip of her coffee. "I'm glad I stayed."

"I miss Lawrence so much. More than I ever thought I could." Jana bit into her bagel.

"That's a natural feeling when you love someone," Graciela said.

"We've been arguing over crazy stuff."

"You haven't been married that long," Robyn pointed out. "You're still getting to know the man. Arguments are going to happen."

Jana didn't mention that all of their fights stemmed from the topic of sex. She didn't dare say that Lawrence had taken her to a sex club. She was concerned that they would get the wrong idea about her husband.

It was important to make them believe that she had made the right choice in marrying Lawrence. Jana wasn't sure why, but it was the way she felt.

Our marriage isn't that bad, she told herself. Lawrence was a wonderful man, and he took care of her. He treated her like a queen.

Their marriage was worth fighting for—she knew it in her heart. Divorce was not an option.

• • •

J ANA RAN INTO LAWRENCE'S arms as soon as he entered the house. "I'm so glad you're home. I missed you so much."

She planted kisses all over his face.

"Maybe I should start traveling more often," he teased. "I like this type of welcome." She rose on tiptoe to meet her husband's lips. He kissed her hungrily.

"I missed you too," he whispered. "You were all that I thought about."

He retrieved a brightly wrapped gift box from his jacket. "I have something for you."

"What is it?" she asked.

"Babe, just open it and see for yourself."

Jana tore the wrapping off her gift.

"Lawrence, this is stunning!" Jana exclaimed, holding up a sapphire and diamond tennis bracelet. "I love it."

"I know how much you love those sapphire and diamond earrings that belonged to your mother. When I saw this, I thought it would be perfect with them."

"You are so thoughtful," Jana murmured. "Thank you."

"I love you," Lawrence declared. "I know things between us have been a little rough, but my feelings haven't changed. I love you, and I wouldn't put you in harm's way ever."

Jana could read the sincerity in his expression. "I love you too."

"I want our marriage to work, sweetheart."

"So do I," Jana confirmed. "There's nothing I want more."

Lawrence continued to hold her snugly in his arms. "What we have is special, Jana. It's definitely worth fighting for."

She couldn't agree more.

Chapter 20

JANA WAITED UNTIL LAWRENCE was asleep, then she eased out of bed. She tiptoed to the bathroom and turned on the shower.

She wanted so much to please her husband, but the demands he placed on her only made her feel dirty.

Tears filled her eyes and rolled down her cheeks.

Alone in the shower, she prayed over her situation. Jana also thought about her conversation with Graciela and Robyn.

"I can't do all those things that Lawrence wants me to do, Father God," she whispered. "It just doesn't feel right in my spirit."

Lawrence was awake when she strolled back into the bedroom. He sat up in bed and turned on a nearby lamp. Studying her face, he asked, "Babe, what's going on?"

"I hope I didn't wake you," Jana responded. "I just wanted to take a shower. I thought it might help me sleep."

"It's much more than that," Lawrence said. "Jana, please be honest with me. Tell me what's bothering you."

She climbed back into bed. "What exactly is a liberated Christian? Please explain that to me."

He yawned, then glanced over at the clock on the nightstand. "Do you really want to discuss this now?"

Jana nodded. "I know it's late, but it's been on my mind. I've heard you refer to yourself as one, and so have Pastor Laney and Ron."

"Okay," Lawrence mumbled. "Liberated Christians are people who are free from the control of rigid theologies or authoritarian churches. We have separated ourselves from sexually repressed religion."

"Like my sexual beliefs?"

He shrugged. "We can learn a lot about God by studying how He made and designed the animal kingdom, including animal sexuality and patterns of living. We should believe God when He said everything He made was good. Animals are not ashamed of their nudity or sexuality. Do you think that we should be? Adam and Eve walked around without clothes until sin separated them from God."

Jana didn't respond.

"When God said it was good, He was also talking about our sexuality too—our bodies, our sex organs, our sexual fantasies and our sexual enjoyment—everything. It was all designed by a pure and Holy God. Basically, liberated Christians live under the law of love."

"I'm having a really hard time thinking of this as biblical," Jana admitted.

"We don't turn our minds off when we read the Bible," Lawrence told her. "You have to read the whole Bible to see the whole picture and not just take a few verses out of context and let that define your sexuality."

"I do agree with that part," Jana interjected. "You shouldn't twist the scriptures to serve your own purpose. I've studied the Bible, and Lawrence, I haven't come across anything in there to support what you've told me."

"It's in the Old Testament, in the book of Esther," Lawrence stated. "The king's queen—"

Jana cut him off. "Queen Vashti."

"Yeah. Remember that Queen Vashti was told to come join her husband with just a crown on her head. He wanted his wife to show off her beauty to his guests so they could admire her sexy body. The queen refused to come, and what happened because of her disobedience? She was dethroned as queen. She disrespected a man who had given her everything. She did not submit to her husband."

"I've been doing a study on her," Jana said. She shifted her position in bed. "According to Wesley's notes, the way I understand it is that by the law of Persia, it was customary to keep men's wives—especially queens— from the view of other men. Initially, I thought the same way that you did. I thought she disrespected her husband until I read that. Now I believe that Queen Vashti felt that her beauty should have been reserved for her husband only. I can understand that because that's how I feel—we've discussed this before, remember? I had to grow up with men trying to grope me or get me into bed. I didn't feel loved. I felt like they only wanted me to be a receptacle for their lust."

Lawrence said, "Okay . . . well, let's move on. The king needed a new wife, so they gathered up all the virgins and gave them all beauty treatments for a year, as well as prepared them for a night of sex play and great sex with the king. The king's eunuchs were castrated so they would not get the wives of the king pregnant. They would prepare and teach the virgins how to please the king sexually. The most beautiful and sexiest in bed with the king became the new queen." He paused before making his point. "Esther won the position as the queen. Most of the people of the Old Testament probably would've been thrown out of the churches we have today."

"God ordained that Esther would marry the king so that she could save the Jews," Jana said.

"Well, she won the sex contest, and that's why she became queen. You just admitted yourself that God designed it for her to win this sex contest. King David—think about him. He would've been kicked out of the church too."

"Those were different times, Lawrence—" Jana began.

Lawrence interrupted her. "Then there's Abraham, who married his sister and gave his wife to two different kings so they could have sex with her. Jacob had sex with another woman on his wedding night and a week later married his second wife. He was having sex with two women and their handmaidens. One time, his first wife actually paid the second wife so that she could have a turn to have sex with Jacob."

Jana shook her head, fighting back tears. It was heartbreaking to hear just how misguided Lawrence was. She knew that he actually believed the crap he was spouting. He sounded just like Pastor Laney.

She inhaled deeply, then exhaled slowly. "The reason men had concubines and multiple wives back in those days was because religion and the law were intertwined. Lawrence, you know that it's not the same today. Religion and law are separate. If you refer to Romans 13, the scriptures tell us to obey the rule of law."

Lawrence opened his mouth to speak, but Jana held up her hand to stop him. "Please, just let me finish. You can't have more than one wife outside of Utah because it's the law. You're right that the Bible doesn't come right out and say yes or no about certain issues, but I can't find anywhere it specifically says that God gave us sexual freedom. Lawrence, He gave us the freedom to love, but that Eros love only comes in the covenant of marriage. Marriage is the union between two people—not three or four."

"Babe, I disagree, and there's something you need to know about me," Lawrence said, becoming very still all of a sudden. "Maybe I should've mentioned it sooner, but I didn't want to drive you away."

"What do you have to tell me?" she asked.

"When Gia and I were married, we were swingers."

"Excuse me," Jana cried. "What did you just say?" She felt like she had just been punched in the stomach.

"Just hear me out," Lawrence pleaded. "Swinging married couples allow their spouses to expand their sexual love to others. I think that you should also know that swingers have stronger marriages than those that don't partake of the lifestyle."

"Yeah, right . . ." Jana swung her legs outward. She got up and began pacing the floor. "I can't believe what I'm hearing."

"These strict religious marriages do nothing but create feelings of slavery, bondage, and jealousy."

Jana turned to face him. "Because people like me don't want to share."

Lawrence climbed out of bed and walked over to where she was standing. "Did you know that the term 'swinging' was first used by a minister?"

Her mouth dropped open in her surprise. "You're kidding, right?"

Lawrence shook his head. "One Sunday he announced to his congregation that there were people swinging back and forth from bed to bed. He compared it to monkeys."

Jana nodded in understanding. "I can certainly see why he'd say that."

"Read your Bible again, because it was acceptable for men to have more than one wife and several concubines for their sexual pleasure. Africa, Egypt, China, and other countries have lived the lifestyle for centuries. Swinging has roots deep in our military history from World War Two and the Korean War. In 1957 the media got hold of what was going on and dubbed it wife-swapping."

"I appreciate your little history lesson, Lawrence, but I still don't agree with the behavior. It's totally wrong." Jana rubbed her arms to ward off the sudden chill she felt. "Dear Lord God . . ." She put her hands to her face.

He tried to pry her hands apart. "I love you, Jana, but you're way too uptight. I'm going to find a way to loosen you up some."

His warning caused a new thought to pop into her head. "Lawrence, I have to know something," Jana began. "Are you still swinging? Since we've been together?"

He shook his head.

Tears running down her face, Jana shouted, "No, you don't get to just shake your head. You give me an answer right now. Have you cheated on me? You tell me."

"I haven't cheated on you, Jana."

When Lawrence reached out for her, she took a step backward. "I'm sorry," she whispered. "I have a lot to process."

"Jana, I love you."

"I don't doubt that," she responded, wiping her tears away with the back of her hand. "Why didn't you tell me about your, ah, your habits before we got married? I believe I had a right to know."

"Because I wasn't sure how you'd react. I didn't want to lose you, sweetheart."

Jana cringed at the use of that endearment. It sure sounded strange right now. She glanced over at the clock. "It's getting late. You have to be in court tomorrow."

"Don't worry about me—I'll be fine," Lawrence told her. "I think we need to talk this through some more. Jana, I'm sorry about keeping this from you."

"Let's try and get some sleep," she said loudly, although she knew that she would be awake for most of the night. "I can't talk about this anymore."

"I want to finish our discussion," Lawrence said. "Whenever you're ready to talk, I'm ready."

Jana nodded.

She made her way back to the bed and climbed in.

Jana buried herself beneath the covers and positioned herself as far away from Lawrence as she could. She released a soft sigh of relief when he joined her in bed but didn't bother to touch her.

Tonight was probably the worst night of her life.

LAWRENCE HATED LYING TO Jana, but she still couldn't handle the truth. She was still too fragile. Even in their dimly lit bedroom, he could see how freaked out she'd been by the idea of swinging.

She's just in shock.

He would broach the subject again in a few days. Lawrence was trying to be patient and understanding, but he was long past ready to take their relationship to the next level. Ron and Lela were waiting on him to have Jana prepped and ready for an encounter.

There was nothing wrong with swinging. It wasn't adultery. A lot of people thought it was, but they had nothing to do but sit in judgment of others.

I have faith in you, Jana. You just have to have faith in me too. I need you to trust that I wouldn't do anything to harm you or our marriage.

She would come around.

That's what Lawrence kept telling himself. Now that she knew the truth and had some time to accept it, Jana would soon be the ideal wife in every way possible.

Chapter 21

SHE WAS MARRIED TO a former swinger.

Jana wasn't sure what to do with this piece of news. Her emotions ran rampant. She felt a sense of betrayal, as if she didn't know Lawrence at all; Jana felt so many things all at once.

One part of her brain told her that most men had multiple lovers at some point in their lives. Even some women kept a count of the notches on their headboards. What made what Lawrence did any different?

Yet if he considered himself a swinger, that meant he must have participated in group sex or orgies. Jana really had a hard time wrapping her mind around this. She couldn't picture her husband—sweet, loving, almost-always-too-serious Lawrence—in a mass of groping hands and bodies.

All of this had taken place while he'd been married to Gia. *It has nothing to do with me, so how do I get past this?* she wondered. *He still should have mentioned it to me. Lawrence should have told me the truth about himself.*

A new burst of anger coursed through Jana. What else didn't she know about Lawrence? Did he have a criminal record? Was Lawrence Maxwell Collins even his real name?

Walking briskly to the door, Jana grabbed her car keys and purse. She needed to get out of that house.

She ended up driving over to the boutique.

Robyn was thrilled to see her. "I'm going to look at this building I think will be perfect for the new store. Want to come along?"

Jana nodded.

She rode with her sister.

"This place has so much potential," Robyn was saying. "It used to be a maternity shop, but it went out of business when the owner died."

Jana wasn't really listening to her sister; her mind was plagued with the nightmare that had suddenly become her life. She wanted something more out of their marriage than just sex. She'd thought they were on solid ground, only to find out they weren't.

Robyn parked the car. When they got out, she glanced over at Jana and said, "Why are you so quiet? Are you feeling okay?"

"I'm okay," Jana lied.

"Are you sure? You look like something's bothering you."

Jana plastered on a smile. "Robyn, I'm fine. C'mon and let's see if this place is as perfect as you keep saying."

Jana could feel her sister's gaze on her, but she pretended not to notice.

They were given a tour by the real estate broker. Jana walked around the space and made some notes while Robyn and the agent talked.

When they were back in the car, Robyn asked, "Well, what do you think?"

"It's nice, and I think it could work, but I'm not completely sold on the place. Robyn, I think we should keep looking."

"Jana, why won't you tell me what's going on with you?"

"Robyn, I'll be okay. It's not anything that you can do—just a phase that Lawrence and I are going through."

"Are you sure?" Robyn wanted to know.

"Trust me," Jana said. "There's nothing you can do. It's up to me and Lawrence."

AWRENCE WALKED DOWNSTAIRS AND into the family room, waving a small white flag. "I come in peace. I don't want to fight anymore."

Jana laid her book down on the sofa. "It's not on my agenda either."

He sat down beside her. "I love you more than I love my own life, babe. For the first time in a long time, I'm afraid of losing someone I truly care about." Lawrence met her gaze. "I don't want to lose you."

She had seen that earnest look before. "I feel as if I don't really know you, Lawrence."

"You know me," he countered. "Your heart knows me. I'm still the same man that you dated, fell in love with, and married. I have a past—a colorful one, but it's my past. I won't sit here and tell you that I regret any of it, because then I would be lying. My ex-wife and I had an open marriage, and it suited us both."

"But you think that swinging is okay, that it's not a sin, right?"

"I'm afraid that I don't, Jana." Lawrence rose to his feet. "I believe as strongly as you do—we're just on opposite sides of the coin. So I guess it comes back to what do we do now?"

"Maybe we should try counseling," Jana suggested after a brief pause.

"I can call Pastor Laney tomorrow morning."

Jana shook her head vehemently. "I'd rather we find someone else."

"You want Daniel to counsel us."

It wasn't a question. Jana could tell that Lawrence wasn't pleased with the idea, so she responded, "No. I think it should be someone who doesn't know either one of us."

She wouldn't dream of going to Daniel with something like this. Jana hoped that her sister and brother-in-law never found out.

Lawrence considered the idea, deliberately, like a lawyer. At last he said, "Tell me something, Jana. What are you hoping to accomplish by going to counseling? The only problem we have is that our beliefs about sex don't line up."

"That's an important part of marriage, don't you think?" Jana asked.

"You're just not as open-minded as I am."

"You're right about that," she confirmed. "Lawrence, right now I'm really confused. I know what feels right to me . . ." Jana released a long sigh. "I just don't know what to do or how we can get past this. We need some help."

"Why won't you trust me?" he wanted to know.

"I did trust you, Lawrence. But I've just found out that you have secrets. Secrets that I'm still trying to deal with. I don't really know what to believe now because I don't know who you really are."

"That's why you should try and discern for yourself what's right and wrong, honey. Forget what you heard in church all those years. Study the Bible for yourself."

"I'd like to resolve this once and for all," Jana stated. "But even if we lay your secrets to rest, I have to be honest with you, Lawrence. I won't ever be comfortable with sex clubs and all that stuff. It's just not me."

"Honey, I was just like you at one time. But then I had a talk with Pastor Laney, and then I studied the Bible for myself."

Jana wasn't sure what to do. Lawrence had been brainwashed, and no amount of talking would change his mind or his beliefs.

Lawrence tried to make a joke. "We could practice sex your way. I mean right now."

"I'm sorry," she told him. "I've still got a lot on my mind. I can't."

A flash of anger passed over his face, but he kept his mouth closed.

"I don't see how you can expect me to just move past everything you've told me—I need time to digest all of this, Lawrence."

"I understand," he said after a moment. "I'll give you the space that you need."

He headed for the door.

"Where are you going?" she asked.

"I need to get out of here for a couple of hours."

He picked up his keys, pausing long enough to say "Good night."

"Wait," Jana said. "When will you be back?"

"An hour . . . two hours . . . I don't know."

He left the room, slamming the doors behind him.

Jana felt like she was living in the twilight zone.

She checked the clock an hour later, then again at midnight. Lawrence had been gone almost three hours.

Jana sat up in bed and tried calling his cell phone. It went straight to voice mail. *He's avoiding me now.*

Jana couldn't sleep, so she picked up her Bible and opened it to a random page. She read scriptures until her eyelids became heavy. She put the book back on her nightstand and lay back down.

A lone tear slipped from her tired eyes.

T HE NEXT MORNING, LAWRENCE was still hopeful that soon Jana would understand. He didn't want to force Jana into the lifestyle after what had happened with his first wife. Gia had never been able to find her comfort zone until she'd downed several glasses of Jack Daniel's. Soon she'd been drinking twenty-four seven and taking pills for depression. When she'd collapsed at a charity function, Lawrence had known that his marriage had been over.

He had never liked women who drank heavily—they turned him off completely. Still, he'd tried to end the relationship on friendly terms.

He'd paid her a hefty settlement and sent her on her way. He believed that Gia was still bitter about their breakup and his subsequent marriage, so he made a point of avoiding her at all costs.

Lawrence had gone to Le Luxure Manoir the night before. He had placed a call to Rhoda as soon as he'd gotten into his car and had asked her to meet him there. They'd had a nice little foursome with Lenny and Angie.

He felt a thread of guilt but brushed it off. He wouldn't have had to go behind Jana's back if she'd been more cooperative. It was her fault that he had been forced to commit adultery.

Ron stuck his head inside his office. "Hey, want to grab a bite to eat?" he asked, cutting into Lawrence's thoughts.

They went down to the Italian restaurant across the street, a place with red-and-white checkered tablecloths.

"Are things any better at home?" Ron asked.

Lawrence gave a slight shrug. "Not really."

"Take her away," Ron suggested. "Go to that spa in Arizona. The one Angie and Lenny go to all the time. Make it a romantic weekend."

The idea sounded appealing. "But that still doesn't get us any closer to doing what I want."

"Listen to me," Ron said. "The first thing you need to do is get Jana comfortable with her own body. Have the his-and-her body massages. Walk around in the buff while you're in the room. Put a little X in her drink . . . man, you know . . ."

Lawrence was struck by that idea. "I hadn't thought of that. Yeah, I could try some X to get her to relax." He recalled that that's how he'd gotten Gia to participate her first time. It had worked like a charm.

The more he considered the idea the more he liked it. Lawrence had his secretary make the necessary arrangements for the spa.

Later at home, he told Jana, "Don't make any plans for next weekend."

She glanced up from the book she was reading. "What's up?"

"I have a surprise for you," Lawrence said, smiling broadly.

Jana looked skeptical, so he pulled an envelope out of his pocket. "This is Sanctuary Spa in Arizona. I'm sure you've heard Lela rave about it. I thought we might need to get away for a couple of days just to relax and enjoy each other."

Jana looked pleased as she looked over the brochure. "This place sounds heavenly. I can't wait to get there."

"We have two nights in a luxurious casita, access to the meditation garden, steam baths and vitality pools, spa treatments, and"—Lawrence added with a grin—"very romantic evenings."

Jana gave him a wary look. "Okay, Lawrence. Is it just going to be the two of us, or will others be joining us?"

"It's just you and me—I want this trip to be about us."

That's what she wanted to hear. "You're right," she said with a grin. "I'm beginning to think that we just might need this vacation as well."

"Oh, I didn't book separate rooms, Jana."

"It's fine," she said, a little confused. "I didn't expect that you would. Besides, separate bedrooms don't help a marriage."

"Does that mean . . . ," he said.

She shrugged and replied honestly, "I don't know. I just want to take it one day at a time. I'm not going there closed-minded, though. I'm hoping this trip will be a stepping stone toward our future."

"That's my plan exactly. It won't fix our problems, but I just believe that after this weekend, we'll be able to move forward."

Chapter 22

JANA AND GRACIELA WENT shopping for her upcoming weekend.

"That spa sounds wonderful, *mi'ja*. I don't know what's been going on with you two, but you don't sound as stressed as you were before."

"We've been having some problems, which is why I'm looking forward to getting away," Jana admitted. She felt a little queasy and placed her hand to her stomach.

"Hey, what's wrong?" Graciela asked. "Are you okay?"

The feeling grew worse, climbing up into her throat. Jana leaned against a nearby wall. "I feel nauseated."

"Really? Do you think you could be pregnant?"

Jana shook her head in denial. "Graciela, I don't think so. I'm on birth control."

"That's never stopped anything," she responded. "My sister was on birth control when she got pregnant with the twins."

Pregnancy would be all she needed. "I don't think I have to worry about that." The nausea passed and Jana began to feel much better.

"Maybe you just need to eat something. I get that way when I don't eat regularly." Graciela surveyed her face. "When did you last eat?"

"Last night. I wasn't hungry earlier."

"C'mon, *mi'ja*. We can shop after we put something in that stomach of yours."

After a quick lunch of hamburgers and French fries, Graciela helped Jana pick out some new lingerie.

"What do you think?" Jana asked her friend.

"That's way too tame." Graciela picked up something else. "Now, this will make Poppy stand to attention, if you know what I mean."

Jana laughed. "What am I going to do with you?"

They left the Beverly Center two hours later. Graciela went back to her office to pick up some work, while Jana drove home.

She was struck with another bout of nausea when she came home. Jana rushed off to the bathroom. She fell to her knees and vomited up the contents of her stomach.

"You okay?" Lawrence asked, instantly at her side.

"It's just a nervous stomach," she responded. "I don't think that hamburger I had for lunch agreed with me."

"Maybe you should lie down and take a nap," he suggested.

Jana felt weak as she tried to stand. "I think I will."

Lawrence helped her to their bedroom. He turned down the covers and assisted her into bed, then he closed the drapes to darken the room.

"I'll be in the living room if you need me," he told her.

She nodded, closing her eyes, hoping that her stomach would stop churning. She had no idea why she was suddenly so nauseated.

The thought of being pregnant rose up in her.

Was it possible?

Jana made a mental note to purchase a pregnancy test. She didn't really believe that she was carrying a baby, but she decided to take the test just to be sure. In some cases, birth control failed. She had started her birth control a month before her wedding, but shortly after the wedding her doctor had lowered her dosage because she'd been complaining about headaches. During one month, her cycle had started three times.

She wanted a baby, but she and Lawrence had decided to wait. How would he feel if she was pregnant? She had to buy that test when they got back.

• • •

J ANA COULD HARDLY CONTAIN her excitement as the limo driver pulled up in front of the Sanctuary on Camelback Mountain Resort & Spa, a luxury resort nestled in the mountains.

"Oh, Lawrence, it's beautiful," she murmured.

He nodded.

Hand in hand, they walked through the lobby and up to the front desk to check in.

The clerk gave Lawrence the keys to a mountain vista suite, featuring a living area and private balcony, state-of-the-art technology, and parquet flooring throughout. The separate bedroom boasted an inviting king-size bed and a huge dressing area with a floor-to-ceiling mirror and ottoman.

Jana couldn't wait to jump into the shower in the travertine marble bathroom. She wanted to wash away the weariness she felt from their travel.

She accepted the glass of wine he offered when she strolled out of the bathroom. "Thank you, honey."

She took a sip, then another.

Jana suddenly felt a peacefulness fall over her. Lawrence was watching her and smiling.

"What?" she asked with a giggle. She couldn't resist touching him. It just felt right.

"How are you feeling, baby?" he inquired.

"Great," Jana responded brightly. "I don't think I've ever felt this wonderful."

Lawrence kissed her fingers. "I love you so much."

She grinned. "I love you back."

He took the wineglass from her. "Why don't we get comfortable? I missed being with you. Making love . . ."

Jana stroked his cheek. "I've missed you too."

Lawrence picked her up and carried her to the master bedroom, kicking the door closed behind him.

• • •

"YOU WERE LIKE A different woman," Lawrence told Jana the next morning.

"Yeah, I know," she said lazily. "I don't know what came over me. It must have been the wine." She ran her fingers through her hair, silently noting that she needed to schedule an appointment for a perm and to get her extensions redone.

"Then I need to take home a case of whatever we had," Lawrence responded with a chuckle. "It's been a while since we've had a night like that."

They spent the day checking out the city, where they purchased souvenirs before returning to the hotel for massages and facials.

"Are you having fun?" Lawrence asked her.

"I am," Jana confirmed. "I feel the same way I felt when we were on our honeymoon." She glanced over at him. "I thought we were going away for the weekend. I didn't know that you took the entire week off from the firm."

"Our marriage is more important than any job."

"Thanks so much for this," Jana told him. She kissed his lips.

That evening, they sat in front of the fireplace drinking champagne and snacking on fruit and cheese.

"I don't know what it is about this champagne or that red wine we had last night, but it really makes me . . ." She giggled. "You know . . ."

"I am not complaining," Lawrence said. "I'm loving this new side of you."

She grinned. "Really?"

"See how much fun we can have when you let your hair down?"

Jana reached up and released the barrette holding her ponytail together. She shook her head. "Now I've truly let my hair down."

Grinning, Lawrence murmured, "Yes, you have. But don't stop now . . ."

Chapter 23

A FEW DAYS AFTER THEY got back from their trip, Lawrence and Jana had dinner with Ron and Lela.

Jana wanted to cancel because she was still feeling a little nauseated. She called her doctor, who said it could just be the birth control pills. She had an appointment to come in on Friday.

Lela wasn't much of a cook, so they had a chef come in to prepare their meals whenever they had guests. Other times, they spent a lot of money eating out. Ron made no bones about the fact that he hadn't married Lela for her cooking skills.

Ron poured Jana a glass of champagne.

"Thank you," she murmured, wishing he'd stop looking at her with that hungry look in his eyes. If anything, it seemed more wolfish tonight than ever before.

Ron handed Lawrence a glass of champagne, and the two men lapsed into a conversation about golf.

"At least they're not talking law," Lela whispered.

Jana agreed as she sipped her champagne.

They sat down to dinner. The steaming dish the chef brought in smelled heavenly.

"The lobster ravioli is delicious," Jana complimented.

Lawrence laughed. "My wife loves seafood."

"I do," she confirmed, leaning away from the hot food. She felt a little warm.

Jana accepted a second glass of champagne with dessert. She noticed that Lela was looking more and more uncomfortable. Usually chatty, she'd said barely a word during dinner.

They left the table and settled in the family room.

Jana wasn't feeling much better; in fact, she began to feel strange. She became transfixed on every sound, as if trying to capture its very essence. For a brief moment her vision blurred, and she rubbed her arms to ward off a chill.

Jana glanced over at her husband. "I think something is wrong with me," she whispered.

"Honey, you're fine," he whispered back. "Just sit back and relax." He picked up a bottle and said, "Have some more champagne."

For a moment, Jana felt her heart racing, but it subsided as quickly as it had come. Her body started to settle down to a more natural rhythm. She refused the offer of champagne, though. "I think I've had enough to drink, honey."

Her vision blurred again. She felt like she was roaming around the room even though she was still sitting down. She felt transported—that was it, she decided. She fell back in and out of her body all at once.

She was barely aware of Lawrence getting up and walking over to the love seat where Lela was sitting. Jana felt a moment of confusion as she tried to focus. She felt, rather than saw, the person who sat down beside her.

Jana could hear voices. She tried to speak, but it was hard to concentrate.

Did Lawrence put something in my drink? The thought crossed her mind but left quickly. *No, of course not. Why would he do something like that?*

Jana glanced across the room, trying to find her husband. Through a drug-induced haze, she watched in disbelief as Lawrence undressed Lela.

Before Jana could protest, she was pulled into a set of muscular arms— arms that weren't familiar. She trained her eyes on his face.

"What are you d-doing?" she asked Ron.

He began kissing her.

Jana struggled in his arms, trying to push him away from her. "S-stop . . ."

Her stomach churned nervously. "Get away f-from me," she managed to say while struggling to get away from him. She looked over to Lawrence for help, but he was in the throes of passion with Lela.

Jana became extremely nauseated and threw up the contents of her stomach. She was feeling too ill to delight in the horrified expression on Ron Boykin's face.

Scared and humiliated, Jana got up as quickly as she could and staggered toward the front door. She held her shirt together as she stumbled out of the house and scrabbled through her purse, trying to find her car keys.

Half dressed, Lawrence ran out of the house after her.

Jana promptly climbed in the car and locked the doors.

"What are you doing?" he shouted at her, beating on the glass window. "Get out of this car right now, Jana."

"Leave me alone," she shouted back. "Lawrence, if you don't move I will run you over."

"This is my car."

"You can pick it up tomorrow, but there's no way I'm staying here a moment longer. You and your friends are a bunch of perverts. Ron tried to rape me and you were going to let him."

He leaned down, nearly pressing his face against the window. "Jana, calm down. Ron wasn't trying to rape you, babe. I wouldn't let something like that happen. Look, you're just upset right now—it's the ecstasy."

Her mouth dropped open in shock. "You gave me ecstasy? Oh Lord . . . I've got to get away from here."

"Jana, you shouldn't be driving in this condition," Lawrence said. "Open the door and I'll take you home."

"No," Jana shouted as she turned on the ignition. "Leave me alone!"

She backed out of the driveway, narrowly missing the mailbox.

The world looked too strange as she drove. *Concentrate*, she told herself. *Keep your eyes on the road.*

With agonizing slowness, Jana drove off into the night.

Chapter 24

ROBYN WAS SHOCKED TO see her sister standing at her front door so late in the evening. "Jana, what's wrong?"

"I don't want to talk about it right now," she responded, brushing past her sister. "Robyn, I just need to stay here for a few days if you and Daniel don't mind."

Smelling Jana's clothes, Robyn crinkled her nose. "Of course we don't mind."

Jana made her way to her old bedroom. She removed her soiled dress and crossed the room in quick strides to the bathroom.

In the shower, she tried to rub her skin raw to rid herself of feeling so dirty.

Jana couldn't erase the images of her husband having sex with Lela. How could he do that to her? How could Lela?

Still feeling very high, she left the bathroom and sat down on her bed.

Robyn knocked before opening the door. "I made you some tea," she announced as she entered the room. She sat down beside Jana.

"I'm sure you're wondering what happened between me and Lawrence, but I'm just not ready to talk about it."

"That's fine," Robyn responded. "I'll be here if you need me."

Jana nodded. "Thank you."

She was grateful that her sister wasn't pushing the issue. Jana needed some time to process all that had transpired.

She felt sick to her stomach. Lurching to her feet, she ran to the bathroom and vomited a second time. Then she climbed into bed and sobbed until she was all cried out. Her cell rang until she turned it off, then she heard the phone ring in the house.

Robyn came back to her room. This time she stuck her head inside and said, "Do you want to talk to Lawrence?"

Jana shook her head furiously.

"Okay, I'll let him know."

Jana was calmer when her sister returned. "I'm sorry for coming here so late. I just didn't have anywhere else to go."

"Sweetie, this is your home too. You can come anytime you need to do so. You still have your key, don't you?"

Jana nodded. "I didn't want to scare you or catch you and Daniel . . . anyway, I figured I'd better knock instead of just walking in."

"Are you hungry?"

"I'm fine, Robyn. I just need a place where I can be safe for now."

Her sister wrapped her strong arms around her. "I don't know what happened, but you are safe here. You don't have to worry about that."

"Robyn's right," Daniel announced from behind them. "Nobody, and I do mean nobody, will bother you while you're in this house."

Jana walked over and hugged her brother-in-law. "Thank you."

He made sure Jana was fine, then left the sisters alone to talk.

"Did Lawrence do something to you?" Robyn asked.

Jana swallowed hard. "It's not something I can talk about right now. I hope that you can understand. I just can't talk about it yet."

JANA DIDN'T SLEEP WELL. She had a terrible headache, which had started around midnight and plagued her now. Her dry mouth and throat added to her misery. She experienced some light cramping and assumed her cycle was about to start.

"I didn't know you were up," Robyn said when Jana entered the kitchen. "How did you sleep?"

"I didn't," Jana responded. "Where's Daniel?"

"He had a breakfast meeting this morning, so he's already gone. It's just the two of us."

Jana sat down at the breakfast table.

"Lawrence called again this morning," Robyn announced. "I told him that you were still sleeping."

"Thank you. Robyn, I don't think I can talk to him right now."

Robyn handed Jana a cup of hot tea. "Are you hungry?"

Jana shook her head. "I feel nauseous."

Robyn drew back at this news. "How long have you been feeling that way?"

"About a week—it comes and goes," Jana stated. "I'm not pregnant, though. I had a light period, but it only lasted for half a day. I guess my body's still adjusting to my new birth control pills." A lone tear slipped down her cheek. "I'm sorry."

"You don't have to apologize, Jana."

"Love isn't supposed to hurt," she told Robyn. "I did everything that I could to be a good wife to Lawrence."

A look of puzzlement came over Robyn's face. "Sweetie, did he hit you?"

Jana shook her head. "Of course not. Robyn . . ."

Robyn stood up and walked over to her sister, embracing her. "I'm so sorry. It breaks my heart to see you like this." Her eyes grew bright with unshed tears.

Jana broke down crying.

"Sweetie, what did he do to you? Was he having an affair?"

Jana couldn't respond.

"I'm not going to press you, but I'm here if you want to talk," Robyn said. "Why don't you go back to your room and lie down," she suggested.

Jana opened her mouth to speak, but then doubled over in pain. She groaned in agony. "Robyn, there's something wrong," she said in a strangled voice. She waited a heartbeat before saying, "I'm bleeding, but it doesn't feel like my cycle."

Robyn glanced toward the phone. "I need to get you to a hospital."

"I need to clean myself up first," Jana said.

"Sweetie, we're not gonna worry about that until we get you to the hospital."

Robyn practically carried Jana to the car, then drove as quickly as she could. She didn't stop until she was in front of the emergency room entrance. "My sister needs help," she screamed.

Everything happened in a blur for Jana.

She was taken to one of the rooms and poked and prodded. A nurse rattled off questions, wanting to know when she'd had her last period, if she was on birth control, and if there was a possibility of her being pregnant.

The doctor came in after a while to speak to her.

Robyn got up to leave, but Jana said meekly, like a child, "No, I want you here with me."

"Mrs. Collins, you were pregnant, but the embryo did not implant itself into the womb properly. The pregnancy terminated on its own."

Jana glanced over at Robyn. She thought about all the wine and champagne she'd consumed and the pills Lawrence had put in her drink. She should have taken the pregnancy test before she'd left. If the pregnancy hadn't terminated on its own, she didn't dare consider the danger she'd have unknowingly placed her child in. "I was going to have a baby," she said in a low voice.

Her sister embraced her.

The doctor assured her that she would be able to get pregnant again in the future. He gave her after-care instructions and gave the okay for her to be discharged.

"Thank you," Jana said.

"Let's get you back home," Robyn stated.

Numb, Jana eased out of the hospital bed and dressed in the pair of sweats her sister pulled out of a tote bag.

"They were in the car," Robyn told her.

During the drive home, Jana stared out of the window. When she spoke, all she said was, "Lawrence and I were going to have a baby."

Chapter 25

ROBYN OPENED THE FRONT door.

"I'm here to see my wife," Lawrence stated without preamble, ignoring the peeved expression on her face. "I came by here earlier, but nobody came to the door."

"Did it ever occur to you that maybe we weren't home, Lawrence? Humph! You're supposed to be so intelligent, but I'm not so sure about that, since you don't seem to know a good thing when you find it." She took a step backward and said, "Come on inside. My sister is sitting on the patio."

"I don't know what Jana told you, but—"

Robyn cut him off by saying, "Jana hasn't told me anything, Lawrence. I don't know what you've done, so you should consider yourself lucky. If I did know, you'd be sorry, I can promise you that."

Lawrence scowled at her. "And here I thought you were so saved and sanctified."

"Being saved, sanctified, and baptized in the Holy Spirit don't mean that I won't crown you one good time. You do anything to hurt my sister or upset her any more than you already have and you may be seeing Jesus long before you thought."

Lawrence stared down the petite woman, but she didn't flinch. He was the one who looked away first.

"Jana's had an emotional day, so don't upset her."

He gave a slight nod, then walked toward the back of the house.

Jana was outside, a Bible on her lap.

"I can't believe you embarrassed me like that," he uttered, taking a seat beside her.

She gave him a look of pure venom. "And I can't believe you actually drugged me so that another man could take advantage of me." Jana suddenly had another realization. "You gave me ecstasy while we were on vacation too, didn't you? That's why I—"

"Keep your voice down, please." Lawrence stole a peek over his shoulder. "Jana, I was simply trying to help you relax."

"You almost got me raped."

"Ron wouldn't have raped you. No means no."

She glared at him. "*Oh, really?* Then why did you feel the need to drug me? Why didn't you tell me that you were taking me over there for an orgy?"

Lawrence reached for her, but Jana slapped his hands away. "You're being irrational," he said. "Please, just calm down."

"I don't want to calm down." Her voice rose up an octave. "Lawrence, I had to go to the hospital earlier. I had a miscarriage."

His eyebrows rose in surprise. "What?"

"I lost our baby. Lawrence, I was pregnant."

"But how? You were on birth control."

"The dosage had to be lowered, remember? Well, it must have been too low. I don't know how it happened, but the fact is that I was pregnant."

He looked horrified. "Did the miscarriage happen because of the ecstasy?"

She denied the possibility. "No, the embryo never implanted itself in my womb properly. The miscarriage would've happened no matter what. The doctor told me that the pregnancy wasn't viable."

Lawrence was looking terribly guilty. "Jana, had I known . . . I never would've given you anything like X. I hope you know that."

"I do," she responded, not as hostile. "But you never should've drugged me no matter what."

"You're right," he conceded. He looked over his shoulder, then back at her. "You're my wife. Why don't you come home with me, Jana? We'll work it all out in the privacy of our own home."

"Oh, no, I don't think so," she replied forcefully. "Lawrence, I don't trust you anymore. You betrayed me in the worst way."

Lawrence sighed in resignation.

Jana bore in on him. "Do you have any idea how much it hurt me to see you with Lela? How could you do this to me, Lawrence?"

His voice was flat. "I don't have your hang-ups."

"What you did was wrong. I'm never going to share something so intimate. If you want to be a pervert, do it and leave me out of it."

"I could do this behind your back, but then it would be cheating," he protested. "I have tried very hard to be honest with you about what I want. I thought you wanted to submit to me like the Bible says," he added with more of an edge.

Jana dismissed that idea out of her head. "God calls for women to be submissive to their husbands, but if the women are requested or demanded by their husbands to do something immoral or illegal, God doesn't want them to obey."

Lawrence rose to his feet, defeated. "Jana, I'm sorry about the baby. I'd really like for you to come home with me so that we can finish our conversation there."

Jana had no intention of doing that. "I can't go back there right now."

"If you don't, then our marriage is over."

Her eyes rose in surprise. "Now you have the nerve to threaten me?" she said weakly. "Lawrence, please leave. I really can't deal with you right now. I've lost my baby, I have a terrible headache, and I can't seem to get it together."

"It was an error in judgment about the ecstasy. I'm sorry, Jana."

"But you're not sorry about your partner trying to rape me?"

"Jana, he wouldn't have raped you," Lawrence assured her. "You don't need to go around saying things like that—especially because you're angry with me."

She saw his legal mind at work. "You're more concerned about your partner than you are for me. That's just great, Lawrence."

"Jana—"

"*Please, just leave.*"

He pointed a threatening finger at her. "I'm not going to beg you to come home with me. I'll give you one day to make a decision. If you're not home within twenty-four hours, then I'm filing for divorce."

She glared at Lawrence. "Do what you feel you must, that's what I'm going to do."

When he left, Jana collapsed into her chair. She had what felt like an oncoming migraine.

She was still stunned over the fact that Lawrence had given her an ultimatum when he was the one who'd broken their marriage vows. Jana had suffered a miscarriage, and now she was grieved for the child she would never get to know.

"Lord, I feel so alone," she whispered. "My body hurts; my heart hurts," she whispered. On a normal day, she truly believed that sitting in a tranquil place did wonders for the soul. Her sister's backyard was leafy and green, surrounded by high ivy-covered walls. It also had a beautiful rose garden. Jana used to come out here whenever she was troubled. God had always met her in this tiny oasis, and Jana needed him now.

Heal my heart, Father God. Please stop this pain. Help me get through the loss of my baby and my husband. It's just too much for me to handle right now.

Queen Vashti refused to compromise her values. Because of her refusal, she lost her husband in the process. This must have been how it felt to Queen Vashti. *Some good came out of her heartbreak, but what good can come out of mine?*

GRACIELA ARRIVED SHORTLY AFTER two. Robyn must have called and told her what happened. Jana was still sitting on the patio when she arrived.

"*¿Cómo te sientes?*" she asked.

"I'm okay, I guess," Jana responded. "Mostly I feel numb."

Robyn joined them. "I don't know what's going on between you two, but Lawrence looked like he was ready to spit nails when he left."

Jana's eyes filled with tears, and she struggled to piece together the shards of strength she had left within her. "I need to talk to you two. You deserve to know the truth about what happened between me and Lawrence."

She took a deep breath and released it slowly.

"It's okay, sweetie," Robyn murmured, rubbing her neck and shoulders. "We can wait until you're ready to talk about this."

Graciela agreed.

"I need to do this now," Jana responded. "It's just that it's so hard."

She began to cry.

Graciela handed her a tissue.

Jana wiped her face and blew her nose. "I hurt so badly. I can't even describe to you how terrible I feel." She took a moment to gather herself.

"The reason I was so upset last night is because Lawrence took me to Ron and Lela Boykin's house for dinner. I thought we were just going to have dinner with friends and then go home, but they had other plans. Plans I didn't know about."

Robyn frowned. "Sweetie, what are you talking about? What other plans?"

"Lawrence put ecstasy in my drink."

"But why would he do that?" Robyn asked, shocked.

"He wanted me to relax. At least that's what he told me."

"Relax for what?" Graciela demanded.

"He wanted . . . h-he . . ." Jana couldn't talk because of the sobs clogging her throat from her grief. Her sister handed her another tissue.

Graciela got up and embraced her. "It's gonna be fine, sweetie. Everything will be fine."

After Jana wiped her face with the tissue, she said, "I'm so sorry for bawling like that. I just couldn't hold it in any longer."

"Honey, it's okay," Robyn assured her.

"Do you want to tell us what happened last night?" Graciela asked. "You don't have to if you're not ready."

"Lawrence threatened to divorce me if I didn't go home with him today. Right now I'm not sure I want to be married to him either." Jana released a long sigh. "He cheated on me. Lawrence cheated right in front of me."

"Huh?" Graciela uttered.

"After dinner, we were all in the family room. I started to feel strange, and then before I knew it, Lawrence was across the room with Lela. They were kissing and undressing each other."

"Oh, my goodness!" Robyn whispered. "How could he do something like that to you?"

"Apparently, I'm not enough woman for him. He needs more."

Robyn was still in shock, but Graciela's mood veered to anger. "What a complete jerk!" She got up and began pacing back and forth as she lapsed into a round of Spanish curses.

"There's more," Jana stated. "While my husband was getting it on with Lela, Ron tried to put the moves on me."

"Ron Boykin?" Robyn shook her head in disbelief. "Lord, what is this world coming to?"

"You should file a complaint against them both," Graciela suggested hotly.

"I can't help thinking that I should've taken a pregnancy test before we left for the spa—at least then I wouldn't have been drinking wine or champagne. You were right, Graciela. I was pregnant and didn't know it. I lost the baby earlier today."

Graciela's mouth dropped open in shock. "Oh, *mi'ja*, I'm so sorry. Is it because of the drugs?"

"No, I can't put that on him. The baby didn't implant in my womb the way it should, so the pregnancy wasn't viable." Jana shook her head. "If Ron Boykin had succeeded, then yes, I'd press charges and everything, but the truth is that Ron didn't approach me without my husband's permission. That's what I find so unforgivable."

Robyn was furious. "I think it's horrible. How could Lawrence claim to love you and put you in a position like that?"

"I agree with your sister," Graciela cried. "It's one thing if you're agreeable to something like that, but to drug you and— You should press charges against Lawrence."

Jana hung her head miserably. "I can't get the image of him and Lela out of my mind. Every time I close my eyes I can see them. I hate it."

"I told you they were all into some freaky stuff."

Jana nodded in agreement. "Graciela, you were right."

"You are welcome to stay here with me and Daniel for as long as you need," Robyn said.

"Thank you," Jana replied. "Because I don't have anywhere else to go. I have so much on my mind right now. I need some time to think about what happens next."

Chapter 26

"HOW ARE YOU FEELING?" Graciela asked when she stopped by Robyn's house to see Jana the following week. "Are you sleeping any better?"

Jana turned around, wiping away her tears. "Today isn't such a good day for me. I've been crying on and off like this for most of the afternoon. Graciela, I never thought . . . how can Lawrence be a part of something like that? That law firm is nothing but a den of perversion. I just don't get it."

"It was probably a gradual thing for him," Graciela observed. "The same way he was gradually seducing you into that lifestyle."

Jana's eyes met Graciela's. "What are you talking about?"

"Look at the way you're dressing now. Lawrence was slowly changing you into the woman he thought you should be. He introduced you to porn, and you said yourself that some of his friends didn't seem to mind *performing*, for lack of a better word, in front of you all. Then he takes you to a sex club. . . . All of this was leading up to one thing: your induction into the lifestyle."

Jana could see what she meant. "I wanted to please him, but I just can't do what he wants. I don't want to share him with another woman, and I certainly don't want to give myself to another man, even though Lawrence doesn't mind."

"Jana, there's nothing wrong with your feeling that way."

"Then why is Lawrence so furious with me, Graciela?" Jana asked. "He says he's going to divorce me unless I get with the program."

Graciela didn't betray her feeling. "How do you feel about this?"

Jana was bewildered. "I don't know, Graciela. I still love Lawrence. He's my husband. I'm angry with him for putting me in that position, but I'm not ready to give up on my marriage. Lawrence has a problem—a sexual addiction. That's what I believe, and I know that God can fix this. It might be a good idea if we start seeing a counselor. Our marriage is more than sex."

Graciela didn't respond.

"Just say it," Jana insisted. "You tried to tell me that there was something going on with Lawrence from the moment you met him. You have never really liked him."

"I like him even less now," she muttered. "*Mi'ja*, I don't like what he did to you."

"The thing is that Lawrence has this mind-set that swinging is not a sin. He really believes this, Graciela. I love him so much and I don't want to give up on him, but this is crazy. How do I get Lawrence to understand that this lifestyle is wrong?"

"Do you still want to be with him after everything that has happened?" Graciela asked. "Have you forgiven Lawrence?"

Jana didn't respond right away.

But when she did, she answered, "I'm not ready to move back into our home yet. I'm still upset and very angry, but I'm trying to give this all to God. Lawrence is going to have to fight for me if he wants me back—that's all I can say for right now. I know that Lawrence cheated on me because he doesn't consider it cheating. He has been brainwashed to believe that swinging is just a lifestyle. He believes that since the Bible doesn't speak specifically against swinging and wife-swapping, it's okay."

Jana surveyed Graciela's face. "What do you think I should do?"

"I think you should hang him by his—"

Jana interrupted her friend. "I don't know why I asked you that. I already knew the answer."

"It's your marriage, so I don't have a right to say anything, Jana. As your BFF, I have to support you no matter what." She quickly corrected herself. "Well, as long as you're not doing anything illegal or really crazy."

Jana saw her point. "I'm not saying that Lawrence and I are getting back together. Graciela, I do need to talk to him. If our marriage can be saved, then I think we should at least try."

"I know, *mi'ja*," Graciela said. "But I don't think you should rush into any kind of decision about anything. You just lost your baby. You're grieving."

Jana's eyes filled with tears. "I really wanted to have a baby with Lawrence."

Graciela nodded. "I know what that feels like. Enrique and I want children, but after my third miscarriage, I just couldn't set myself up for heartbreak again."

"How do you get past the pain?"

Graciela gave her a sad smile. "Through prayer."

"Will you pray with me right now?" Jana asked.

Graciela took Jana's hands in her own. They closed their eyes as Jana began to pray.

"I CAME BY THE HOUSE today, but I couldn't get inside," Jana announced when she entered Lawrence's office. "I assume you had the locks changed. The reason I went by there is because I think we need to talk."

"There is nothing to talk about," Lawrence stated without emotion. "Now, if you will excuse me, I have a client waiting. One with an appointment."

Jana met his gaze straight on. "I'm not your client. I'm your wife, Lawrence, and right now our marriage is very fragile. I would think that would be your priority."

"Wife . . . that's a joke," Lawrence grunted. "Any wife of mine would want to please me. She would willingly do whatever I asked, because I've given her the world and because she loves me. She wouldn't try to use something like the loss of a child to make me feel worse than I do."

"And no husband should ask his wife to commit adultery," Jana shot back. "That's what you were asking me to do, and when I wouldn't just lie down and say jump right in, the water's fine, you decided you'd give me drugs and take away my right to say no."

Lawrence looked imperious behind his huge walnut desk. "I admit that I was wrong to give you the X and I regret my actions, Jana. I really am sorry. I'm sorry about the baby, but we had no idea that you were pregnant." He leaned back in his chair. "However, there are a lot of couples like me, who enjoy watching their mates experience sexual pleasure with someone else, without jealousy or fear of loss. Jana, swinging is only considered cheating by people who really don't understand that the practice was intended to promote a more stable and open marriage."

Jana shook her head in denial.

"You may not know this, but swingers have a much higher success rate as it relates to marriage than those who are not part of the lifestyle," Lawrence explained. "If we are open and honest with each other, then our marriage has survived the first test—communication. You need to stop worrying about what society or the church tells you is right or wrong. There was a time when it was thought that sex was just for the purpose of reproduction."

Jana could hardly believe what she was hearing. This was not the Lawrence she'd fallen in love with and married. *Who was this man?*

"I didn't stand up before God, my family, and friends and vow until death do *us all* part. Nor did I agree never to commit adultery against you plus all of our lovers on the side." She kept her voice tightly under control. "Maybe we should have gotten married by a minister who accepts these types of marriage arrangements, and then we could've had them added to our marriage vows. That should make it sort of acceptable."

"No need to be sarcastic, Jana."

"Tell me something, Lawrence. If you want to sleep with other women, then why get married at all?"

"I loved you."

That did not faze her at all. "Apparently, I'm not enough for you. For the record, one of the Ten Commandments actually states thou shall not commit adultery against thy wife."

"It's not adultery if two people agree. Jana, the Bible has been misquoted and mistranslated to falsely suppress sexuality."

"Well, I don't agree," she remarked. "If we can just ignore God's law so easily, then crime should be made legal too. You're working on a case now for a building owner accused of telling someone that it's okay to burn his warehouse down. So is it okay because they both agreed to it?"

Lawrence didn't respond.

"Just because you have two people who say it's okay doesn't make it right."

Leaning back in his chair, Lawrence said loftily, "I'm bored with this conversation and I've kept my client waiting long enough. Jana, I'm not going to force you into the lifestyle."

She folded her arms across her chest. "So what are you going to do?"

"I'm going to divorce you," he stated. "If you don't love me enough to do this for me, then I don't see the need to stay married, because like you, I don't want to cheat on my spouse."

Jana slowly recovered from her shock. She took a deep breath and exhaled slowly before saying, "So instead of giving up that lifestyle, you'd rather divorce me."

Lawrence calmly rose to his feet. "You'll be hearing from my attorney with the details. I'll walk you out."

"I don't need you to escort me to the door," Jana snapped. "I can find my own way out of this den of hell."

"Have a nice life, however boring it may be," Lawrence said. "By the way, I've already had Sofia pack up your stuff. Your boxes will be dropped off at your sister's house. There's no need for you to ever come to my house again."

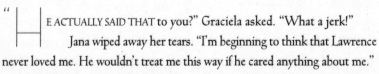E ACTUALLY SAID THAT to you?" Graciela asked. "What a jerk!"

Jana wiped away her tears. "I'm beginning to think that Lawrence never loved me. He wouldn't treat me this way if he cared anything about me."

"So what are you going to do?"

Jana shrugged. "Well, he's already locked me out of the house, so I'll start by finding an apartment. Robyn and Daniel don't mind me staying with them, but I want my own space. After I get an apartment, I guess I'll go back to college and finish my degree—something I should've done in the first place."

"Good for you."

A pang of sadness came over Jana. "I still love him, Graciela," she confessed. "How do I get over him?"

"By taking it one day at a time." Graciela broke into a big grin. "Or finding yourself a real man."

Jana laughed in spite of herself. "Only you."

"I shouldn't be flip. I'm sorry. Jana, I can only imagine how much you're hurting. *Mi'ja*, your heart is breaking, and it bothers me that I don't have the right words and there is nothing that I can do to stop this pain you're feeling."

"I really thought that Lawrence wanted me, Graciela. I really thought he loved me so much that he would choose me."

"Maybe he's testing you," Graciela suggested. "Lawrence could be playing hardball with you because he's trying to force you into doing what he wants—agreeing to be in the lifestyle. He probably thinks that you love him so much that you'd be willing to do just about anything to be with him."

"He was so cold to me. I don't know."

"I can't believe I'm saying this about that jerk, but I guess you're rubbing off on me. Lawrence is just as upset over what happened too. I'm sure he feels terrible about hurting you and then the loss of the baby—it's a lot to deal with. Just pray and give Lawrence some time. You never know how God will work on his heart."

"Maybe God should just work on my heart," Jana said quietly. She sounded resigned. "The man told me that he had his housekeeper pack up my stuff. He had it taken to my sister's house. Lawrence couldn't get me out of his house fast enough. These are not the actions of someone wanting to save his marriage. If my marriage is over, then I need to accept it and try to move on. The first thing I'm going to do is go back to work with Robyn in the shop."

Chapter 27

JANA STARED DOWN AT the legal documents in her hands. "I can't believe this," she murmured. "Lawrence just had me served with divorce papers. He had them serve me in the boutique. This could have been done when I was at home. He's really trying to humiliate me. Lawrence is the one who ruined our marriage."

Robyn embraced her. "Are you okay?"

"I don't know," Jana responded, wiping away her tears. She strode over to the phone and picked it up.

She could hear the phone ringing on the other end, but she hung up before anyone answered. "Robyn, I need to leave for an hour or two. This is a conversation I need to have with Lawrence in person."

"I agree," Robyn responded. "You and Lawrence should really sit down and talk this thing out. You've only been separated for a couple of weeks. Before you go, let's have some prayer."

She turned to her assistant. "Minnie, can you watch the front while Jana and I go to the office for a minute? We won't be long."

They went into Robyn's office, closed the door, and prayed.

When it was over, Jana grabbed her car keys and purse and left the store. "I'll be back as soon as I can."

"Take your time," Robyn stated. "Do you want Daniel to meet you there?"

Jana shook her head no. "I'll be fine."

She drove to the Beverly Hills law office, where she walked past Rhoda, straight through the double doors leading into her soon-to-be-ex-husband's corner office. "I can't believe you're actually planning to go through with the divorce. Don't you think we need to talk about this at all? Did our marriage mean anything to you?"

"Mr. Collins, I tried to stop her," his secretary blurted, sounding flustered. This same woman used to greet Jana with a smile. She was just as fickle as Lawrence was, apparently. That's probably why they worked so well together.

"Rhoda, I am still his wife," Jana informed her. "I don't need an appointment to see him."

"I was given strict orders to—"

"It's okay, Rhoda," Lawrence interjected. "Just close the doors behind you, please, and hold my calls."

"What did you tell her?" Jana questioned. "Did you tell Rhoda not to let me into your office? Have I been banned from the building?"

A flush of guilt appeared on his face. "I simply told Rhoda that I didn't want to be disturbed. It had nothing to do with you."

"Did you ever love me, Lawrence?" Jana asked with her hands on her hips.

"You know the answer to that," he responded. "But I want a wife who believes in making her husband happy."

Jana sent him a sharp glare. "I don't believe in being unfaithful—even if it's with your permission, Lawrence. I actually thought we were happy until you decided you wanted to share me with your friends."

He sounded bored. "We want two different things out of this marriage."

"So why bother getting married, Lawrence?" she asked. "Wouldn't it be less complicated for you if you just jumped into bed with any and every woman you see without worrying about a wife?"

"It's no longer your concern."

Jana sighed in resignation. "You're right. It's not. I don't know why I even bothered to come here to try to communicate with you. It's like talking to a brick wall when I talk to you."

"Jana, I'm sorry it didn't work out between us."

She glared at him. "Whatever . . ."

"What's with the attitude?" Lawrence asked. "There's no need for us to be enemies."

His indifference was infuriating. "There's even less for us to pretend to be friends."

"Why are you so angry? You don't want to participate in the lifestyle, and I want a wife who will. I've released you of that obligation. What more do you want from me?"

She approached his desk, towering over him. "Why didn't you tell me about this lifestyle *before* we got married? Why did you marry me and rob me of my virginity when you knew this is what you were really about? I should've been told before our wedding."

"We had this conversation already—at least I thought we had," Lawrence uttered, sighing. "Jana, you were a virgin. I knew you had no experience, and I figured once we got together, you'd be all for it. I was wrong. And for the record, I didn't rob you of anything. I was your husband—it was mine to take."

"You were nothing more than a mistake, Lawrence. Don't get it twisted." Jana picked up her purse and walked through the double doors. As a parting shot she added, "I'm still waiting to meet my true partner for life."

She could hear Lawrence calling her, but Jana kept her pace brisk and steady despite the way her body trembled in nervous energy.

Her marriage was over, and it was time to move toward her future.

J ANA CALLED GRACIELA WHEN she was back in the Ford Explorer. Lawrence had taken the BMW away from her. She gave her friend a quick recap of what happened.

"Did you really tell him that?" Graciela asked with a chuckle.

Jana nodded. "I wanted to hurt him the same way he's hurt me. I know it's wrong, but I meant every word."

"I like it. Poppy deserves that and so much more. He'd better not let me see him. I got some words for him in English and Spanish."

Jana laughed, tickled by the idea. "It wouldn't bother Lawrence. Besides, he's not worth it, Graciela, so don't waste your time."

"He probably knows that he's wrong, Jana. Lawrence is being nasty so he doesn't have to deal with the fact that he's a first-class jerk."

"You always know how to make me feel better," Jana said with a smile. She was starting to feel a little better. "I'll call you later. I need to get back to the store so that Robyn can leave for her appointment."

"Are you working in the boutique again?"

"Yeah," Jana responded. "I'm pretty sure I won't be getting my two-thousand-dollar allowances anymore. In the meantime, I need to make a living. I don't want to stay with Robyn and Daniel any longer than I have to, you know? I want to get my own place."

"I know you're excited about opening the second boutique," Graciela said.

Jana smiled. "We still have to find the right location before we can move forward."

SHE RETURNED TO THE shop in time for Robyn to rush out. "Thanks so much for closing for me."

"Not a problem," Jana responded.

Her cell phone rang. It was Lawrence, so she let it go straight to voice mail. There wasn't anything nice that Jana could say to him right now; she was too angry and hurt.

She felt like a knife had been stuck through her heart. He was giving no thought to all she had gone through with losing the baby—his only thought was to toss her aside because she didn't want to sleep with other men.

How she made it through the next three hours, Jana had no idea. It could only be that she was numb from the shock of their last conversation.

But by the time she made it home, the numbness had worn off.

The house was empty, as Daniel was at the church for the men's Bible study and Robyn had had to meet with the committee for an upcoming women's retreat. Jana hurried to her bedroom and shut the door. She fell on the floor in a fetal position, pounding the floor and crying. She cried uncontrollably, repeating, "No! No! No!"

We were happy. How could this be happening to us?

Jana went through so many different emotions. She felt used. She didn't feel like a woman anymore. She felt dirty. She felt ugly.

Crushed. Devastated. Lost.

Her future, which had once been so clear, was now filled with despair.

Chapter 28

LOOKING BACK TWO DAYS later, Jana realized that she didn't remember much of that evening except that she hadn't slept well. It had felt like a nightmare, and she'd figured that when she awoke in the morning, it would all be over and everything would be back to normal.

But it wasn't. Her life would never be the same again.

Nobody knew what was going on inside her. The visits and phone calls from her closest friends were meant to be encouraging, hopeful, and soothing, but they were happy, and in a good place in their lives, and didn't understand that the pain she felt was so indescribable that she wanted to die. Jana wasn't suicidal, but she didn't want to do anything but sleep her life away.

The next morning, Robyn strolled into her room, saying, "Okay, that's enough! I let you stay home for the past two days in those same ol' tired pajamas. It's time for you to take a good shower and get into some clean clothes."

"I don't feel good," Jana moaned. "Why doesn't anybody understand that?"

"Sweetie, I do understand," Robyn responded. "But I'm not going to let you bury yourself in depression. Jana, you stink, your hair is dirty, and all you've been doing is lying around in bed. I know that you don't want to, but you need to get up. Get dressed and take a walk or sit out on the patio. You need to get some fresh air. It'll do wonders for you."

Jana groaned in response.

Robyn walked into the bathroom, and Jana heard her turn on the shower. Her sister wasn't going to go away, she knew that. Feeling so tired, she sat up in bed and swung her legs outward.

"I really don't feel that great," Jana said when Robyn came back into the bedroom.

"You'll feel better after you shower and put some food in your stomach. You need to eat."

Jana made her way into the bathroom. She removed her clothing, wrinkling her nose at her own musty scent. Robyn was right—she definitely needed a shower.

The hot water felt good against her skin. She poured her favorite shower gel onto a sea sponge and slowly massaged her body with it, removing any traces of lingering stress and exhaustion.

Jana felt much better when she stepped out of the shower. She dried off with a huge fluffy body sheet, brushed her teeth, and wandered into the bedroom. Robyn had changed her bedding while she was taking care of her personal hygiene.

Jana sat down on the edge of the bed and moisturized her body with shea butter lotion. Then she sat down to do something with her hair.

The first thing I'm going to do is get this weave taken out. I'm getting my hair cut short. I like it short, and that's the way I'm wearing it. I'm no longer Lawrence's wife. It's long past time that I get back to being the real me.

Jana pulled her hair up into a ponytail. After dressing in a pair of jeans and a tank top, Jana left her bedroom.

Daniel smiled when he saw her enter the kitchen. "It's good to see you."

"I guess I had a moment," Jana allowed. "I just didn't have the energy to get out of bed." She accepted a cup of tea from her sister, then sat down across from Daniel.

He laid down his newspaper and said, "When you have moments like that, you can't give in to them, hon. I know that you're going through a difficult time right now, but Jana, you will survive. You're a strong woman."

"There are days when I'm not so sure," she admitted.

Robyn put a plate of toast and scrambled eggs in front of her. "Eat."

"Yes, ma'am," Jana murmured.

Robyn picked up two more plates and set them down on the table. She sat down beside her husband. Holding hands, the trio bowed their heads in prayer.

Jana bit into her toast. She couldn't remember the last time she had eaten anything. She still didn't have much of an appetite, but Robyn was right—she needed food in order to rebuild her strength.

"Daniel, what do you think I should do?" Jana asked.

"Go back to college and get that degree." He settled back in his chair. "You were so excited about becoming a Christian counselor. I remember when you came to me and told me that God placed it on your heart. You told me that it was your calling. Then you met Lawrence and you put your calling aside."

"I fell in love."

"There's nothing wrong with that," Daniel said. "I just don't think you should've dropped out of school."

"Do you think that's why my marriage didn't work?" she asked. "Because I put a man before my calling? Was Lawrence placed in my life just to be a distraction?" Jana stuck a forkful of scrambled eggs in her mouth.

"I don't know," Daniel said. "We don't know the mind of God."

"I really believed that Lawrence was the man for me," Jana stated.

"I'm not saying that he wasn't," Daniel replied. "I think that you need to spend some time with the Lord. Let Him guide you."

She had been doing that. It was good advice. "Thanks, Daniel."

"Your sister and I love you as if you were our own child," he said warmly. "You're a very special woman, and one day the right man will come. If Lawrence ever comes to his senses and commits to working on his marriage, then you'll know that this is the man God has chosen for you."

"I'm not going to focus on Lawrence. Although," she confessed, "it's not easy to think about anything else right now. I'm going to seek God's face. I want to spend time in His presence. If you don't see me much in the next couple of days, it's not because I've gone back into my depression. I'm planning to spend a lot of time with the Lord. If anybody can heal a broken heart, it's God."

J ANA FILLED OUT HER paperwork to complete her registration at the Los Angeles Bible College. She was thrilled about going back to school to finish her degree.

This was such a difficult time in Jana's personal walk with God. Each day it seemed that her prayers were going unanswered. Her faith was weakening, but then she realized it was because she expected God to do things her way.

She was doing all the right things. She was praying. She was fasting. Fasting was easy for her because she didn't really have an appetite.

Jana was still struggling with depression. Some days she did not want to leave her bed. She felt so alone, so much that it hurt.

Please help, God. Please hold me!

Jana lost almost fifteen pounds.

Her emotions continued to run the gamut. Times of anger. Times of depression. Times of guilt and loneliness.

During the times when she felt as if she couldn't make it another day, Jana would sing the hymn "Great Is Thy Faithfulness."

She walked around reciting Jeremiah 29:11. "God knows the plans he has for us; plans to prosper us and not to harm us, plans to give us hope and a future. . . ."

Jana prayed that each day would take her closer to that future.

R OBYN AND JANA PORED over their business proposal for the new boutique.

"This is going to be a really nice store," Jana stated. "Now if we can just find the right location."

"We will," Robyn assured her. "I think you should manage that one.

You're more of a fashionista than I am. I want to bring in some of the high-end designers and keep Robyn's I as is."

"Then we need to bring over your designs too," Jana told her. "Make the second store more of a couture fashion boutique."

Robyn got up and walked into the kitchen to stir the turnip greens. Jana followed her into the kitchen to check on the cornbread.

While they prepared the rest of their dinner, they continued discussing their expansion plans.

After dinner, Daniel and Robyn went to the church for a meeting. Jana cleaned the kitchen, then settled down in the family room to watch TV.

Her cell phone rang. It was Angie.

Jana ignored the call. She didn't want to talk to anyone who was tied to Lawrence. For all she knew, he had probably slept with her too.

A wave of anger washed through her. Jana could imagine how they must have laughed at her stupidity. She had gone against her gut feelings and allowed these uppity women into her life.

Never again, she vowed silently.

Jana picked up her journal, which she'd brought into the room with her. Since her split from Lawrence, she had begun writing more and more. It was a safe place for her to process her thoughts and feelings.

This week is much better than last week. I've stopped crying and I can say his name without choking up. I've even stopped praying for God to punish Lawrence for the way he treated me. I'm sure in his own crazy way, my soon-to-be ex believes he is doing the honorable thing by leaving me. He didn't want to cheat on me—at least he didn't want to do it behind my back. He'd much rather do it right in my face.

Me, I prefer the old-fashioned way, if given a choice. Just do it and then lie to me and let me find out. . . .

Okay, I'm losing it.

Cheating in any form is hurtful. The truth is that I would rather have my marriage. I stood before God and everyone and vowed to remain in my marriage until death. Lawrence apparently didn't mean a word of his vows.

Have I forgiven him? Some days I think so, but then on other days, I'm not so sure. Right now I'm focusing on me and my needs, because I want to survive with my sanity intact.

Lawrence can drop dead for all that I care!

P.S. Apparently, I still have some anger issues.

Chapter 29

LAWRENCE WAS IN A bad mood. He had been snapping at everyone all day long.

"Hey, what's going on with you?" Ron questioned. "You haven't been yourself for the past couple of days."

"I miss my wife," Lawrence said, then he thumped his desk with his fist. "I really miss Jana. What we had together was special."

"Los Angeles is full of beautiful women," Ron said dismissively. "A man in your position can have any one he wants. But this time you might want to pick one who doesn't have a problem with our lifestyle."

Lawrence sighed in resignation. "I guess you're right."

"I know I am. Life is too short, Lawrence. There's nothing wrong with what we do. You just have to have the right woman. Jana didn't trust you, man. And she was jealous and insecure. You went through that with Gia. Why go through it again?"

Lawrence settled back against the soft leather of his chair and silently considered Ron's words.

Ron sputtered, "She's not worth it."

"Don't go there," Lawrence warned. He was well aware how angry Ron was that Jana had refused his advances. "Jana is a wonderful person—she thinks differently when it comes to sex."

Ron looked at him in disbelief for a moment. "So? And sex is everything." He then walked out of Lawrence's office.

Lawrence muttered a string of profanities. He hated that Jana was constantly on his mind.

An hour later, still unable to work, he got up and left his office. Lawrence needed a break. He ran into Ron's wife in the reception area. "Lela, hello."

"Hi, Lawrence," she responded. "I came to surprise my husband for lunch, but I guess I was too late."

"He had a meeting with a client."

"How are you doing?" she asked. "I haven't seen you in a couple of weeks."

"I'm fine."

Lela lowered her voice to a whisper. "I didn't mean to upset Jana. I thought she was okay with the lifestyle."

"I pushed her too soon," Lawrence murmured, gesturing for her to follow him back to his office. "She wasn't ready."

"I don't think Jana will ever be ready," Lela said, taking a seat in one of the visitor chairs facing his mahogany desk. "She's not like us, Lawrence."

"No, she isn't," he admitted. He also knew how guilty Lela felt about that disastrous night. She really liked Jana.

Lela leaned forward slightly. "If you love her, then why don't you go get your wife? The lifestyle isn't worth losing the woman you love."

"I shouldn't have to change my life, Lela," Lawrence argued. "We haven't done anything wrong, and I'm not going to let her believe otherwise. I love her, but I have no reason to go running after her."

Lela made a move of impatience. "For what it's worth, I think you're making a huge mistake. The lifestyle isn't about breaking up marriages. It's supposed to bring us closer to our spouses because everything is out and in the open."

"I'm not willing to give up my sex life," Lawrence insisted. "I enjoy it too much. I don't want to lie to Jana and start going out behind her back. That's not the type of life that I want."

"So you'd rather just give up on your marriage?"

Lawrence didn't respond.

Lela rose to her feet. "Would you tell my husband that I stopped by?"

He nodded.

"I'll see you around."

Lawrence's eyes traveled from her face, stopping briefly at her neck before moving downward.

Before he could voice his thoughts, Lela said crisply, "Enjoy the rest of your day."

"I HEAR YOU'RE ABOUT TO become the second ex–Mrs. Collins."

Jana looked up to find Lawrence's former wife standing at the counter. Tall, beautiful, and curvy, the woman looked exactly like she did in her photos. She was dressed in a pair of jeans and a long-sleeved white silk shirt.

"I'm Gia Collins."

"I recognize you from your pictures," Jana said, offering the woman her hand. "It's nice to meet you."

Gia smiled as she shook Jana's hand. "This certainly wasn't the type of reception I expected. Thank you for being so pleasant."

"I don't have an issue with you."

"Same here," Gia agreed. "I came by here to see if you had a moment to talk. We were both married to Lawrence, and we know . . ." She lowered her voice to a whisper. "We both know his particular tastes when it comes to sex. I thought you might need someone to talk to who's been through it."

Jana surveyed Gia's face and read the sincerity in her eyes. "I appreciate your coming here. Just give me a few minutes for my sister to come back to the store. We can talk then."

Soon, Robyn strolled in, carrying a stack of mail. "I'm back," she announced.

"Gia, this is my sister, Robyn." To her sister, Jana said, "This is Gia Collins. She was Lawrence's first wife."

Robyn did a slight double take but said, "It's very nice to meet you."

"I'm going to take a break so that Gia and I can talk."

"Take your time," Robyn told her.

The two women headed next door to the coffee shop.

Gia initiated the conversation as they ordered. "I was really shocked to hear that you two were divorcing. I thought maybe you were the one he would stay with forever."

"Why is that?"

"I saw you and Lawrence once. You were having lunch at the country club and you looked so happy. I'd never seen him look at anyone the way that he was looking at you—he certainly never looked at me that way."

"I realize now that I really didn't know Lawrence as well as I thought," Jana replied.

Gia picked up her iced tea and took a sip. "I take it you didn't know that he was into the lifestyle."

Troubled, Jana met Gia's gaze. "Did you know when you and Lawrence married, or was this something that happened later?"

"Lawrence has been into the lifestyle for years. I think all the way back to his college days."

"And you?"

"He introduced me to it," she said cautiously. "Initially, I was open to trying new things. I wanted to keep the spice in my marriage." She frowned at the memories. "It got old pretty quick for me. It bothered me seeing him with other women, and I didn't care for some of the men. I used to have to take something or drink just to be able to go through with it. Lawrence told me that I was too insecure and jealous; he said that I was becoming an ugly drunk and that I was making his life miserable. One day when I came home, the locks had been changed and my stuff packed up."

"I see he's not very original."

Gia nodded, seeing what she meant. "So what did he tell you about me? That it was my idea for us to try swinging? Did he tell you that I was an alcoholic?"

Jana nodded.

Gia gave a short laugh. "Of course he would. I don't even know why I asked that question."

"You're not an alcoholic, then? It was all a lie?"

She nodded. "Jana, I used to drink just to deal with what I had to do to keep my husband, but then I started drinking more and more. I grew up with an alcoholic father. I was not about to travel down that road. I went away for a long weekend to clear my mind and figure out what I needed to do. I had already decided to end my marriage, but then I came home to find that I no longer had a home."

"Do you still love him?" Jana wanted to know.

"No, I don't think so. I'm not real sure that I even like the man, and I definitely resent him for all that happened."

Gia took a sip of her tea, then another. "I'm in a relationship with a wonderful man now, but when it comes to sex, I just can't do it. I feel so dirty. After all these years, I still feel dirty. I'm in therapy now."

"I guess it's going to take time," Jana said. "I thank God every day that it didn't get that far with me."

Gia's eyes grew big in her surprise. "You never—"

Jana cut her off. "No. One night Lawrence gave me ecstasy, and while he was having sex with Lela, Ron Boykin tried to undress me, but I threw up all over him. The drugs made me sick." She didn't want to tell Gia about the pregnancy.

Gia burst into laughter. "Serves him right. I never liked Ron."

"I still feel just as unclean, though," Jana lamented. "My body's sore from all the scrubbing I've done in the shower."

"I totally understand."

"Lawrence called me earlier today," Jana said. "He wants to meet with me, but I'm not ready."

"He won't leave the lifestyle," Gia warned Jana. "Lawrence loves it too much. He really believes that it's God's will for us to explore our sexual freedom. You can thank Pastor Laney for that. That man calls himself a pastor, but he's a big freak, if you know what I mean."

"He's into the lifestyle?" Jana asked, although she had a feeling that she already knew the answer.

"Yeah. He and his wife were our first couple—I guess I should say my first couple. Lawrence thought they would put me at ease."

Jana felt sick to her stomach. "How awful for you, Gia. I'm so sorry for what you had to endure. He made me believe that he hadn't done anything until that night with Ron and Lela."

"I hope you don't believe that," Gia uttered. "All those nights that Lawrence claimed to be working late, he was at a sex club. Oh, and his secretary Rhoda. He's been sleeping with her for years."

Jana couldn't believe what she was hearing. "How do you know that?"

"That's his MO, Jana. Lawrence really loves sex and he's not gonna miss out—no matter what."

Thrown by Gia's words, Jana didn't know how to respond. Lawrence had been cheating on her the entire time they'd been married?

She felt a renewed wave of anger. Lela had never been her friend. She'd known all along the kind of man that Lawrence was. She'd known everything and yet she'd said nothing.

"Lawrence is a good man, and for the most part, he's a wonderful husband," Gia pointed out in his defense.

"I guess that depends on your definition of a good husband," Jana said, offended. "It sounds to me like Lawrence was nothing but a cheating dog."

Gia didn't respond to Jana's outburst of anger right away. She put her hand over Jana's. "I'm sorry you got caught up in this madness."

Jana slipped her hand free. "I don't mean to be rude, but why are you telling me all this?"

"The answer is very simple. Because I felt betrayed by people that I thought were friends. I needed someone to talk to, but I was too ashamed to tell my close friends and family. I felt that you didn't deserve to go through that."

Jana gave her a warm smile. "Thank you, Gia. I appreciate this. And you're right—this is not something I can discuss with everybody. I'd like to pray for you," Jana announced. "God just put it in my spirit."

Gia smiled. "Prayer's good anytime, and I need all that I can get."

◆ ◆ ◆

N SATURDAY, JANA BUMPED into Lawrence—literally—when she was at a charity event. She was in line at the buffet table, and, apparently, so was he.

"Jana, I didn't know you'd be here," Lawrence said, acting surprised. "I've been calling you."

"I know," Jana responded. "I wasn't ready to talk to you. I'm not so sure we have anything to say to each other."

"We're adults. You don't have to avoid me," Lawrence said while putting chilled shrimp on his plate.

His reasonable act did not wash with her. "You're not running things anymore. If I don't feel like talking to you or anyone else, I don't have to answer my phone."

He had the nerve to look stunned. "What? Why all the attitude?"

Jana faced him, one hand on her hip. "Lawrence, tell me something—just how many times did you cheat on me?"

He looked surprised by her question. "Excuse me? What did you just ask me?"

"You heard me."

Lawrence nervously pulled at the neckline of his shirt. "Why would you ask me something like that?"

"Just be honest with me, Lawrence. I already know that you weren't working late like you told me. And I know that you and your little secretary have been getting it on for years."

He was about to deny it, but then he sighed. "What does it matter now?" he wanted to know.

"I guess I already have my answer," Jana said as she walked away from him without looking back.

"Who have you been talking to?" Lawrence asked, following behind her.

Jana stopped in her tracks and turned around to face him. "I guess you forgot that I have a brain."

Lawrence wasn't buying that. "You would've said something earlier," he told her. "So you spoke to someone recently. It's not Lela, because you're still upset with her. I don't think it's Angie, so who is it?"

"I don't have time for this. I'll see you later, Lawrence."

"Jana, stop . . ."

She stopped walking and turned around. "What, Lawrence? What do you want?"

"I am trying to have a civil conversation with you. Now is not the time to play the bitter ex-wife."

How easily he categorized her. "Comments like that don't win me over, Lawrence."

He was not apologetic. "That's the way you're acting, Jana."

"Well then, the play's over, Lawrence. I'm done." She left him standing there.

Chapter 30

THE FOLLOWING WEEKEND, GRACIELA and another friend convinced Jana to join them for a girls'-night-out dinner.

"Claire, I can't remember the last time I saw you," Jana said after giving her a hug. "You've lost all of your pregnancy weight. You look great."

When they were seated at their table, Claire pulled out pictures of her four-month-old daughter.

"She's getting so big," Jana said. "They seem to grow up so fast."

"Oh no, he didn't . . . ," Graciela muttered. "Jana . . ."

"What's wrong?" she asked, following her friend's gaze. Jana stiffened when she spotted Lawrence with a date.

"He is such a jerk!"

"Graciela, c'mon," Jana said softly. "Lawrence is out of my life, so I don't want to spend another second even thinking about him."

"Well, I hope he catches something he can't get rid of. Look at that *thing* he's got draped all over him. And that dress looks like it was painted on her."

"She's actually wearing fishnet stockings," Claire exclaimed.

Jana met Lawrence's gaze briefly—long enough to feel the heat of his hate-filled stare. Confused, she turned away from him. Why was he angry with her? He was the one with the problem. "Let's just enjoy ourselves," she suggested without emotion.

"He knows this is your favorite restaurant. That's why he brought her here," Graciela said, steaming. "He's just trying to hurt you."

"Don't worry," Jana responded. "He'll never get a reaction from me. Now do me a favor and don't let him get one from any of you. I don't want him to think he's winning."

The women nodded in agreement.

Smiling, Lawrence paused at the table and said, "Hello, ladies."

Graciela broke into a big, cheesy grin. "How are you, Lawrence? I hope you took care of that little you-know-what situation. The penicillin worked like a charm, didn't it? Now don't forget to go back for your follow-up. And for goodness' sake—refrain from all that sleeping around, because you could catch it again or something worse."

His date gasped. "What is she talking about, Lawrence?"

He muttered a string of profanities at Graciela before stomping away. Jana could hear the woman questioning him about his health.

She glanced over at Graciela and said, "That was so wrong."

"Sorry, I'm not as saved as you are, Jana."

Everyone burst into laughter at the table.

"It was wrong," Jana repeated, "but I have to admit that I enjoyed every minute of it. Lawrence is furious right now."

"They're over there arguing," Claire announced with a short laugh. "I think that chick is a little concerned about her health."

"Then she at least has some scruples," Graciela observed. "I would've already walked out on him, though, if it were me."

Just then Lawrence's date blew by them, heading straight for the exit.

"Maybe she had to go to the bathroom," Jana suggested innocently.

"Naaw," Graciela responded. "That chick is gone."

Lawrence got up and walked over to their table. "Jana, I'd like to speak with you."

"We have nothing to discuss," she replied coolly. "If you hurry, you can catch your date."

He glared at Graciela. "I could sue."

She smiled. "Go ahead . . ."

"You had no right to go into my medical records."

Jana's mouth dropped open in shock, and so did Graciela's.

"It was true?" Jana asked. "She just said it to embarrass you . . . Graciela, did you look through his records? How could you have looked at them?"

"Yeah, she did," he stated. "She probably knows somebody in my doctor's office."

Graciela was offended. "Poppy, I don't have a clue who your doctor is—I was giving you what you deserved for the way you treated my girl. You just outed yourself."

Lawrence swallowed hard, then rushed out of the restaurant.

"OMIGOODNESS! It's true," Jana blurted. "Lawrence really did catch something."

"Too bad his you-know-what didn't fall off. Poppy better be careful."

"I don't know if I feel bad for him or if I'm about to jump for joy. I actually have mixed feelings about this." Jana picked up her water glass.

"I'd be doing a praise dance myself," Graciela uttered. "Lawrence got exactly what he deserved."

"You wrong and you know it."

"You were always too nice, Jana." Graciela laughed. "*Mi'ja*, it's a good thing you got out of that marriage when you did."

When it looked like Lawrence wouldn't be returning, Jana relaxed in her seat, laughing with her friends.

While they waited for the server to come take their orders, Claire told them her thoughts and feelings on being a first-time mom. Jana scanned her menu, pretending to be engrossed in the offerings. She didn't want Claire to see a hint of sadness in her eyes. She still grieved for the child she had lost.

ANA GOT OUT OF her car and made her way quickly up the steps. She heard footsteps behind her.

"Jana, wait . . ."

Her heart racing, she turned around, her hand to her chest. "Lawrence, you scared me! What are you doing out here?"

"What have you told that bigmouth friend of yours? I could sue her for slander, you know."

Jana shrugged at the empty threat. "Graciela doesn't scare easy. Besides, if I were you, I wouldn't go there, especially after drugging me and allowing your partner to paw me . . . all of this without my permission, mind you. As for what I told her, I told Graciela the truth."

Lawrence looked extremely angry. "Jana, I wasn't trying to hurt you."

"That's debatable."

"Look, I didn't appreciate being humiliated like that."

Jana folded her arms across her chest. "Oh, so it's okay to humiliate me, but when it's turned on you, you can't handle it."

"Do you hate me this much?"

"I don't hate you, Lawrence," Jana said icily. "In fact, I don't even think about you or have any feelings whatsoever where you're concerned. I just don't feel anything when it comes to you."

He was taken aback by her words. "What is your problem?"

"You're at my home, Lawrence. You can leave anytime you want."

"Oh, this is about tonight. You're jealous."

"Of what?" Jana demanded. "You having an STD? I don't think so. Maybe if you weren't sleeping with anything with a skirt on . . ."

Lawrence waved off her words with his hand. "Jana, you need to stop being such a prude. Sharing the flesh is very different than sharing the mind and soul. For me sex is sex . . . *period*. I didn't want to share my day-to-day life with anyone but you. That's why I married you. Swinging has nothing to do with the loving, caring, and respectful relationship I wanted to have with you. It's simply pleasure of the flesh that I enjoy."

"Lawrence, you're sick," she uttered in disgust. "I am not in the mood for yet another debate on sexuality, free love, and all that. Please leave."

"Jana . . ."

She unlocked the door to her sister's house. "Good night, Lawrence."

"You're turning into a shrew," he said before leaving.

"Whatever," she responded.

As Jana closed the door behind her, she realized that she did not really know the man she'd married. Lawrence had kept secrets from her. She understood why, for if she'd known the truth, she wouldn't have stayed with him.

They most likely would never have made it down the aisle.

Jana still loved him—that was the crazy part. Maybe she should pray that God remove any feelings she still had. He was divorcing her, and Jana no longer wanted to be in love with him.

She needed a complete fresh start.

Chapter 31

"DANIEL PREACHED YESTERDAY," JANA stated. "I was in tears by the time he finished."

Robyn agreed. "He did, didn't he? My honey had been working on his sermon all week, but then Saturday, he came to me and said God told him to talk about something else. I told him to just let the Holy Spirit guide him. Sweetie, how are you doing really?" Robyn asked. She wiped down the glass countertop.

"I'm okay. Graciela and I saw Lawrence Friday night. He and a date were at Southern Style."

"I still can't believe what a pathetic jerk he turned out to be." Robyn shook her head sadly. "I hate that he hurt you."

"Pain is a part of life," Jana replied. "I'll be fine."

"Sweetie, I know how much you loved him."

"I still love him," she confessed. "But I've accepted that my marriage is over. Now it's time for me to move on."

"Jana," Robyn interjected as she gestured toward the door.

Jana followed her sister's gaze. "Lawrence? What are you doing here? I thought we'd said everything we needed to say to each other."

"There's more we need to discuss," he said. "Do you have a minute to talk?"

Lawrence nodded a greeting to Robyn. "I won't keep you long."

A look passed between the two sisters. "I can take a break." Jana stepped from behind the counter. "Robyn, can we use your office?"

"Sure."

Lawrence followed Jana through the stockroom to the back, where her sister's office was located.

"I'm surprised to see you," Jana said, a little flustered by seeing him again so soon. "I thought we said everything that needed to be said already."

"I came here to apologize to you. Jana, I'm sorry."

"Lawrence, aren't you tired of doing this—apologizing for your rude comments and harsh words? Why don't we just stay away from each other?" she suggested. "That way no one has to apologize for anything."

"I didn't just come to apologize, Jana. The other reason I came was because I wanted to discuss your living arrangements. You can't live with your sister forever."

She grew more confused. "I know that. Graciela and I will be looking for a place for me this weekend." She gave him a sidelong glance. "Why do you care where I live?"

"I want to buy a house for you," Lawrence announced.

Jana didn't hide her surprise. "Why?"

"I feel like I owe you that much."

"Thanks for the offer, Lawrence. But no thanks." Jana rose to her feet. "I can take care of myself."

"Jana, don't be stubborn," he said. "You're my wife, and even though our marriage didn't work out, I'd like to make sure that you have a nice place to live. I'm not the kind of man who would leave you out in the cold like that."

"I appreciate your concern," Jana replied smoothly, "but I have it all under control. Lawrence, this separation and the divorce have been hard on me. I need a clean break from you."

"So you want nothing to do with me? That's what you're saying, right?"

"I think it's best."

"If that's what you want, that's fine," Lawrence said. "But let me help you buy a home. I owe you this much."

Jana didn't know where this was coming from. "Can I think about it? I don't think I'm going to accept your offer, but I will think about it."

"That's all I ask."

Lawrence turned on his heel and left the store.

"Are you okay?" Robyn asked when Jana walked out of the stockroom.

She nodded, still in a daze. "Lawrence offered to buy me a house. He says that he owes me that much."

Robyn didn't respond.

"What?" Jana asked at last. "Out with it. I know you have something to say."

"I think he's right," Robyn said.

Jana didn't agree at all. "I turned him down. I don't want anything from Lawrence."

"Jana, don't get crazy. Let the man buy you a house. After all he's done to you, he needs to buy you a mansion."

The two sisters smiled at each other, then Jana laughed.

"LAWRENCE OFFERED TO BUY a place for me," Jana announced as they strolled through one of the models in a new community. "I turned him down."

Graciela stopped in her tracks. "Now, why would you do a fool thing like that?"

"I don't want anything from him."

Graciela echoed Robyn's view. "He owes you that much, mi'ja. If Lawrence wants to buy you a house, let him do it. And don't settle for just anything. Get something you really want."

The fact that Graciela thought so too made Jana hesitate. "I don't know, Graciela. I really need to pray about this."

"Prayer is good, but in this situation you need to use just some plain common sense. You don't want to live with Daniel and Robyn for the rest of your life."

"I hope that won't be the case," Jana said. "I saved some money from my allowance, maybe enough for a down payment for a . . ." Her voice died away. "I guess I can just rent an apartment until I get a decent job."

"Or you can let Lawrence help you. He owes you that."

"I'll think about it, Graciela."

Her friend lapsed into Spanish, then back to English. "I don't know what's to think about. The man is rich. He can buy you an entire island. But noooo . . . you would rather live in a shoebox. I thought I'd trained you right, but obviously . . ."

Jana laughed. "Okay, I will meet with Lawrence just to make sure he's serious about this. I'm not about to get my hopes up until I have something in writing."

"Now that's my girl."

JANA ARRANGED TO MEET Lawrence for dinner.

"How have you been?" he asked.

"Fine," Jana responded. She picked up the menu and scanned the selections.

"I never thought we would be eating together again."

Jana agreed.

"Have you made a decision about the house?" Lawrence wanted to know.

She was glad he'd brought it up first. "I think I want a condo—it's about all that I need. I don't have a family, and I'm about to be single again."

"You can have whatever you want, Jana. I'm serious about this."

Their meal passed pleasantly enough, though they fell silent too many times. Finally, Lawrence said, "I was thinking that maybe we could go back to the house. I really miss you, Jana."

She shook her head. "I hope your offer isn't tied to my having sex with you, because it's not going to happen, Lawrence."

He put up both hands to make himself clear. "One has nothing to do with the other."

Jana settled back in her chair. "I hope you're sincere about that."

"I know you may not think so after my actions, but sweetheart, you *can* trust me."

He was always so persuasive. "It's not that easy, Lawrence. A lot has happened."

"I still love you."

Jana did not respond.

"I hope that one day we'll be able to be friends, if nothing more," Lawrence said. "I really care about you."

She looked him dead in the eye. "I can't promise you anything, Lawrence. I'm sorry."

Chapter 32

JANA LEFT HER CLASS and drove to the boutique.

Another huge shipment had come in for the upcoming Thanksgiving holiday sale. By the time she arrived, the other two employees had already unpacked two boxes. She put away her stuff and dove in, pulling the clothes out and putting them on plastic hangers.

Robyn stayed out front assisting customers, while Jana and her staff put away the new inventory.

Jana held a pair of pants up to her waist. "I've lost so much weight. I think I need to go a size smaller."

"I wish I had that problem," one of the other women said. "I've been trying to lose some weight forever."

At the end of the day, Jana volunteered to stay and close for Robyn. "You've been here since nine this morning. You need to go home and spend some time with Daniel," she told her sister.

Robyn protested. "I'm sure you have some studying to do."

"I do," Jana confirmed. "But it's not something I can't handle when I get home. Now no more excuses, Robyn. Go home to your man. Take advantage of the fact that I'm here working and you and Daniel will be home *alone*."

Robyn caught the hint and grinned. "I'll see you later."

Jana laughed. "Have fun."

She felt a certain sadness that she was now alone and would soon be a single woman again. To tell the truth, Jana hadn't been crazy about it the first time around. She had always dreamed of being married, and she'd loved her time as Lawrence's wife.

She also wasn't looking forward to the holidays this year. She and Lawrence had made so many plans together. They were supposed to have visited his family in northern California and then flown to North Carolina to visit her aunt and uncle along with Daniel and Robyn.

After closing up shop, Jana decided to head down the block to see a film. Outside the theater, she called Robyn from her cell phone. "I decided to see a movie because I wanted to give you and Daniel some more time alone. I'll talk to you later. Tell Daniel to save me some of that bread pudding."

She hung up before Robyn could say anything. Jana was reaching for the door leading into the theater when she heard her name being called. She turned around.

"Hey, Jana, it's so good to see you," Lela said, delighted. "I've called you a couple of times, but I kept getting your voice mail."

"That's because I didn't want to talk to you," Jana responded coldly. "I still don't."

"Please, Jana . . ."

"Lela, I'm doing everything in my power not to taint my walk as a Christian. Get out of my way and just leave me alone. I thought you were my friend," she said harshly. "You and Ron both are going to bust hell wide open if you don't get right with God. That stuff that Pastor Laney is saying is wrong!"

Lela was contrite. "I never wanted to hurt you, Jana. Lawrence told Ron and me that you were ready. We didn't know that you'd get so upset. I'm so sorry."

"You're sorry. Fine."

Jana proceeded to walk inside, but Lela followed her, asking, "What can I do to make this up to you?"

"Nothing," she responded. "Actually, I take that back. You can stay away from me. If you ever see me again, do me a favor and cross to the other side." Her nostrils flared with fury. "I want nothing to do with you, Lela."

"I feel terrible about this, Jana," Lela said quietly. "I miss our friendship so much."

Jana looked over her shoulder at Lela. "We can never be friends. Especially after seeing you with my husband and then finding out how you knew what he was doing all this time behind my back. You were never my friend."

Lela's eyes filled with tears. "You will never know how sorry I am."

Disgusted, Jana strode to the box office window.

J ANA SHOULD HAVE KNOWN there would be a reaction. The next day Lawrence invited her out to lunch.

"Why did you want me to meet you here?" Jana asked after sitting down in the chair he pulled out for her.

"Ron mentioned that Lela came home crying. I guess you two ran into each other. He said she was really upset."

She settled back in her chair. "And?"

"Well, what happened between you two?" Lawrence wanted to know.

Jana let out a sharp breath. "Why don't you ask her? I'm sure she'll give it to you straight."

The waiter came to take their drink order.

When he left, Lawrence said, "None of this is her fault, Jana. If you want to be angry with someone, take it out on me."

"She had sex with my husband. I have every right to be furious with both of you."

"Despite all that's happened, Jana, I want you to know that I still love you," Lawrence pleaded. "I thought that you were ready to embrace the lifestyle."

She found his words hard to believe. "I don't need to hear this, Lawrence."

"Jana, apparently I was wrong. What can I say?"

"I really don't want to hear another apology from you or Lela." Jana folded her arms across her chest. "No, Lawrence . . . I haven't gotten over it. In fact, I'm still furious with you. I hate what you did to me, and if you're waiting on me to crumble and just fall apart, you'll have a long wait. I'm hurt by what you did, but I refuse to let it stop me from following my path."

The waiter reappeared with their drinks.

Lawrence stared down at the table. "I hate what I did to you, Jana. I never should've tried to drug you like that. I was wrong and I know it. I have no excuse."

"I still have nightmares of that night," she told him. "I trusted you, Lawrence. I trusted you to keep me safe."

He didn't respond.

She took a sip of her water, then informed him, "If you called me here to discuss Lela, then I won't bother staying for lunch. I don't want to keep looking back. I'm trying to move on with my life."

"I called to see if you'd given any more thought to my offer," he replied. "I'm having my attorney draw up a settlement for you. I misled you on some things, so it's only fair that I compensate you for your heartache."

She didn't want that. "No amount of money can ever repay me for the hurt you caused."

"How about a million dollars?" Lawrence said.

Jana almost choked on her water. "What did you just say?"

"I'm willing to give you a settlement of one million dollars and whatever the cost of your new home is."

"Why?" Jana exclaimed. "We weren't even married a year."

"Jana, I lied to you. I cheated on you and I even put drugs in your drink. That's not me, and it's not the man I wanted to be—not in your eyes. You lost our baby. . . ."

His generosity left her speechless.

"You are a good woman, Jana. Don't think that I don't know what I had in you. I love you, but I had to let you go." He added, "As for my lifestyle, I don't believe I've sinned against God or anything like that. I am a liberated Christian and I'm proud of it."

She had heard this song before. "If you were so liberated, why did you hide your lifestyle from me?"

"I didn't think you were able to handle the truth," Lawrence stated. "I will always love you, Jana."

"I will probably always love you too." Jana finished off her water, then restarted the conversation on a nicer note. "Thank you for the settlement. I'm blown away."

He nodded vigorously. "If you're okay with it, then I'll have my attorney draw up the papers and get them over to your attorney. I believe that my offer is more than fair."

Jana agreed. "You've been very generous. Thank you, Lawrence."

"I want you to have a very nice life."

"I want the same for you, Lawrence."

The waiter delivered their meals, breaking the united moment, but Lawrence and Jana had a pleasant time talking as they ate their lunch.

"So what are you planning to do for the holidays?" he asked her. "You're still welcome to come with me. My mom would love to see you."

Her fork stopped halfway to her mouth. "Lawrence, I can't do that. I don't know what I'd say to her if she asked me why we're not together." Jana gave him a sideways look. "She does know that we're getting a divorce, right?"

"Yeah, I told her."

"What did you tell her was the reason?" Jana questioned. "You didn't tell her that I was on drugs or an alcoholic, did you?"

Discomfited, Lawrence put his napkin on the table. "Okay, where did that come from?"

Jana leaned back in her seat. "Did you tell me the truth about your breakup with Gia?"

"I embellished some, I admit it." Lawrence leaned forward. "How did you know?"

"I met her."

Surprise siphoned the blood from his face. "You met who? Gia? When did this happen?"

"It doesn't matter," Jana responded. "Lawrence, why did you tell those awful lies on her? She didn't deserve that."

Lawrence said, annoyed, "She got a nice little settlement for her trouble."

Jana stiffened.

"Hey, you know that I didn't mean it the way that it came out. I wanted to do right by her after everything that happened."

Jana knew by now not to believe him. "So what did you tell your mother about our split, Lawrence?"

"I told her that you were too good for me. I told her that I was the reason we weren't together. That's it."

Jana folded her arms across her chest. "Uh-huh."

"I did," Lawrence protested.

She laughed. "You're so full of it. You probably told her that I had an affair or that I'd run off with the mailman or something."

"I would never tell anyone that a woman left me for another man," Lawrence said. "My ego couldn't handle it."

"You know what? I believe that," she responded with a chuckle.

Finally, his look of self-righteousness melted. "It's good to see you laugh again."

Jana wiped her mouth with her napkin, then said, "It feels good to be able to laugh."

Chapter 33

Jana and Graciela found the perfect place.

It was around the sixteenth place the realtor had taken them to see. She'd liked a couple of them, but this one really felt like home.

"This is it," Jana stated. She placed a phone call to Robyn to meet them at the location.

"My sister's going to be here in about ten minutes," she told the real estate agent.

Graciela pulled her off to the side. "This place is beautiful, but it's on the pricey side. Do you think that Lawrence is going to be okay with this?"

Jana hadn't told her sister or Graciela anything until her attorney had confirmed that he had received the settlement offer and it had been signed off on. Lawrence had kept his word: He would buy a home of her choosing in addition to giving her one million dollars.

After Robyn arrived, she fell in love with the luxury two-bedroom condominium. Like Graciela, she was concerned about the five-hundred-thousand-dollar price.

"I have something to tell you both," Jana announced.

"What is it?" Robyn asked warily. "Are you and Lawrence getting back together?"

Jana shook her head no. "It's not that. We actually just signed our settlement papers. Lawrence offered to buy the house of my choosing—this one—and he's also giving me a million dollars."

Graciela fell back against the wall, clutching her chest. She started sputtering words in Spanish, while Robyn sounded like she was speaking in tongues. She pulled out a bottle of oil and began walking from room to room, anointing the condominium.

"Poppy's all right with me," Graciela vowed. "He's all right with me."

"It was a nice gesture," Jana said. "I was shocked when he told me he was doing this for me. He loved me—this much I know."

Robyn nodded in agreement. "He just didn't love you enough to walk away from that sinful lifestyle."

Jana nodded, then jabbed her friend out the front door. "I guess I need to tell the real estate agent something. We've kept her out there waiting all this time."

"*Mi'ja,* she's earned her money. Congratulations, Jana. You are a millionaire now."

Jana gave her a sad smile. "The money is nice, but I'd rather have my husband back."

"I thank God that he's trying to do right by you, Jana. I wonder if he's doing it because you could've had him disbarred. Him and that no-good friend of his. Maybe that's why Lawrence is trying to be so nice."

Jana hadn't considered that. "I don't know—maybe."

"Or it's that he really and truly loves you," Robyn stated. "That's what I choose to believe."

Jana nodded in agreement. "Me too."

She did not want to consider that Lawrence had used her yet again.

THE TELEPHONE RANG, INTERRUPTING her studies. Without taking her eyes off her notes, Jana reached for the phone.

"Hello," she mumbled.

After a brief pause, a timid voice said, "Jana, this is Lela. Please don't hang up."

"How did you get this number?" Jana demanded.

"Lawrence gave it to me. I really need to talk to you."

"I told you before that we don't have anything to talk about, Lela. Now don't call my house again, because I want nothing to do with you."

"I'm begging you," Lela pleaded. "I can't talk about this with anyone else. They won't understand about the swinging."

"I don't really care," Jana cried.

"Jana, I need you to hear me out. If you want nothing to do with me after we talk, then that's fine."

"You don't call the shots here."

A different tone entered Lela's voice. "I got to know you pretty well, and this coldness—it's not you."

Jana resisted the urge to slam the phone down in Lela's ear. "You and your fancy friends don't know me at all."

"I'm begging you, Jana. Ever since that night, and seeing how upset you were, I've been feeling differently about the lifestyle. Something that I saw in your face changed me that night, and things haven't been right since then."

"I can't imagine why," Jana uttered sarcastically.

"You can treat me like a dog if you like, but the truth is that you are a Christian and I know that your heart is good. You really care about people even if they let you down. You were my friend even when I wasn't such a great friend to you, Jana. Right now I need a friend—someone who will tell me the truth. *God's truth.*"

Jana wasn't in a sympathetic mood, though. "If you need a word from the Lord, then you need to pray and ask Him to speak to your heart."

Lela began to cry. "I need to talk to you."

Her tears weakened Jana's resolve. "I can meet you around three."

"Thank y-you," she mumbled. "I really appreciate this."

"See you at three," Jana stated flatly, then hung up the phone.

Chapter 34

"TELL ME ONE MORE time why you are meeting with that tramp," Graciela stated. "You know Lawrence probably had her call to try and get into your business."

"Well, he sent the wrong person," Jana replied. "I haven't forgotten what they did to me." After hearing from Lela, she'd gone to see Graciela at her office.

"I wouldn't waste my time meeting with her, *mi'ja*."

Jana folded her arms across her chest. "Actually, there are some things I need to say to Mrs. Lela Boykin. Things I should've said a long time ago."

"Maybe I should go with you—you might need me to referee or post bail, which I'd be more than happy to do. You know I have your back."

Laughing, Jana shook her head. "Thanks for the offer, but I don't think I'll need bail."

"You have me on speed dial, so holla." Graciela rose to her feet. "I have to get back to work, but like I said, call me if you need some backup."

"I will," Jana promised. She picked up her purse and headed toward the door. "I'll call you later."

"You better."

She walked to the elevator, whispering a soft prayer. "Lord, help me keep my cool during this meeting. Please guard my mouth so that I don't have to repent later."

She arrived first, so she sat in her car until Lela arrived.

"Jana, thank you for agreeing to meet with me."

"Against my better judgment," she muttered. "Say whatever it is that you came to say so that we can get this over with."

"I don't blame you for being angry with me," Lela stated. "Lawrence told us that you were ready—"

"I never agreed to be a part of your little perversion."

Lela nodded. "I see that now. I was sorry to hear about the baby."

Jana bristled at Lela's words. Lawrence had had no right to tell her anything about their child. "Why did you want to meet?" she wanted to know. "There's really nothing you can say to me—"

"I wanted to apologize again," Lela quickly interjected. "I'm so sorry for my part in the breakup of your marriage. If I'd known—"

"Known what, Lela? Did you know that you're committing adultery?" Jana questioned. "Did you know that it's wrong to sleep with married men even with your husband's permission? And speaking of prior knowledge— you knew all along that Lawrence was going to sex clubs. You knew it, and so did Angie."

"Lawrence didn't want us telling you anything. He wanted to tell you himself. In his defense, he was waiting for the right time."

"That's crap and you know it," Jana said.

Lela bowed her head. "I'm not that different from you. I never wanted this type of lifestyle," she confessed. "I'm not thrilled with my husband having sex with other women, and I don't care to have sex with other men. That's the truth."

"Then why are you living it?"

The anguish in Lela's face showed how much she had wrestled with the issue. "I loved Ron more than my own life and I didn't want to lose him. I'm not as brave as you. He made it clear when we first got married that if I didn't submit to him, he would leave me because he didn't want to cheat on me. Besides, I believed it couldn't be too bad after talking with Pastor Laney."

"Did you ever think about seeking God for yourself?"

"I thought I did," Lela answered quietly. "Jana, I know now that God isn't happy with what I've done. He's punishing me because of it."

"What do you mean that you're being punished?"

"Now Ron wants me to have sex with other women. It's not enough to pass me around to his friends." Tears formed in Lela's eyes. "It's not enough that I got an STD and now, because of it, I can't conceive. I'll never be able to have a child. We had fertility tests done, and I got the news yesterday."

Jana felt a thread of pity for Lela.

"I was trying to be a submissive wife, but I have no interest in being with other women or men. I wanted a normal marriage with Ron. That's all I ever wanted. He wanted more, and I didn't want to risk losing him."

Jana reached out to her. "Lela, I've heard you use the words 'submit' and 'submissive' a few times. Do you know what being submissive truly means?"

"The Bible tells us that we have to submit to our husbands."

"Yes, it does," Jana agreed. "But it also tells us that we can refuse to do anything immoral or illegal, Lela."

She wiped her face. "I never heard that."

"That's why it's important to study the Word for yourself. Colossians 3:18 tells us to submit to our husbands as is fitting to the Lord. Adultery is not fitting to God."

Lela could see the point. "I love my husband, but I can't stay in the lifestyle."

"Have you told Ron that?" Jana asked.

"I've tried," Lela said, starting to fret. "He won't listen to me. Ron wants what he wants and that's it. He takes any argument as a sign of disrespect."

Jana settled back in her chair. "So I guess the question is, What are you prepared to do?"

Lela looked up at her hopefully. "Jana, that's why I really needed to talk to you. I don't know what to do."

"Lela, only you can make a decision regarding your marriage and your salvation."

The words came out almost in a whisper. "I feel like I need to leave Ron."

Chapter 35

"I KEEP THINKING ABOUT LELA," Jana told Robyn. "I'm still so angry with her, but I also feel bad for her." Her sister had come over to help her unpack some of her stuff.

"She needs to leave that man."

Jana eyed her sister with curiosity. "I can't believe you just said that."

"It's control," Robyn said. She took a stack of towels out of the carton and laid them on top of Jana's new coffee table.

Jana agreed. "You know, I've been thinking of starting a support group for women like Lela. Like us. Women caught up in doing whatever to please a man. It could be group sex, wife swapping, drugs—even prostitution. I remember how torn and confused I felt. I remember how dirty I felt at times. It was like I'd never feel clean again."

Robyn smiled at Jana's proposal. "I think it's a wonderful idea. Why don't you discuss it with Daniel?"

"I will," Jana responded. "I feel in my spirit that I should do something like this. Maybe we can help some of these women. I might even help myself in the process."

They finished setting up the kitchen and the bathrooms, then moved on to the master bedroom.

"This feels so strange to me," Jana said, feeling a pang of despair. "I have more money than I could ever imagine and I own this place. Robyn, why do I feel so lost?"

"You never saw yourself being alone. In your mind, you are still a married woman. It's going to take some time to transition from that."

"Hopefully by the time my divorce is final," Jana said with a short, rueful laugh. "I'm so pathetic."

Robyn hugged her. "No, you're not. You are a very beautiful and vibrant woman with a call on her life to help other women. Keep your eyes on God and not on your situation."

Jana picked up a tissue and blew her nose. "I feel so alone at times. If I can just get rid of feeling like that, I'll be fine."

J ANA SPENT THE NEXT week fasting and praying until noon each day about her vision. Daniel had been excited about the support program, and he encouraged her to proceed.

Lela popped in Jana's mind during a moment of prayer. Following the prompting of her spirit, Jana picked up the telephone and called the one woman she'd vowed never to see again.

"I want to invite you to a support group that we're having at our church. It's for women like . . . like us. Women involved with swinging, prostitution, or drugs because of our spouses. Women in a hard place in their lives."

"I need that," Lela murmured tearfully. "I'll be there, even if I have to lie to Ron about where I'm going."

Jana gave her the date and time.

"Thank you," Lela said before hanging up.

"Okay, God," Jana whispered. "I know that You know where this is going, but could You give me a little clue?"

H ER FIRST SUPPORT MEETING was held two weeks later. Jana was pleased to have six people attend her first session. Daniel had taken out an ad in the newspaper and announced it on the radio. She and Robyn had passed out flyers.

The chairs were arranged in a semicircle in the room usually reserved for children's church.

Jana greeted everyone and introduced herself.

"One of the reasons I started this group is because I was married to a man who wanted to share me with other men. He was a swinger and he loved the lifestyle more than he loved me. The thing is, he considered himself a Christian—a liberated Christian."

She took a deep breath before continuing. "What the world calls liberty, the Bible teaches us is actually bondage. Second Peter 2:19 says that 'while they promise them liberty, they themselves are the servants of corruption: for of whom a man is overcome, of the same is he brought in bondage,'" Jana stated.

"The Bible is very clear that our sexual natures are to be used only in the context of marriage. Look up the words 'adultery' and 'fornication,' or in the more modern versions, perhaps it might be called sexual immorality or something like that. Hebrews 13:4 tells us that 'marriage is honorable in all, and the bed undefiled: but whoremongers and adulterers God will judge.'"

The women looked at one another.

"You don't have to be embarrassed," Jana assured them. "There is no judgment here in this room. We are all here because we wanted to honor our husbands by submitting to them, but we have to learn what that really means."

"My husband told me that since we weren't doing anything behind the other's back, it wasn't adultery. Everything was out in the open."

"My husband told me the same thing," Lela confirmed. "He even showed me in the scriptures where women were given to other men. I'm confused and . . . I want to please God with my marriage."

"If you are ever in doubt about what God wants, He has been known to promise that He would be found by those who seek Him with all their heart," Jana stated. "The thirty-seventh chapter of Psalms, verses three, four, and five say, 'Trust in the Lord and do good; dwell in the land and enjoy safe pasture. Delight yourself in the Lord and he will give you the desires of your heart. Commit your way to the Lord; trust in him and he will do this . . .'" Jana paused a moment before continuing.

"If you don't take anything else I've said tonight with you, just remember this—what the world calls liberty, God calls sin outside of marriage. When society tells us something different from what God's word says, we must obey *His* word. If you are following your sexual appetites rather than what God has commanded, it's wrong and God will hold you accountable for your actions. God didn't give these commands to be mean to us, but for our own good."

Jana turned to the woman sitting beside her. "How do you feel about the lifestyle?"

"I was never entirely comfortable, but I wanted to please my man," she responded. "He didn't force me to have sex with other people—I did it willingly. But then I woke up one morning and didn't want to do it anymore. It just didn't feel right for me." She glanced around the room. "I can't speak for anybody else."

"The lifestyle cost me more than I ever bargained for," Lela said. "It cost me a child I desperately wanted."

The women focused on Lela, quiet and attentive, waiting for her to continue.

"I contracted an STD early on."

"We always have health checks before we get involved with another couple," the woman sitting beside Jana put in. "And we use protection, of course."

"So did we," Lela countered. "But one night at the club—we were really drunk and just picked up this woman . . ." She cleared her throat nervously. "You can imagine the rest. As far as I'm concerned, it wasn't worth the price I've had to pay."

"My husband and I love sex," a woman named Marcy blurted out. "Since I've become saved, I don't have the urge to swing anymore, but my husband misses it. I'm really afraid that he might fall back into the lifestyle."

"You keep praying for him," Jana replied. "You can't force him to stop. I know, because I gave my husband an ultimatum and he chose the lifestyle."

"My husband and I actually split up over swinging," one of the other women contributed. "He chose the lifestyle too. I was left feeling like I was worthless, unattractive, and not lovable."

"How do you feel about yourself now?" Jana inquired. "Do you still feel like that?"

"Sometimes," the woman admitted.

"You are beautiful," Jana told her. "You have to believe it in here," she said, pointing to her heart. "He's not worthy of you. This is what you have to remember. *It's his loss.*"

A couple of the other women in the group offered up opinions and words of encouragement of their own.

At the end of the meeting, Lela walked over to Jana and said, "Thank you so much for inviting me. This has really helped me. I've been doing a lot of praying and thinking about my life."

"I'm glad," Jana replied neutrally. She was not going to let Lela get close to her ever again. She had forgiven her, but she didn't intend to be her friend.

Jana had seen enough betrayal to last a lifetime.

Chapter 36

"I WASN'T SURE YOU'D LET me come over," Lawrence said when she opened her front door. He'd called her earlier asking to see her.

"I'm in a good mood," she replied. "Plus, I was curious as to why you wanted to see me in the first place."

Lawrence followed her into the living room, looking all about the room. "You've done a great job with the place." He had come to see it before she'd bought the place. Lawrence had wanted to make sure that Jana was getting his money's worth.

Jana sat down in an overstuffed chair. "You said that we needed to talk, so let's talk."

Her directions took him off guard. "How have you been?" he asked.

She folded her arms across her chest. "Lawrence, I know you didn't come all the way over here to find out how I'm doing. Why are you really here?"

A storm passed over his face, working his jaw muscles. Finally he admitted, "Jana, I miss you. I'm finding it harder and harder to get through each day without you."

She didn't respond because she didn't know what to say. She hadn't been expecting this type of declaration. He'd been the one who'd wanted the divorce in the first place.

"Did you hear what I said?" Lawrence asked.

"I heard you," Jana replied faintly. "What do you want me to say? You were the one who filed for the divorce, Lawrence."

"Maybe I was too hasty."

Jana played with the fringe on the square throw pillow, not responding.

"I was hurt, Jana, by the way you acted, but you have to know that I never stopped loving you. I bought you this condo and I gave you a nice little settlement, didn't I?"

"Don't go there with me, Lawrence," she warned. "I'm not going to let you hold anything over my head."

"I'm just saying . . ."

"Lawrence, just tell me the truth. Why are you really here?"

"I've been thinking that maybe we should try again."

Jana met Lawrence's gaze straight on. "And why should we do that? You're still a part of that lifestyle, aren't you?"

"Maybe you're more important to me than that lifestyle," he said reluctantly. "I love you, Jana, and I want you as my wife. *I want you back.*"

Jana wasn't giving in to his momentary whims. "No, you don't. Lawrence, I'm not the type of woman you want to be married to. I'm too much of a prude."

"I never should've said that about you."

"No, you shouldn't have," she said. "But you did, numerous times."

Lawrence got up and walked over to her. Pulling her up, he said, "Let me make it up to you."

He kissed her hungrily.

The touch of his lips on hers ignited a passion she'd thought was buried. "We need to stop," Jana moaned, moving away from him. "We have to settle some stuff before our relationship turns physical."

"This is the best way to get it back on track, sweetheart. I've missed you so much."

Jana pulled away from him. "Lawrence, I said *no.*"

He continued to hold her for a few moments. Then his grasp grew slack. "What's wrong with you?" he demanded. "We're still married, and if you have sex with anyone, it should be me."

"Oh, now you want a monogamous relationship," she mocked. "Lawrence, the only reason you came here is because you want sex. I'm not stupid."

"That's not the only reason," he stated. "Look, I know you must miss me, Jana. I'm your husband."

"Lawrence, we're getting a divorce, and you will soon be my ex-husband. We don't need to be intimate, because it will only confuse things."

She could see him casting about for new options. "Hey, what if I took you on a date? Can we start off with a date just to see how things go?"

Jana eyed him. "Are you serious?"

Lawrence nodded fervently. "I intend to win you back. I love you and I don't want to lose you."

"The divorce is almost final."

"Then we'll just have to get married all over again. Or I can stop the paperwork."

Confused, Jana shook her head. "Now you've decided to try and work things out."

He broke into a smile. "Better late than never—don't you think, babe?" He strode toward the door, filled with new purpose. "I'm leaving before I wear out my welcome."

He still knew how to make her laugh. "Good-bye, Lawrence."

She closed the door, a grin on her face.

"I don't know if I'll ever understand that man."

THE NEXT DAY, JANA brought up the subject of the partnership. "We should open Robyn's Couture."

Her sister clapped her hands. "Great! Jana, you have the second store. You're more suited for what we're planning to do."

"Are you sure about this, Robyn?" Jana asked. "You really want me to be your partner?"

Her sister nodded. "Daniel and I prayed about it, and we feel it's the right decision. You and I are equal partners. Robyn's II will have all of my designs, formal wear, and bridal."

"I love it," Jana exclaimed. "I'm so excited. Have you thought about location?"

"I was thinking it should be in the building across from where you live."

Jana tried to picture her block. "Are you talking about the space right next to the bistro?"

"Yeah," Robyn responded. "What do you think?"

"It's perfect. I was thinking about that location too. I even wrote down the information for you." Jana searched her purse. "Here it is. We should call and make an appointment to see it."

Right away, Robyn pulled out her cell phone. "Do you have time to see it today?"

Jana cracked a smile. "It's right across from where I live, so it's definitely not a problem for me. If we get it, then I can walk to work."

While Robyn was on the phone, Jana pulled out her checkbook.

"How much do I need for capital?" she asked her sister when she put away her cell phone.

"Your share would be fifty thousand dollars for what we want to do with the store." Remembering her sister's new-gotten riches, she added, "I'm still surprised that he didn't have you sign a prenuptial agreement and then just buys you a condo and gives you a million dollars."

"He said that a prenup only means that you're betting your marriage is not going to work." Jana reached over and grabbed her sister's hand. "Robyn, thanks for this. It means a lot to me."

"The business is growing by leaps and bounds. You're very much a part of that. Jana, you have a good eye for fashion, and you know this business probably better than I do. Robyn's is a success because of you. I'm thrilled to have you as my partner."

"If Mama were here today, she'd be so proud of you," Jana said. "She loved to sew, and she wanted to have her own shop one day."

Robyn nodded in agreement. "I know. It was all she talked about—she really wanted a store filled with her designs. She designed outfits for half of Hollywood working with the Fashion House."

Jana had a sudden idea. "Robyn, do we still have any of Mama's designs?"

"Yeah, they're in my studio," she said, not sure where Jana was going with this.

"Pull them out and let's see if maybe we can make some of Mama's dreams come true. You can add your own creative touches to make them more modern."

Robyn's face filled with delight. "That's a fabulous idea. Matter of fact, we can brand them with Mama's name."

Robyn and Jana pored over ideas for the next two hours. Then it was time for them to leave for their appointment.

"I'm telling you, that space is perfect," Jana said as they drove along the freeway.

"I'm so excited about this." Robyn glanced over at her sister. "We're a chain."

They laughed.

Jana sent up a silent prayer of thanksgiving.

LAWRENCE TOOK JANA TO a movie premiere.

As luck would have it, Angie spotted her and came over. "Oh, my goodness! It's so nice to see you, Jana. I hope this means that the two of you are reconciling. It's about time. Lawrence is a good man, and if you don't realize it, there are plenty of women who will."

"Drop it, Angie," Lawrence told her, his tone firm and final.

She sent him a sharp glare before sashaying off to talk to someone else.

"I think this was the wrong place to bring you for our first date," he muttered.

Jana gave him a gentle squeeze on the arm. "It's fine. You work with many of these people. I know we're going to have to face them sooner or later."

The tension left his voice. "Thank you for being so understanding. We won't stay long."

Jana was touched by his sensitivity. It reminded her of when they first met.

Ron and Lela arrived as they were leaving. They were both surprised to see her with Lawrence.

"We're already on our way out," he told Ron. "See you tomorrow."

In the car, Lawrence said, chuckling, "He's going to have a thousand questions tomorrow. I'm not telling him anything because I don't want to jinx it."

Jana laughed. This was the man she had fallen in love with.

They went back to her place, where she made a pot of coffee and served slices of lemon cake.

"Did you make this?" Lawrence asked.

She quickly corrected him. "Robyn made it from scratch. I still haven't mastered the art of cake baking."

"Would you tell her that it's delicious and I wouldn't be opposed to having one delivered to my office or my home? Do you think that she's too mad to make me one?"

"If you really want one, I'll ask her."

Lawrence kissed her. "Thanks, babe."

It was like old times for them as they talked and laughed. Jana was surprised when he finished his cake and coffee that he prepared to leave.

"Believe me, I don't want to leave you, but I know that you're not ready for—"

"I'm not," Jana quickly supplied for him. "Lawrence, I really had a nice time tonight." She struggled with her own desires of the flesh. She knew that if she let him get too close, they would end up in bed together. "Thank you for giving us one more chance. I'm not going to let you down."

Lawrence kissed her. "Then I'd better get out of here while I still can."

Jana walked him to the door, where he turned to her and said, "I'll call you later in the week. I'd like to do something with you on Saturday if your schedule's clear. Maybe we could take a trip to Catalina Island. Separate rooms."

"We'll see," Jana responded.

When he left, she fell back on her couch, grinning from ear to ear.

Chapter 37

WANT MY WIFE BACK.

Lawrence couldn't get Jana out of his mind or his heart. He loved her more than his own life, and if that meant walking away from the lifestyle, he would do so. He found that he was getting bored with it. It no longer satisfied him as it had in the past.

He missed Jana. Nothing was the same without her.

Lawrence got up and walked down to Ron's office.

"I didn't expect to see you and Jana together last night."

He sat down in a chair facing his friend's desk. "She and I attended the premiere together—it was a date."

"Really?" Ron said, intrigued by the notion. "So she couldn't do without you, huh? I told you that you didn't need to give the woman a condo and a million dollars."

Lawrence didn't agree. "I owed Jana that and much more. She was an innocent and I almost destroyed her. She was pregnant when I gave her that X, Ron."

His partner shrugged. "But the pregnancy wasn't viable. It's not your fault what happened."

The telephone rang and Ron answered it. He said into the receiver, "Have them fill out the paperwork and I'll be with them shortly."

When he put the phone back down, he surveyed his friend's face. "You are still in love with Jana. How is she feeling about you?"

"She loves me," Lawrence affirmed. "She just doesn't trust me."

Ron waved his hand at him. "Man, what are you doing? Jana is not going for the lifestyle. What are you going to do about that?"

"I don't know," he admitted honestly. "I want my wife back. If that means that I have to give up the lifestyle, so be it."

Ron shook his head in disbelief. "I don't believe you. You can't give it up. You love it."

"I think I love Jana more."

"ARE YOU AND LAWRENCE getting back together?" Lela asked after the support group meeting ended.

"I don't know," Jana answered honestly. "I'm taking it real slow this time around. I'm not sure he's out of the lifestyle even though he says that he is. He could be lying to me."

"I don't think he is, Jana. He's told Ron the same thing, and he wouldn't lie to his best friend."

Jana was comforted by that news. "I guess he really is trying, then."

Lela switched her purse from one side to the other. "Well, Ron made it clear to me that he wasn't giving up the lifestyle."

"So what are you going to do?"

Lela shrugged. "We've been fighting a lot because I won't go to the club or any of the house parties with him." She flashed a sly smile. "I've been having a lot of headaches. I have a decision to make—I know that and I have to make it soon."

Jana gave her a hug. "I'll keep you lifted in prayer."

"If anybody understands—you do."

They walked out together.

LELA SHOWED UP AT the new boutique, where Jana was unpacking the new fixtures. Lela's eyes were red and swollen.

"Lela, are you okay?" Jana inquired.

"I left Ron."

"Really?"

Lela nodded. "Jana, I just couldn't take it anymore. I don't want to be in that lifestyle for another minute." She stepped further inside the store. "I went to church yesterday, and while I was sitting there, I suddenly heard a voice that said that I needed to flee. It stayed with me; 'you need to flee.' I wasn't sure what that meant exactly. Then this morning, it was clear to me—I had to leave Ron."

Jana embraced her. "I'm so sorry."

"Don't be," Lela responded, trying to be brave. "I'm not. Ron isn't going to want me after I tell him that I'm out of the lifestyle."

"Maybe you should let him decide for himself, Lela," Jana suggested. "He just might surprise you. I know that Lawrence shocked me when he decided to leave it behind. He was the one walking around telling me how scriptural it was and that there was nothing wrong with swinging."

Lela wasn't as hopeful. "Ron is going to want a divorce."

Jana saw how grim Lela was, and she had to agree. Ron wasn't the same type of man as Lawrence. "So what are you going to do now?" Jana questioned.

"I guess I'm going to have to find a job. There's no telling how Ron is going to act during our divorce. He's not going to be as generous as Lawrence was to you."

"I'm really sorry."

Lela pulled fully away. "Jana, it's fine. I love my husband, and yes, I'd like for our marriage to work, but I know deep in my heart that it's over between us." She seemed lighter, almost glad.

"Where are you staying?" Jana asked her.

"In a hotel for now. You know, I've been thinking about the condos where you live. They're gorgeous."

"There's one available in my building," Jana announced. "It's a one-bedroom, though."

"I don't care. I have some money saved, so I'll be able to buy something right away." Lela's eyes filled with tears. "I can't believe I'm doing this. I know it's the right thing to do, but I still can't believe it."

"You don't have to make any rush decisions."

"Jana, I don't like living in a hotel. I need my own home." She stopped, regarding Jana closely. "I know you don't believe me, but I mean it. I'm happy that you and Lawrence are working things out, but Ron and I are getting a divorce. I have no choice but to accept it."

"It sounds as if you've made up your mind."

"When I packed my bags and left the house, the decision had been made. I'm back to being a single woman." Lela shook her head, and her face crumpled with hard lines. "Life sucks, don't it?"

Chapter 38

TODAY WAS THE GRAND opening for Robyn's Couture.

The two sisters rushed about the store, making sure that everything was in place.

Lela walked over to them and said, "Okay, breathe . . . everything is perfect. This is where everyone will find their inner Hollywood Star."

Jana had hired her shortly before the store opened, and they worked well together. She had proven to be a real asset to the boutique.

"Much better than tennis," they both agreed.

Robyn's Couture launched with a boutique filled with limited-edition clothing inspired by Hollywood fashions that offered a creative and fresh look. At Jana's urging, they also offered one-of-a-kind accessories.

A red carpet was placed outside the front door for the Hollywood flair.

As soon as the doors opened, customers burst into the store. They were busy for the next three hours straight. Jana wasn't complaining, and neither was Robyn. Lawrence sent flowers to them, as well as a huge gift basket containing goodies that helped to sustain them since they weren't able to take a lunch break.

When it was time to close, Jana sent up a prayer. She gave thanks for their success, the support group, and for life in general. Then she went home and jumped into the shower after eating a dinner salad she'd picked up from a restaurant on the way home.

Thrilled with the way her day had turned out, Jana fell to her knees and thanked God all over again.

She praised Him until she had no voice left.

L ELA ATTENDED CHURCH WITH her on Sunday.

Jana was surprised when Lela stood up and walked down to the front of the sanctuary to receive the gift of salvation. She couldn't stop her tears from flowing. An odd thought struck Jana—had she not gone through what she had with Lawrence, then the support group wouldn't have been in existence.

And Lela might not have been here today giving her life to the Lord.

After church, they went to a nearby restaurant for a celebratory lunch.

"Jana, I'm so thankful that you allowed me back into your life," Lela said. "I'm so embarrassed over how stupid I've been. I was such a fool."

Jana replied simply, "Now you know better."

Lela nodded. "I'll do better. I can't tell you how I'm feeling right now. I have so much clarity."

Jana smiled. "I'm happy for you. That's how I felt when I recognized the truth. We don't have to twist the scriptures around. God's word stands as is."

"You said that before," Lela said, "but that was when I was listening to Pastor Laney. That man needs to be forced out of the pulpit. People are buying into his lies—Ron and I did. Lawrence did. A lot of others."

"Lawrence told me that he's not going to NVC like he used to. He hasn't really been going to any church. He's really confused, I think." Jana finished off her shrimp scampi and wiped her mouth on the edge of her napkin.

"I can understand why," Lela responded. "We'll keep praying for him. God will show Lawrence the way."

"Amen to that."

• • •

R ON BLEW THROUGH THE doors of the boutique, his hands balled into fists. His eyes flashed red-hot anger. "How dare you tear up my marriage just because you couldn't hold on to Lawrence!" he yelled.

Jana immediately inched closer to the telephone in case she needed to call the police. "I didn't do anything," she responded as calmly as she could manage. "Lela has a mind of her own and she decided to use it. I had nothing to do with that."

He leaned over the counter, as if trying to get in her face. "I want my wife back now."

"Then you need to talk to her," Jana retorted, her eyes never leaving Ron's face. She was not about to let him intimidate her. "She's not here right now, and I don't know when she'll be in, so you need to leave."

"I'll leave when I'm good and ready."

"You'll be leaving right now," a voice said from behind him.

Daniel walked up to Ron, his gaze direct and unwavering. "If Jana has asked you to leave, you need to do as she's requested."

Ron looked Daniel from head to toe, sizing up the six-feet-five, two-hundred-and-fifty-pound man. "My wife works here, so I am staying here until I see her."

Jana tried to use reason. "Ron, she'll call you if she wants to speak to you. Now, I'd really like for you to leave my shop." She couldn't resist adding, "While you can still walk out."

Daniel was a big man, much bigger than Ron, even though as a pastor he strove to live a peaceful life.

Ron glanced over at Daniel, then said nastily to Jana, "Lawrence was right to get rid of you. I knew the moment I saw you that you were trouble. If he has half a brain left, he'll leave you alone for good."

Jana didn't flinch at his words. "Interestingly enough, I didn't think about you one way or the other."

Ron's mouth tightened. "If I don't hear from Lela, I *will* be back."

"I don't want to have to call the police or my brother-in-law on you, Ron, but I will," Jana vowed. "Please don't come back to my store without an invitation."

He muttered a string of profanities as he made his way through the double doors.

"Ron is such a jerk," Jana said warily. "I'm glad you were here, Daniel. I thought I was going to have to pull out my taser."

"Call me if he comes back." Daniel pointed toward the back room. "I have some inventory for you. Robyn's new collection is ready."

Jana clapped her hands, her mood brightening. "Great. I've been waiting for this. She outdid herself this time, Daniel."

He agreed. "I told her that just this morning."

A customer entered the store. While Daniel brought in the cartons containing the new inventory, Jana assisted her client.

"My sister's new collection just came in but won't be on the floor until later this evening," Jana told the woman. "If you have some time, why don't you come back then? I have a feeling we'll find the perfect dress for you."

"I'll do that," the woman said. "But I still want to go on and get these two items now. They may not be here when I come back later."

Jana rang her up. "Your total is four hundred sixty-two dollars."

"Charge it to my American Express."

Jana had just finished with her when another customer entered the store, then another. They were about to get busy. She stole a quick peek at the clock on the wall. Her part-time employee should be arriving soon.

Jana went from one woman to the other, assisting them. Amy arrived and immediately came to Jana's aid.

The shop had a steady flow of customers for the next two hours. Jana wasn't complaining, though. She loved when there was heavy traffic into the boutique. She put out more bottles of water and a fresh batch of fruit trays.

The customers loved that touch.

"Ron was here looking for you," Jana announced when Lela arrived an hour later. "He was very angry and didn't want to leave. Thank goodness Daniel came by when he did."

"He likes to intimidate, but he's all bark and no bite." Lela removed her jacket and laid it behind the counter. "I'm sure he acted like he had some sense when he saw Daniel." She added dryly, "Ron likes to tell people that he's a lover and not a fighter."

"All I know is that I've never seen Ron like that," Jana said. "He was really angry with me."

"He's upset that I had the nerve to leave him, and he's trying to blame you." Lela shrugged in nonchalance. "He'll just have to get over it. I keep telling him that this was my decision. You had nothing to do with it."

"You still love him."

Lela nodded. "I do. I know that you are still very much in love with Lawrence. We'd both rather be with our husbands." She stopped, correcting that notion. "I get angry every time I think about the way I let Ron brainwash me. I was such a fool. Jana, I thank God that He brought you into my life. Had we never met, I'd probably still be over there getting passed around like French fries."

Jana chuckled. "French fries? Really?"

"I couldn't think of anything else." Lela glanced into the stockroom. "We got a new shipment in, I see."

"It's the winter collection of Robyn's designs. She had Daniel bring them over. Wait until you see the clothes. My sister outdid herself this time."

"I can't wait," Lela murmured.

Lawrence stopped by the store at closing to see if Jana wanted to grab a late dinner with him.

Jana was exhausted from the long day, but she said, "I'd love to."

He had been away in Seattle for a week at a conference and had just gotten back a few hours earlier.

"Your buddy came to the shop earlier today," Jana said over dinner. "Ron said some horrible things to me."

Lawrence looked angry. "What did he say?"

"It doesn't matter. Daniel was there and he made him leave. If my brother-in-law hadn't been there, I would've used my taser."

He laughed. "I don't doubt that you would have." Lawrence finished the last of his glass of wine. "I'll have a talk with Ron. He never should've burst in on you like that."

"You don't have to do that, honey. Just let it go. Ron's upset right now because he's lost his wife. He's emotional."

"You make him sound like a woman."

She eyed Lawrence. "No you didn't just say that to me."

He realized what she meant. "It's true."

After dinner, Lawrence followed her to the condo, where they settled in the living room to watch a movie.

"I want you to come home, Jana."

She glanced over at him. "I want that too, but it's still too soon, Lawrence. You may have left the lifestyle, but we're still on different pages when it comes to open marriages. Our beliefs are not the same."

He had an answer ready for that. "You wanted me out of the lifestyle, and I left. Babe, I don't know what you want from me." He held out his hand, making his case like a lawyer. "What I personally believe should not affect our love for each other. You don't believe in abortion, and I do. Should we stay apart because of that?"

"Lawrence, can you please listen to me for a moment?" Jana asked. "Marriage is supposed to be a place of shelter, hope, and strength during difficult times, and a place of deep joy and thankfulness to God for all the goodness we experience. It's my belief that my faith in God defines our relationship and our family."

"I believe in God," Lawrence interjected. "You're not with a non-Christian, babe."

"Lawrence, we talked about having children one day. If we're not on the same page about stuff and children are involved, the complications are even greater. As their father, what you say will have a powerful impact on them."

Lawrence didn't see the difficulty. "I'm sure we can reach a compromise on what we tell our children. Jana, I know that the Bible talks about being unequally yoked. It's my understanding that God is saying that we shouldn't be partners with those who reject God. This is not the case with us."

"I want us to be on the same page spiritually, Lawrence," she stressed. "That's all I'm trying to say to you. I want us to attend church together, and it doesn't have to be Daniel's church. We can find a church that both of us enjoy. I want us to have Bible study together."

He nodded in understanding. "I'm willing to do that. I'm willing to do whatever we need to make our marriage work."

He sidled over on the couch and kissed her.

When Lawrence began to get too touchy, Jana pulled away from him. "We can't."

He groaned. "Babe, why not? I stopped the divorce. We're still married. This is the longest I've ever been without sex. It's killing me. . . ."

Jana gave him a sympathetic look. "I'm sorry, but I don't want to rush into a physical relationship with you, Lawrence. I love you and I want you very much, but we still have some issues to work through."

Lawrence didn't hide his disappointment.

He didn't stay much longer after that; he complained of having to take a cold shower.

She walked him to the door and kissed him good-bye. She then went to her room, undressed, and soaked in her Jacuzzi for a few minutes.

Later, a pajama-clad Jana sat down with her journal and began to write down her thoughts.

> I believe Lawrence is serious about making our marriage work. He has given up the lifestyle but not the belief that it's sinful. Once we find the right church, it is my prayer that he will discover the truth for himself. I think he still considers me sexually repressed, but I appreciate him respecting my wishes.
>
> I love Lawrence and want nothing more than to be his wife. I feel as if I can trust him again, as he's done nothing to betray that trust.
>
> Father God, You honor marriage, and I give my marriage to You. Please show me if this relationship is truly what You have for me. I don't want to open my heart completely only to be hurt once

again by this man. He is good to me, but is this the man that You have for me?

Until I hear from You, Lord, I'm not leaving my condo. I'm staying right here. Lawrence and I still have to discuss the fact that I'm not going to be a housewife—I have a business to run. I know how he feels about working women, but he will have to respect my feelings on this.

Jana put away her journal.

She climbed into bed and propped herself up against a stack of pillows, then flipped through the television channels, looking for something interesting to watch.

The telephone rang.

It was Lawrence.

Jana answered the phone. "Are you home?"

"Yeah. I just got here. I wanted to call you and tell you once more that I love you very much and we will work out any issues that we have."

She smiled. "I love you too."

Chapter 39

"YOU NEED TO TELL Jana to stay out of my marriage," Ron uttered as he strode into Lawrence's office. "She's the reason Lela left me."

Lawrence shot a bored look his way. "Your wife has a mind of her own."

Ron paced back and forth in Lawrence's office. "Jana brainwashed her. Did you know that she's started some type of support group for ex-swingers?"

Surprised, Lawrence turned his attention from his computer monitor. "What are you talking about? She has a support group for women—I know that—but it's not for ex-swingers." He was sure that Jana would've mentioned something to him. She was big on honesty.

"Jana meets with a bunch of women who are unhappy being swingers, prostitutes—something stupid like that."

"She never mentioned it to me," Lawrence said. "How do you know about it?"

"Lela told me about it. Oh, yeah, she's saved now—I guess she wasn't before." Ron scratched the back of his neck. "The woman was always stupid, but she was great in bed."

"Lela loves you," Lawrence reassured Ron. "She'll come back to you."

"Oh, yeah? She just purchased a condo in the same building as Jana. They work together. Those two are joined at the hip now."

Lawrence shrugged upon hearing the news. "Well, it's time for you to move on. Why don't you start taking applications for your next wife?"

"I'm not ready for that," Ron shot back. "Believe it or not, I want Lela back home with me. She's already house-trained, if you know what I mean. Now, you need to follow your own advice. Jana—she was never really a submissive wife to you."

Lawrence sent Ron a warning look. "Like I said earlier, Lela has a mind of her own. She left you of her own accord—don't blame Jana for this. Leave her alone."

Ron stared at Lawrence as if he didn't recognize him. "Jana is to blame for what's happened to my marriage. Lela now believes that what we've been doing is wrong. She didn't get that from anybody but Jana."

"Leave my wife out of this, Ron," Lawrence rumbled.

"Then tell her to stay out of my marriage."

Lawrence met Ron's gaze straight on. "You need to calm down. For the last time, Jana is not to blame for the breakdown of your marriage, so leave her out of this."

"I can't believe that you're defending her." Ron shook his head in disbelief.

"Jana was a good wife to me. We had different beliefs and that's why we're having problems right now. Eventually, she'll come to realize that our love is bigger than anything else. Ron, you don't see me having a meltdown. You won't get Lela back that way."

"You think Jana's coming back to you?" Ron asked.

"I'm not giving up on her," Lawrence responded. "But I'm not going to pressure her either. She will have to come to me on her own."

Ron released a long sigh. "Everything was great until Lela met Jana and started listening to her religious crap. I just want my wife back."

"Man, chill . . . ," Lawrence said. "You're making yourself look desperate. Start showing up around town with another woman on your arm and see what happens. Lela will be running you down after that."

"That didn't work so well for you," Ron reminded him.

"Jana was jealous," Lawrence argued. "She's playing hard to get, but I'm not fooled, she's still very much in love with me."

Ron sat in Lawrence's office for the next twenty minutes, bemoaning the fact that his wife was being difficult and furthermore was entitled to a sizable chunk of his assets.

After making plans with Lawrence to go out for drinks after work, Ron went back to his office down the hall, leaving Lawrence alone with his thoughts of Jana.

Lawrence knew one thing. It had been almost two months since he'd been with a woman, and he was climbing the walls. He didn't want to resort to his old ways, but he needed a physical release. This one time wouldn't hurt, he told himself.

Lawrence couldn't wait much longer.

L AWRENCE LED HIS DATE into the master bedroom. "This is where I'll make all of your dreams come true." He had gone out drinking with Ron, who'd insisted on going to Le Luxure Manoir.

Her giggle brought Lawrence's attention back to her.

"Oh, I hope so. I'm loving this suite. Your house is beautiful."

Lawrence could tell by the way Cindy was looking around, trying to calculate the cost of every object around her, that she was already plotting to make him fall in love with her. Cindy was already planning to be the next Mrs. Collins.

Lawrence chuckled softly. It wasn't going to happen.

He was still in love with Jana and was serious about winning her back. Cindy was just a diversion for now. His eyes scanned her from head to toe.

A very sexy and beautiful diversion.

Lawrence removed his shirt. He tried to ignore the nagging headache he'd had all day.

He glanced at the clock. It was 10:45 p.m. He glanced back over his shoulder to Cindy, who was removing her clothes. He took off his pants.

Just as they settled in bed, his headache seemed to worsen. Lawrence began to experience excessive sweating.

Cindy frowned. "What's going on, baby?"

"I don't know," he managed to say, experiencing a wave of discomfort. "My chest hurts. I think I'm having a heart attack. Call . . ." He couldn't finish his sentence because he was in so much pain.

Cindy dialed 9-1-1, screaming for them to send help.

He wanted to tell her to stop being hysterical, but he couldn't get the words out. He hoped she would at least grab his robe and cover his naked body, but Cindy was too scared. She wouldn't even look at him; she just kept crying and screaming on the telephone.

Lawrence felt like he was about to lose consciousness. He struggled to hang on, praying that God would spare his life. He wasn't ready to die.

They soon heard the sirens.

Cindy grabbed his robe and slipped into it. "Hold on, baby," she told him. "They're here."

She took off, running out of the room and down the stairs.

Lawrence had no idea what happened next; when he opened his eyes, he was in the hospital. His chest still hurt, but it wasn't as painful as before. He was vaguely aware of someone wearing white entering the room and talking about taking some blood.

He didn't care. They could take whatever they needed. Lawrence just wanted the pain to disappear.

Shortly after midnight, his blood work came back from the lab. The doctor walked into his room to explain the results.

It was just as he'd thought. He'd had a heart attack.

Lawrence was transported to the cath lab for an angiogram and angioplasty. He sent up a silent prayer.

Lord, I thank you for letting me live. I won't waste a moment of this gift you've given me. I was wrong for what I was about to do to Jana. Please don't let her find out.

He hadn't seen Cindy, so he assumed she must have gone home. That was fine with him. He needed Jana.

◆ ◆ ◆

JANA HUNG UP THE phone. "OMIGOSH."

She and Graciela were up late planning a surprise anniversary party for Robyn and Daniel.

"What's wrong?" Graciela asked.

Jana glanced over at her friend. "Lawrence is in the hospital. He had a heart attack."

Graciela's mouth dropped open. "When did this happen?"

"Earlier tonight," Jana responded, getting up off the floor. "I've got to get over there."

Graciela rose to her feet. "I'll drive you there. Which hospital?"

"Cedars-Sinai." Jana picked up her purse. "Graciela, you don't have to drive me. I'm sure you want to get home to Enrique."

She shook her head. "I'll call him on the way to Cedars. I'm not leaving you alone to deal with this. You're already shaking."

Jana was relieved by her friend's offer to help. "Thanks."

Jana rushed into the hospital lobby as soon as they parked the car.

"I'm Jana Collins. Someone called and said my husband has been admitted to this hospital. His name is Lawrence Collins."

They directed her upstairs to the fourth floor.

After they stepped off the elevator, Jana and Graciela walked up to the nurses' station. "I'm Jana Collins. My husband was admitted earlier tonight."

The nurse looked past her to a woman standing nearby.

Jana turned around.

"Who are you?" Graciela asked.

She tilted her chin upward and said, "I'm Lawrence's girlfriend."

"Do you have a name?" Jana asked. A wave of anger coursed through her veins. She despised Lawrence for deceiving her again. She noted that the woman was wearing only a robe—her husband's robe. *Guess she didn't have any time to change clothes.*

"My name is Cindy. Cindy Keeler."

Jana turned back around to face the nurse. "I was told that I needed to sign off on some forms. Is there a DNR form for me to sign?" she asked.

Graciela glanced over at her and said, "No—you didn't just ask for a DNR form."

"What's a DNR form?" Cindy asked.

"Do not resuscitate," Jana explained.

Graciela laughed. "That's my girl."

"I don't think you should sign that DNR form," Cindy stated. "Lawrence wouldn't want that."

Jana didn't look up. "Cindy, the best thing for you to do is walk back over to that waiting area and stay out of my business. You may be Lawrence's girlfriend, but I am still his wife, and I have final say over what happens until he is able to speak for himself."

The nurse put a hand to her mouth to hide her chuckles.

Graciela was not as discreet. She cracked up with laughter. "Oops, you might want to pick up the pieces of your face down there on the floor, Mindy."

"Cindy. My name is Cindy."

"Who cares," Graciela uttered.

Jana asked the nurse, "Is this everything you need from me?"

The woman nodded. "Would you like to see your husband now?"

"No, thank you. His girlfriend is here. Let her see him. *I'm done.*"

G RACIELA TOOK HER BACK to the condo. "You have every right to be hurt, *mi'ja.*"

"I can't believe that I fell for his lies a second time," Jana muttered. "I am such a fool."

"No, you're not," Graciela stated. "You just love the wrong man."

There was a knock on her door.

"I'll get it," Graciela told her.

It was Lela.

"I just heard about Lawrence. I didn't expect you to be home—I thought you'd be at the hospital."

"His girlfriend was there," Jana announced. "Did you know he was seeing someone?"

Lela shook her head. "This is the first I've heard of it. I promise, Jana. I didn't know." She pulled out her cell phone. "I'm calling Ron to find out the story."

"You don't have to do that. It's obvious that Lawrence hasn't changed at all. He's still lying to me."

After a while, Jana sent Graciela and Lela home. She wanted to be alone.

Raising her eyes heavenward, she whispered, "This wasn't the answer I wanted, Father God, but I accept it."

Chapter 40

"YOU SHOULD BE HOME, Lawrence," Jana cried when she opened her door to find him standing there.

"I've been cooped up in that house for two weeks. I needed to get out of there for a little while. Don't worry, I cleared it with my doctor."

"Well, I'm glad to see that you're okay." Jana opened the door wider and took a step backward to let Lawrence enter the condominium.

He followed her over to the sofa and sat down.

"So why are you here?" Jana asked.

"I came to say thank you."

Jana was surprised. "For what?"

"For coming to the hospital and being there for me. Cindy lied to you. I only met her earlier that night. She's definitely not the woman for me." His face contorted; he knew how it must look to Jana. "You know, having a heart attack makes you see life a little different. Helps to put things in perspective. Life is short, and I don't want to waste mine—not anymore."

Jana smiled tolerantly. "I'm happy for you."

Lawrence reached over and took her hand in his. "I know I've said a lot of this before, but you have to believe me. My heart attack really changed me, Jana."

"Oh, in what way?"

"I know the only reason I'm not dead is because of the good Lord. When I was having the attack, I felt like I was dying. I've never been so scared of anything, Jana, but then I felt this warmth surround me as if I wasn't alone. I heard a voice say that I wasn't going to die. I had one more chance."

"Chance to do what?" Jana wanted to know.

"I saw my life flash before me like a movie. It was in that instant that I knew you were right about everything. I have a chance to change my life for the better. If I don't, then I might not be so lucky the next time." Lawrence squeezed her hand. "I guess I owe you a huge apology. I hadn't been with another woman since we got back together. I wasn't with Cindy."

"You were going to have sex with her, but you had the heart attack," Jana pointed out. "By the way, you don't owe me anything, Lawrence." Jana removed her hand from his. "I'm glad that you're finding your way."

"I am very clear about what I want, Jana. I've been a fool and I admit that."

Jana's eyes grew wet with unshed tears. "Lawrence, I'm happy about your recovery, but our marriage is over. I don't think that it should have ever begun. I am not the wife for you—I know that now."

It was his turn to look surprised. "How can you say that?"

"You don't need me, Lawrence," Jana said. "Who you need in your life is not necessarily a woman. You need to get away from that so-called pastor and church of yours. You need to get away from that law firm and those partners. Lawrence, you need a real relationship with God."

"Jana, I'm not giving up on you. I want you to know that."

"You really should work on your relationship with the Lord."

"Can you stop saying that?" Lawrence snapped. "All I want is my wife. Look, I made a mistake. Doesn't the Bible tell you that you should forgive?"

"Oh, so now you want to talk about what the Bible says," Jana said. "Lawrence, I care for you, but I can't keep revisiting the past. I don't think you should either. I know that you don't want to hear me say this, but it's the truth. What you need in your life now is Christ. Not me, not any woman."

After a moment, Lawrence replied, "You're probably right, Jana."

"Take some time and just focus on God. Everything else will come, Lawrence."

"I can't believe I was so stupid," he muttered. "I believed everything Pastor Laney said."

"That's why you have to pray for wisdom when reading the Bible. Get understanding for yourself—you once told me that, remember?"

Lawrence nodded. "I was so cocky. I thought I knew everything."

"You wanted to believe him because it made what you were doing okay. People often look to validate whatever they're doing so that they don't have to feel guilty about it. You had Pastor Laney do that for you."

He hung his head in shame. "Jana, do you still love me?"

"I do," she confessed. "But I can't go back to you, Lawrence."

"Why not? I was wrong, Jana. I freely admit that."

She gave a slight shake of her head. "Lawrence, I can't do this with you. Not right now."

"Cindy told me that she met you at the hospital. Is this because of her? If so, I want to reassure you that I'm not in love with her. She was just something to pass the time with. If I'm going to get out of the lifestyle, I can't have her in my life either. Jana, there's something else you should know. I'm leaving the law firm."

She couldn't believe what she was hearing. "Really?"

Lawrence nodded. "I'm serious about changing my life. I need to leave all that stuff behind me, so I'm opening up my own office. I found office space on Wilshire Boulevard."

"That's wonderful, Lawrence."

He chuckled. "I knew you'd be thrilled about it."

"I wish you much success with your new office. But don't go rushing into anything, Lawrence. You need to take better care of yourself." She tapped her heart.

"I will," he promised. "I had really hoped you would be with me on this journey."

"I'm sorry."

Lawrence hugged her. "I will always regret what happened between us. You will make some man a great wife—although I'm still hoping to win you back."

Jana smiled. "Until you meet the next Mrs. Lawrence Maxwell Collins."

"It's you that I want, and I'm not going to give up on you." Lawrence rose to his feet. "I guess I should get back to the house. I promised my doctor I wouldn't be out and about too long."

Jana walked him to the door. "Take care of yourself, Lawrence."

He pulled her into his arms and kissed her. "You too."

She stroked his cheek. "Do what the doctor instructed. I know how you are when it comes to medication."

"I'll always regret losing you, Jana."

She grinned. "Yeah . . . you will."

He kissed her.

They both knew that it was a kiss good-bye.

"LAWRENCE CAME BY EARLIER," Jana announced when Graciela came over.

"He did? What did he want?" Graciela asked.

"He says that he wants me back." Jana gave her friend a recap of the conversation she'd had with Lawrence.

"No big surprise there," Graciela murmured. "I'm sure he means it too. This time it might work, though. His heart can't take all of that extracurricular activity."

Jana laughed. "Lawrence believes that God was giving him a warning with the heart attack. I'd take heed if I were him. The next time could be fatal."

Graciela agreed. "So are you considering going back to him?"

Jana shook her head. "Lawrence needs to focus on God. He doesn't need me or any other woman distracting him right now."

"He ought to be tired of women—all that he's been doing," Graciela commented with a short laugh. "That's why his heart tried to give out."

Jana chuckled. "You know you need to quit."

"On the serious side, I know that you still love him, Jana."

"I do," she admitted. "But that doesn't mean our marriage can be saved. He had sex with another woman while we were married. I forgave him and I let him back into my heart, but when I saw Cindy at the hospital, I just knew that we were over. I forgave him for that too, but—"

Graciela interrupted her. "There are no *buts* in forgiveness, Jana."

She sighed in resignation. "I know."

"Marriages have survived more."

"You know how much I wanted my marriage to work, Graciela. Lawrence hurt me so much. He cheated on me and he tried to change me. I didn't like who I was becoming. I don't want to be that person."

"Poppy wanted you to become his little sex kitten," Graciela teased.

"I think that's what I really can't get past. Lawrence made me feel as if I wasn't enough woman for him. Seeing Cindy made me feel the same way all over again. I still love him, but I don't want to be with him. It's not a healthy relationship—not right now, anyway."

"What if he has truly changed?"

Jana shrugged. "I don't know. I need to focus on my own relationship with God."

Graciela embraced her. "I know what you need, *mi'ja*. A good chick flick."

Jana was glad to stop talking about her husband. "You look and I'll find something for us to snack on."

Jana made sandwiches for them while Graciela scanned the newspaper to check movie times.

It was truly time for Jana to move on.

"SURPRISE," EVERYONE YELLED WHEN Daniel and Robyn entered the condo with Jana.

Robyn looked at her sister. "What have you done?"

"Happy anniversary," she responded. "You and Daniel have been so good to me. I wanted to do something for you both."

She hugged Robyn first and then Daniel. "Thank you for giving me a home and for all of your support."

Graciela and Enrique joined them, offering their congratulations.

Jana eased out on her balcony while the guests of honor were working the room, greeting everyone.

She smiled at the memory of her sister's face when she'd handed her tickets to a fourteen-day cruise. Robyn and Daniel had always dreamed of taking a cruise to the Mediterranean, but they would never have spent that kind of money on themselves. They believed in using their financial blessings to help others less fortunate. Jana was grateful that she could afford to send them on a luxury vacation.

She also felt a thread of sadness that her divorce would soon be final; she'd been touched by Lawrence's gesture, but her marriage was truly over.

A lone tear slid down her face.

She wiped it away when Graciela joined her. "I thought I'd find you out here," Graciela said.

"I love standing out here looking over the city," Jana murmured. "It's so beautiful at night."

"I bet you're out here thinking about Lawrence."

"I am," Jana confirmed. "I can't stop wondering why. Why couldn't our marriage work?"

Graciela embraced her. "You know why. It wasn't your fault, Jana. You were the ideal wife."

Jana did indeed know why: If she hadn't met Lawrence, she would never have started the support group.

"This is a lovely party," Robyn said from behind them. "Thank you so much for everything."

Jana and Graciela turned around to face her.

She held up the tickets. "Jana, this is too much money. Let us pay you back."

"I will not," Jana uttered. "This is my gift to you and Daniel. You've been wanting to take a cruise like this forever. It's long past time for you two to just indulge yourselves. Life is too short. Now go and enjoy. Lela and I can handle the boutiques while you're gone."

They walked back inside the condo.

Graciela and Enrique stayed behind to help Jana clean up after the party. They practically had to run Robyn and Daniel out because they insisted on helping too.

It didn't take long, and soon Jana had her condo to herself.

As she readied for bed, she hummed softly.

The evening had been a success. She still felt pangs of sadness course through her at the thought of her marriage ending so quickly, but God had indeed used her for ministry.

She started to sing, rejoicing in the fact that God had chosen her for this task—the ideal woman.

Author's Note

THANKS SO MUCH FOR reading *The Ideal Wife*. It is my prayer that you enjoyed this story. Anyone familiar with my books knows that biblical characters inspire many of my stories. *The Ideal Wife* was birthed after I read about Queen Vashti (Esther 1). She was the wife of King Ahasuerus of Persia. Her name in Hebrew derives from the Persian word for "beautiful woman."

Ironically, her beauty ended her marriage. Queen Vashti refused her husband's demand to parade before the people while wearing her royal crown. Most believe the king wanted her to appear wearing only her crown. If this theory is correct, then her husband had treated his wife as though she'd been a harlot.

It has also been said that Queen Vashti prized modesty in a woman above all else, and that this was the act not of a rebellious woman but of a regal queen who refused to display herself and her position to shame. However, there are others who view Queen Vashti's actions as disobedience; they assert she wasn't being a submissive wife.

We can speculate, but the facts are that Vashti was removed as queen and Esther took her place. This act allowed Queen Esther to save the Jews. The other fact is that a woman only has to be submissive to her husband if what he is asking is godly.

Women DO NOT have to be submissive in anything that goes against God. Colossians 3:18 tells us: "Wives, submit to your husbands, as is fitting in the Lord." Men should love their wives as Christ loved the Church.

In that light, a godly man would never ask his wife to do something that goes against her dignity or would dishonor the Lord.

Readers Club Guide for

THE IDEAL WIFE

by Jacquelin Thomas

SUMMARY

Young newlywed Jana is settling into married life with her handsome
husband, Lawrence, after a whirlwind courtship and wedding. But soon
after their honeymoon, it becomes apparent that in order to adapt to her
successful husband's world, Jana will need to change. Her new circle of
friends includes the wives of Lawrence's partners at his law firm, who spend
their days shopping, having lunch, and working on charity committees. Jana
tries her best to be the ideal wife, but it soon becomes clear that her husband
has voracious and somewhat unusual sexual appetites and, although she
strives to please him, Jana is having trouble reconciling his uninhibited
lifestyle with her faith. Will she be forced to choose between her husband
and her God?

QUESTIONS FOR DISCUSSION

1. Why do you think the author opens the novel with the epigraph from the book of Esther? What tone does this set?

2. In trying to reconcile her husband's wants with her strong faith, Jana relates to the biblical story of Queen Vashti: "My first impression of Queen Vashti after reading the scripture was that of a rude and undisciplined woman. Now I'm beginning to think differently. . . ." (pp. 51–52) Why does the queen's story strike such a chord with Jana?

3. Do you think Jana's reaction to Lawrence when he wants to watch the "blue" movie is justified? How would you have reacted in this situation?

4. What do you think of Lawrence's requests concerning their intimate life? Is there a way he could have broached the subject better and possibly reached a compromise?

5. Both Jana and Lawrence make strong arguments citing biblical scripture in defense of their own opinions concerning marital intimacy. Whose is more convincing? How important a role does sex play in marriage?

6. What is the significance of the title, *The Ideal Wife*?

7. Since Lawrence knew his wife was not comfortable with his adventurous sex, were you surprised when he brought her to the swingers' club?

Why do you think he decided to do that? How do you feel about Jana's reaction?

8. Pastor Lacey defines adultery in this way: "The original meaning of adultery stemmed from the fact that women were considered property in the Old Testament . . . so adultery was having sex with a man's wife without his consent. In our society, women are definitely far from being called property, but I still believe the definition should be essentially the same. Having sex with a married person without their partner's consent is adultery but if that person doesn't mind, then there's been no harm done." Do you agree or disagree with his explanation?

9. As they are finalizing their divorce, Lawrence offers to buy Jana a house and give her a million dollars. Should she accept this offer or do you think there will be strings attached? Do you think Lawrence is a changed man at the end of the story?

10. How does Jana try to utilize her difficult experiences to help others? How has what she's been through changed her as a person?

11. Have you ever been in a relationship in which you've been asked to compromise your principles?

A CONVERSATION WITH JACQUELIN THOMAS

Q. You start off *The Ideal Wife* with a scripture passage from Esther 1:8–12. Why did you choose this particular passage and how does it relate to the story?

A. There isn't a whole lot on Queen Vashti in the Bible, but she inspired me to write *The Ideal Wife*. The scripture reference sets the tone for the story. Here is a man proud of his wife's beauty and he wants to show her off to the men in his court, much like Lawrence does with Jana. Only Lawrence takes it a step further—he wants his wife to sleep with other men.

Q. Your novel discusses the difficulty women might face when trying to juggle a modern marriage and their faith. What inspired you to write a novel that addresses such an issue?

A. I was inspired by Queen Vashti, but also by conversations I've had with other women. There are women who want to know just how far to go when it comes to satisfying their husbands, and hopefully this novel will spark open conversation between couples.

Q. Forgiveness plays a big part in *The Ideal Wife*. Was this intentional? What message are you trying to convey to your readers?

A. I think forgiveness comes into play in any Christian novel, but yes, it was intentional. In order to move forward with your life, you have to forgive past hurts. If you don't, you run the risk of bitterness setting in.

Q. You wear so many hats as a writer—romance author, Christian fiction author, young-adult author. How do you decide what to write next? What are the differences, if any, in writing for different genres?

A. I love writing, and God has given me so many stories I find it's hard to keep up at times. I love romance and I'm married to my very own Hero, so writing romance is just a celebration of love. With writing Christian fiction, it's more of a ministry for me, and with YA, I have a heart for teens so I wanted to write books that spoke to their issues. There really isn't any difference between them as I always strive to tell a good story. The teen books are geared toward ages twelve to eighteen. None of my books have profanity or graphic sexual situations.

Q. Can you walk us through your writing regime? Do you have a set outline that you follow, or do you go where the narrative takes you?

A. I write from an outline, which changes from time to time, but for the first draft, I tend to keep it close to my initial notes. The rewriting phase is when I really flesh out my scenes and let the characters tell me where to take the story.

Q. How important is it to incorporate your faith into your work? What does your faith bring to your life?

A. It's very important as my writing is a gift from God. I didn't just decide to be a writer—it is what I was born to do, and I truly believe this. God wants us to use our gifts to glorify Him and that's what I want to do. Without Him, none of this would be possible.

Q. What would you like readers to take away from *The Ideal Wife*?

A. That it's important to search the Word of God for yourself. You can't just lean unto someone else's interpretation of what the scriptures say. People will twist scripture to suit their purposes. If you're doing something that is not in the will of God, He will convict your spirit.

Q. What can we expect from you next?

A. My next book will be a modern-day adaptation of Samson and Delilah's story.

ENHANCE YOUR BOOK CLUB

1. To find out more about author Jacquelin Thomas, check out her official site, www.jacquelinthomas.com, which includes information about her other titles as well as biographical information about the author.

2. Jana's favorite restaurant in the novel is an establishment called Southern Style. Have each member of your book group make a Southern-style dish to bring to your next meeting, or meet in a Southern-style restaurant.

3. The author's inspiration for *The Ideal Wife* is from the book of Esther, mainly the story of Queen Vashti. Have each member of your book group discuss a story from the Bible that has given them inspiration.